The Theatre of the

Worldbreaker

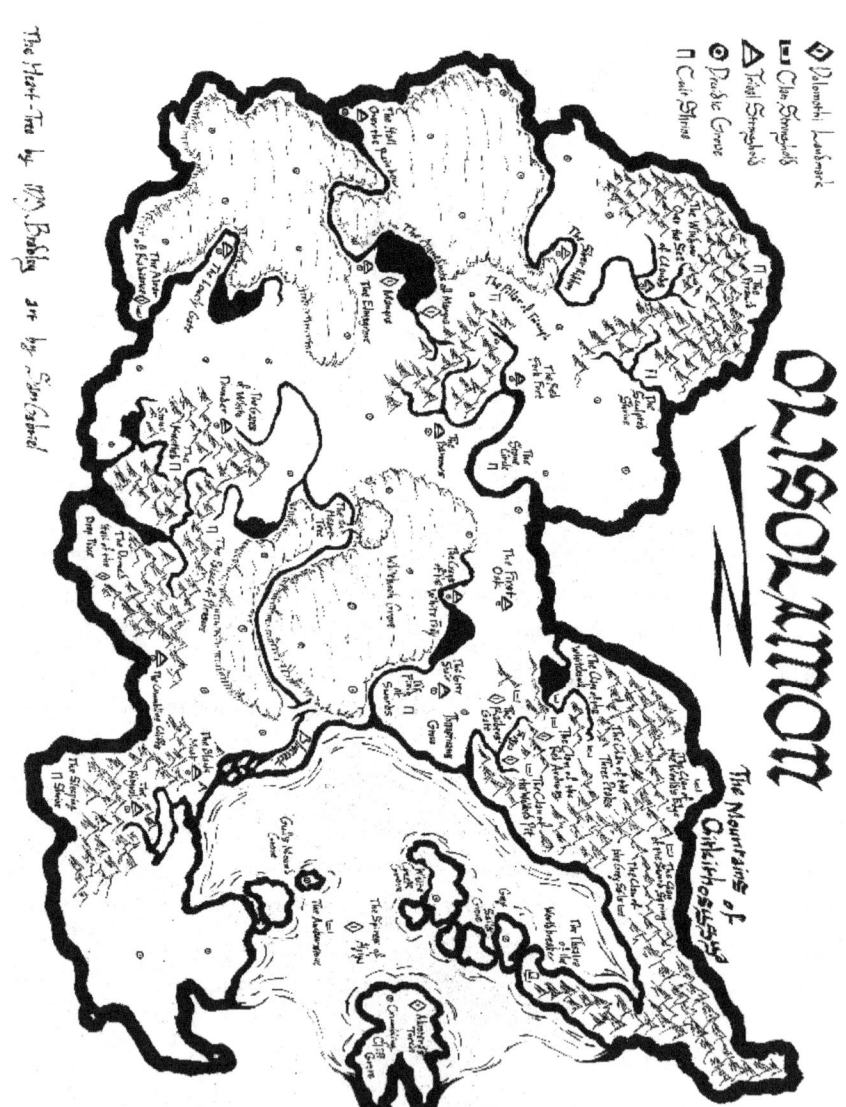

OLISOLAMON

The Mountains of Ciliothos

1

Pronunciation Guide

Abantakus — *Ab-an-ta-kus*
Adotakus — *Ad-o-tak-us*
Akrotera — Ak-ro-ter-ah
Anastagus — *An-ast-ag-us*
Aoife — *Aow-fi*
Athoëasir/Athoëasirki — *Ath-oh-eas-ir/Ath-oh-eas-ir-ki*
Atíko — At-ee-ko
Azaki Kathal — *Aza-ki Kath-al*
Eniku — *En-i-ku*
Eobin — *Ay-o-bin*
Eorl — Ay-orl
Estrif — *Es-trif*
Falaïré — *Fal-ah-ear-ay*
Getitakus — Get-it-ak-us
Gatali — *Ga-ta-li*
Ithani — Ith-an-ee
Iothe — *Ee-oth*
Íriniel — *Eer-in-iel*
Itaki — *It-aki*
Keorl — Kay-orl
Kerkam — Ker-kam
Kogodakus — *Kog-o-dak-us*
Manastakus — Man-ast-ak-us
Mernak — *Mur-nak*
Mūru — *Muu-ru*
Neméstakus — Nem-eh-sta-kus
Nemotakus — Nem-oh-tak-us
Nerevoréoatho/Nerevoréoathoki — *Ne-re-vor-eh-oh-ath-oh/Ne-re-vor-eh-oh-ath-oh-ki*
Niriyen — *Ni-ri-yen*
Okertes — Ok-er-tees
Olisolamon — *Oh-lis-oh-lam-on*
Omotakus — Om-oh-tak-us
Otuko Danaz — *Ot-uk-oh Dan-az*
Oudi — Oo-di
Prasatakus — *Pra-sa-ta-kus*
Qitkithosygya — *Kit-kith-o-sig-ia*
Siade — See-ad
Soekus — *So-kus*
Thiokezöeasiä — *Thi-oh-kes-oh-eas-ih-ah*
Togastakus — *Tog-ast-a-kus*
Tutakus — *Tu-ta-kus.*
Ulika — Oo-lik-ah
Urrakityál — Uur-ah-kit-yahl

2

Utháki Tol — *Ooth-ah-ki Tol*
Valia — *Var-lia*
Veleda — *Vel-ed-ah*
Vogitakus — *Vog-it-ah-kus*
Volõeskryf — *Vol-oo-esk-rif*
Volõmothí — *Vol-oo-moth-ee*
Volõmotistí — *Vol-oo-mot-ist-ee*
Volõvyf — *Vol-oo-vif*
Vyfaesiä — *Vif-ee-si-ah*
Yanastakus — *Yan-ast -ak-us*
Voréoatho/Voréoathoki — *Vor-eh-oh-ath-oh/Vor-eh-oh-ath-oh-ki*
Voréöeasiä/Voréöeasiäki — *Vor-eh-oh-eas-ih-ah/Vor-eh-oh-eas-ih-ah-ki*
Vunti — *Vun-ti*

The tarn glistened smooth and clear as glass beyond the jagged peak's looming shadow. Countless bronze blades' hilts thrust from the waters, knifing through the steam curling off the lake's surface. Neck-deep snow rose from the tarn's edge to the thick ice encrusting the ridge's summit and a single vast white cloud veiled the sun.

'Come, Duratakus.' His master stood before it all, an ebony silhouette at the end of the shallow, weathered steps carved into the mountainside. 'There is no need to linger down there.'

He hurried up the stair, slipping on the slick, melted snow and tugging his brown fur cloak tighter about his shoulders. 'Master?' He stopped two steps from the top.

'Did you know the Volõeskryf take the swords of worthy enemies and bring them back here to this hot spring as a way of gaining Estrif's favour?' Anastagus tucked his thiokezöeasiä under his arm. 'I am of a mind to try something similar with the seed of the Heart-Tree.'

'Casting it into the lake?' Duratakus asked. 'Is Estrif's favour worth giving up its power, master?'

His master held the seed up on his palm, the glossy red fruit standing out before the white world like blood on cotton. 'I have yet to find a way to make use of that power. It is… *stubborn*. I fear it knows the purpose it was grown for and its power is far greater than my own.'

'I'm sure you'll succeed eventually, master.'

Snowflakes the size of coins drifted down around them, resting on the steep snow banks and fading into the wisps of steam curling off the the tarn.

Anastagus watched one melt on the palm of his black glove. 'Perhaps, but if Vyfaesiä decides to prevent me, there is little I can do.'

'Will the Lady of Lies not help, master? Does it have to be Estrif?'

'It's unwise to rely on fickle aid. Estrif is more straightforward in his dealings with mortals.' His master closed his fist over the seed. 'Are *you* ready to help, Duratakus?'

'Of course.' Duratakus drew himself up and pulled his thiokezöeasiä tight to his chest. 'I won't fail you, master.'

'You will have all the longships of the Clan of the Sword Spring. Yanastakus will have those of the Clan of the Grey Sails.' Anastagus rested a long finger on the winged crown of Duratakus' thiokezöeasiä. 'You will also take your new apprentice.'

'Master…' Duratakus swallowed bile. 'That boy'll ruin your plan. He's a complete idiot. I'm not sure he knows a *single* spell beyond the one we chose him for. I *am* sure the thiokezöeasiä he carries around is just a stick he's picked up.'

The corner of Anastagus's mouth twitched. 'Do you trust my judgement, Duratakus?'

'Of course, master.'

'Then take him with you. He will either prove his worth or die,' his master said as his thiokezöeasiä's crown uncurled, its long tendrils groping at the seed of the Heart Tree, closing over the red fruit and clutching it tight. 'Besides, not so long ago, they said similar things about you.'

'Yes, master. I'll do my best.'

'I know you will,' Anastagus said. 'Take the longships downriver to the lake at the world's edge. Yanastakus's ships will join you at the Anchorstone, where the sunken spires of the Volōmothí city ruined in the Sundering reach the lake's surface.'

'And then, master?'

'Burn everything you can easily reach along the coast. Drive the people to the great fortified lighthouse in the far east, then besiege it. It is a great prize and will win us Estrif's favour.' His master steepled his long fingers. 'You must at least make sure to bring back captives and raiding prizes, Duratakus.'

'I will.'

Is that all? Duratakus frowned at the steaming tarn and the swords rising out of the warm water. *His plans are never so simple.*

'Is something amiss, Duratakus?'

He fiddled with the black leather girdle round his waist. 'It's just – I was hoping, master, you'd share the full plan with me this time.'

Anastagus rested a hand upon his shoulder. 'One day, Duratakus. Be patient. I've entrusted you with the most important part of this plan.'

'Thank you, master,' he murmured. 'Would you tell me… again?'

A small smile played across his master's face and he pulled back his hand. 'If you will tell me why you are so fond of hearing it.'

Duratakus shuffled his feet on the ancient step. 'It reminds me how lucky I am. I get to touch greatness.'

'You should have more faith in yourself.' Anastagus's voice turned soft as the snow falling around them. 'You will play a vital role in what we accomplish, Duratakus.'

'Still, master, would you tell me again?'

His master smiled. 'From the beginning?'

'From your moment of realisation, master, if that's ok?'

'In my search for the truth of the world I learnt much. Terrible things.' His master's expression turned distant and dark. 'After, I travelled between the groves, trying to cling to old lies, trying to convince myself it was better if I pretended I didn't know or that what I knew didn't change anything. One day, while I wandered in thought far to the South at the world's edge, a snowstorm crept up on me and I became lost. A woman saved me and led me to shelter while the blizzard raged. She listened to me spill out my heart and helped me realise how important knowing the truth is, not just to me, but to everyone.'

Duratakus frowned and studied the gaping Spider's maw carved upon his master's armguard. 'You never mentioned her before, master. Who was she?'

'She never told me her name, but I went back to thank her in the spring.' The corner of Anastagus's lips twitched. 'Her home was deserted and had clearly been empty for many decades. All I found was a spider, dangling from the ceiling on its thread.'

Duratakus' jaw dropped. 'The Lady of Desire herself? I thought—'

'I am not sure how real it was. Perhaps she merely let me dream the whole thing and sent the spider so I didn't doubt the truth of what she'd showed me.'

'The truth's the most important thing.'

'Understanding the truth is the most important thing,' Anastagus replied. 'To appreciate the beauty of the stars, you must understand they are out of reach.'

'And the Heart-Tree—'

'I do not pretend to know why Vyfaesiä keeps the truth from us. Death should be a welcome rest for people who've lived a full, honest life, but for those of us trapped beneath the Heart-Tree's shade, it is our first and last moment of clarity. An instant in which to realise we

5

have wasted all the time we will ever have. A lifetime spent watching shadows move on the wall of the cave instead of in the sunlight is worse than no life at all. I cannot fail to free this world fragment from it, no matter the cost.'

'You'll succeed, master. I know you will.'

Anastagus turned from the Sword Spring. 'Does it truly matter to you, Duratakus?'

Duratakus held his gaze with a great, hot swell of pride. 'It matters to me, because it matters to you, master. You saved me. Even if you wanted to destroy this world, I'd follow you 'til I drowned in the blood.'

'That is why I have chosen you to be the lynchpin of my plan. Nobody else is as trustworthy.'

'You should've let me lead the attack on the Heart-Tree, master. I wouldn't have failed you like Kogodakus did.'

'But then I would have had to sacrifice you,' his master said.

'You knew he was going to fail?'

'I knew he would die. That is not necessarily failure. It is the fate of all pawns to be sacrificed, Duratakus.'

Duratakus winced. 'Of course, master. It's just…'

'You dislike my sacrifice of him.' Anastagus watched the snow melt on his longer fingers and flicked the drops away into the steaming tarn. 'I know. It is because, deep down, you fear you may be next. All loyal people fear betrayal, for all people fear what they cannot understand and control.'

'If you wished me to sacrifice myself, I would without hesitation, master,' Duratakus said. 'But not if it was only to fail you.'

Anastagus closed his eyes and exhaled. 'Remember, Duratakus, that *our* goal is to free the world from Vyfaesiä's lies. Kogodakus's goal was Valia… and self-destruction.'

'He was weak of heart. He let her twist his mind. He didn't deserve to be your Companion.'

'He pursued his goal with everything he was and in so doing aided our purpose too.' Anastagus offered a black-gloved hand, raising Duratakus up onto the step beside him. 'Do you see the Sword Spring?'

'I do.'

His master pointed a finger at the steaming tarn. 'Everything you need to understand about the warriors you're going to lead you can see here. Study it carefully, you must know them well to lead them to victory.'

'Of course, master.'

Anastagus turned back down the long, ancient stair to the fjord. 'And Duratakus?'

'Yes, master?'

'They will, of course, send aid from the Heart-Tree.'

'Soekus the Lifebringer?'

Anastagus brushed the snow from his shoulders. 'Unlikely. He will be forced to travel to restore the lost groves.'

'Valia, then.' Duratakus raised his chin. 'I won't fail, not even against her.'

His master smiled. 'Not her, either. We have spread them thin. There are few Voréöeasiäki left at the Heart-Tree. I studied them all. They will choose a young, promising Voréöeasiäki, I think. One who carries a falcata. Do not kill him.'

'Master?'

Anastagus dusted snow from the squares of spider carapace covering his chest. 'He may well prove useful once more. Any other Voréöeasiäki are either to be killed, or captured and returned as tribute to Estrif.'

'I understand, master.'

'I will see you again at the Theatre of the Worldbreaker.'

Duratakus watched his master stride down the steps to where the longships' masts rose from the fjord like winter trunks. He turned back to the steaming tarn, touching his fingertips to the hilt of the nearest longsword. His skin turned pale against the biting cold of the blade, his nails purple and dark before the bronze. 'If you're listening, Prince of Bloodshed. Don't let me fail him.'

Thin, angular, black letters lay on the page like plucked spider legs; two words scratched into vellum.

Azaki Kathal.

Azaki watched the letter flutter beside the bright, grass green eyes of the Heart-Tree's image in the amber-topped table. The gentle, white light of the glowing veins in the ebony walls of the High Hall seemed to sink into the dark of the ink like the river into the depths of the Webbed Pit.

Soekus leant forward and folded it in half. 'It would seem Anastagus has noticed you, newest minion.' The crinkles about his eyes faded and his smile slipped away. 'Be wary, Azaki. If he wanted you dead, he wouldn't have sent a warning. He has something else in mind for you.'

'Fantastic.' Azaki pulled a grin across his face as his stomach knotted itself tight. 'Should I write him a reply? Something about the colour of his eyes? Or do you think that's too much?' He chuckled. 'Can you imagine the look on his face when he reads it?'

'You're *not* sending pretend love notes to Anastagus.' Íri's eyes blazed. 'I don't care if you think it'll be funny!'

'Íri,' Itaki chimed. 'Íri.'

She balled up her fist. 'That chicken is *begging* to be roasted. One more Íri out of him and it won't matter how cute he is…'

Azaki tapped the parrot on the beak with a fingertip. 'Quiet, you.'

'Hush.' Itaki bobbed his head up and down and prowled further along Azaki's shoulder. 'Hush, Itaki.'

He grinned and fished out a walnut. 'See how well Itaki's learning? I'm so proud of him.'

'We've no way of replying regardless.' Soekus raised his voice over the satisfied whistles as Itaki demolished the walnut in a shower of crumbs. 'This is just a warning Anastagus is up to something, it may even be complete misdirection on his part.'

'More than likely,' Valia murmured, soft as summer frost.

Kogodakus's seared, ruined face and outstretched stub of an arm flashed through Azaki's mind. *Heartless.* He shivered at the memory of the shrill, eerie shriek of her thorned wind chimes. *If I'd met her in Soekus's stead, I'd be dust and this place would be ashes.*

'Anastagus has already proven cunning.' The shadows on Soekus's face grew deep and dark. 'However, he has the seed of the Heart-Tree and we *must* recover it.'

Valia put a hand on Soekus's shoulder. 'He can't use it. The Heart-Tree won't allow it.'

'We don't know that for sure.' Íriniel's father eased Valia's hand off. 'We can't risk it. Eleven years the seed's been growing here. She had a purpose for it. We can't let Anastagus twist its power to his own ends.'

Azaki bent forward and retrieved the note as Soekus and Valia's debate dropped to tense whispers. He unfolded it, turned it over, twisted it around, and held it up to the light.

Nothing. He crumpled it up into a ball and gave it to Itaki. *That's good, I suppose.*

The parrot clutched it in his toes, lifting it up and down before a narrowed eye and dropping it to the floor.

'There's just no pleasing you sometimes, tiny fiend.' Azaki retrieved the ball and stuck it in his pocket. 'I'm curious, was his handwriting always so... spidery?'

Soekus turned away from Valia and chuckled into his beard. 'Anastagus's bad handwriting has been the subject of jokes for over thirty years, Azaki. They used to say one day he'd discover a great truth, but nobody else would ever be able to read it.'

'There's far more than just that one note,' Valia said. 'We've over two dozen missives from Voréöeasiäki and villages east of here. Anastagus has sent forth the longships of the Volōeskryf to harry and burn anything close to the waterways of the lake at the edge of the world. Most of the Volōvyf have fled to the stronghold upon the islands far to the east or the one near the lake's western shore.'

Only longships? Azaki patted the ball of paper in his pocket, a chill crawling along his spine. *What about all the other clans? What about the Webbed Pit? What about Otuko and Utháki?*

Soekus ran his fingers through his beard. 'The Beacon at the End of the World is so far east it's almost completely isolated. That ancient lighthouse is heavily fortified, but will be easily cut off by Anastagus's raiders' fast ships. The people will soon starve, even if they hold out against assault.'

'There are four groves on the lake's islands too,' Valia said. 'Without them, the Nerevoréoathoki's power will be able to touch our world there...'

'Someone needs to go,' Soekus said. ·

Valia folded her hands on her lap. 'Niriyen is at the Grey Stair stronghold not far from the lake's edge. They will hold, but the Crags of the White Folly further west aren't defended by a Voréöeasiäki strong enough to stop Anastagus.'

'Father?' Íri whispered.

'I must travel to restore the groves lost to Kogodakus's invasion and then pursue Anastagus and the seed,' Soekus said. 'The power it contains is greater than all the Hands of the Heart-Tree combined. He *can't* be allowed to make use of it or we simply won't have a chance of stopping him.'

Íri shot Aazki a sharp look, her eyes full of fire.

A cold fist seized Azaki's heart. *Don't tell them, Íri. You're the only good thing I've got left right now.*

'Even when everyone else has betrayed you, you'll still have me,' Falaïré whispered, her fingertips ghosting across his cheek. 'If we want the seed back, my Azi, then let's take it.'

Íriniel turned to Valia. 'Then—'

'The road from the Crags of the White Folly leads not just to the Heart-Tree, but to countless other settlements too,' Valia said. 'I must go there.'

'And Mernak is in the far north defending the way west from the mountains,' Soekus said. 'It'll have to be another Voréöeasiäki. We'll have to call someone back from one of the groves and hope they can get out there quickly enough.'

Íri glanced between Valia and her father. 'I'll go. I held my own against Kogodakus, I can do it.'

Great. Azaki scowled down at the Voréoatho depicted within the table's top.

Her grass green eyes stared back, piercing right through his and dragging him down into an endless, emerald well.

A faint prickle crawled across the skin between his shoulder blades. *Íri's going to get herself killed if she goes off alone.*

'Are you sure, darling?' Soekus asked. 'You could replace the Voréöeasiäki who goes to the lake instead? One of the Erudite could go.'

'There's no time for that, father. You know there's not. I'm a Voréöeasiäki. I'll fight for the Heart-Tree and the world. It's why I was chosen.'

A shadow loomed in Soekus' eyes; a long, deep darkness. 'Your mother would've said just the same.'

Íri turned to Azaki.

'Promises, promises,' Falaïré murmured in his ear.

He put a finger between Itaki's beak and his other earlobe. 'Fine... I suppose I'll come with you. Itaki will get upset if his mother's gone away for ages and he might annoy me.'

Íri shook her head at him.

Soekus smiled, crinkles creasing the corners of his eyes. 'Thank you, Azaki.'

'Go to Gull's Mound Grove first, children,' Valia said. 'It's at the most southerly point of the lake and the safest place to sail from.'

'The people come before the groves,' Soekus told them. 'If you have to choose, darling, choose the people. I can regrow groves from the smallest splinter of the sacred tree. I can't bring back people.'

Íri swallowed and nodded. 'Come on, Azaki. We need to pack, then leave.'

Azaki gave the two Hands of the Heart-Tree a cheerful wave. 'If I don't come back, it was probably Íri, not Anastagus.'

Soekus chuckled. 'I'm sure you would've deserved it.'

Beyond the entrance to the council room, the light was dim and rain pattered upon the canopy above. Íri's green tunic shrunk toward the far side of the bridge.

Azaki caught her right at the end of it and matched her smaller strides. 'Why so keen? We only just got out of one fight for our lives...'

'It's what we're *meant* to do.' She clutched her thiokezöeasiä to her chest. 'All those people in the Beacon at the End of the World are depending on *us*.'

'Don't you think they ought to be able to look after themselves? Is it really fair for them to always be hiding behind you?'

Íri paused mid-step. 'Of course it's fair.' She fixed him with a piercing stare, a fierce glint in her eyes. 'The Heart-Tree made us stronger so we could help protect this world, we've got to keep our part of the pact.'

He stared up at the canopy. 'Seems too nice to be true. In my experience, people just take for themselves. The stronger they are, the more they can take. If you're seen as weak, or unworthy, you're left to starve, or freeze, or any number of unpleasant fates.'

Fire flashed in her eyes and the blood rose in her cheeks. 'If you believe that, *Azaki of the Webbed Pit,* then why're you coming?'

He shrugged. 'You're going.'

'Shouldn't I be strong enough to do it on my own?' Íri's voice turned tart and sharp as split flint.

Azaki smiled. 'It's complicated. I guess I'm not that bothered by those people all the way over there, but I've grown fond of all this green and teasing you...'

He touched a finger to his lips. *And I should find a way back to Otuko. Utháki's had time to calm down now.*

Íri glanced away, pink fading on her cheeks. 'Maybe you just need to see them.' She started forward down the steps of the path towards her home. 'You didn't care for the Heart-Tree and the glades until you'd seen them.'

'Maybe... Or maybe I just thought you'd get lost without me to hold your hand.'

Itaki nibbled at Azaki's hair all the way to Íri's little home, then fluttered off Azaki's shoulder and in through the window.

He chuckled. 'You might want to…'

Íri sighed. 'I know, he seems to have developed a taste for books.' She glared at him and crossed her arms. 'Something I'm beginning to suspect you deliberately taught him.'

'If only I'd thought of it.' Azaki peered in through the window as Íri murmured some phrase to unseal her door. 'He's vanished, that can't be good.'

'Well go find him.' She dragged him in after her by the wrist, stopped and cocked her head. 'I can't hear him whistling or talking, so he's probably chewing something he shouldn't be.'

Azaki laughed. 'Itaki!'

The bird prowled out from under Íriniel's blankets, tilting his head this way and that.

'Damn. You got there first, you sneaky chicken. Togastakus is going to be very upset.'

Íri snorted and began pulling things out of drawers. 'Rather him than Togastakus. Or you, Azaki.'

'Me too.' He settled himself on the end of her bed and rolled Itaki over onto his back to tickle his feet. 'You'd just steal all the blankets, ball yourself up, and leave me to freeze.'

'You don't even sleep under the blankets,' she accused, piling a small stack of things on the floor beside her. 'You sprawl out on your face basically naked.'

Azaki grinned at her until she flushed. 'It's warmer down here. I'm used to nearly freezing.' He glanced at the rising pile as she dropped a stack of green tunics atop it. 'You're not actually taking all of that are you?'

Íri blinked. 'Yes. Waxed-leather shelter. Blankets. Spare tunics. Spare boot leather. Parchment. Ink bottle. Quills. Quill-making knife. Map. And…'

He glanced at the small pile of white cotton. 'And?'

She huffed. 'You know what they are.'

'Well, maybe bring the map, but the rest…'

Íri glared at him and started folding all her tunics into rough squares. 'This better not be some sneaky plan to try to get me out of my tunic under the pretence of washing our only clothes or something like that.'

Azaki flopped back on her bed and laughed over the rustle of her folding. 'Otuko would never forgive me.'

Íri pressed the last tunic down onto the stack, a small frown creasing her brow. 'Why not?'

Idiot. All his mirth drained away. *She knows you. You mustn't let her realise you have to go back to Otuko.*

Íri stood up. 'Azaki?'

'Old in-joke... Sorry.'

'Right...' She dropped the map on his face. 'Look at that, then.'

Azaki held it up far enough away to see.

Four green circles were carefully inked onto the islands of the great lake.

'Four groves?' he asked.

'Yes,' Íri replied. 'Gull's Mound Grove is the one at the far south. Crumbling Cliff Grove is part of the Beacon at the Edge of the World.'

He sat up and studied the small trios of black huts inked here and there along the lakeshore. 'We ought to stay clear of the coast for as long as possible. The river, too. The raiders will go after everything they can sail near. We can get a boat from this village, Bluecreek, it's closest to that southern grove.'

'We'll be ok on the river for a bit.' She stood up holding her pile. 'The bridge where the Marsh Road crosses the river stops any big boats sailing further up.'

Azaki traced the blue line from the Heart-Tree down to the little black arch where the road crossed it. 'So we sail to there, follow the road south through what appears to be some kind of huge bog, then go east to Bluecreek.'

Íri stuffed her things into a leather bag and dropped it beside him on the bed. 'What do you know about these Volōeskryf longships?'

He glanced out the window and lowered his voice. 'I don't know for sure, but I'd assume they're from the Clan of the Sword Spring and the Clan of the Grey Sails. They're sister clans, sworn to Estrif, and prefer to raid across the lake than over land.'

'What does sworn to Estrif mean?'

'It means they'll try to honour Estrif more than most raiders. Sacrifices after raids, raiding prizes taken to take back to offer to him upon their safe return, things like that.'

Íri paled. 'They sacrifice *people?*'

Azaki shook his head. 'Not really. If you slaughter your goats, you don't get any more milk, so most sacrifices are just prizes from their raids. That said, they'd be keen to kill any proper warriors or soldiers to gain Estrif's attention and favour.'

'And Voréöeasiäki?'

'To them, you're elite warriors. They don't see you as trusted guardians and mediators like the soft-folk do. Killing a Voréöeasiäki would be a huge scalp, like killing the enemy keorl leading a raid.'

Íri swung her pack onto her back. 'So they'll go after the groves.'

'Other raiders probably wouldn't risk it if Anastagus wasn't ordering them, but they would. They'd probably wait 'til they'd done all their other raiding in case they lose, though.'

'Do you want to pack some stuff before we go?'

'I'm actually either wearing or holding everything I own.' He ruffled Itaki's head with one finger and scooped the bird up. 'Plus this troublesome chicken.'

'Oh.' Íri crooked a finger at him and moved to the door. 'You know you can take stuff from the storerooms, Azaki. You're a Voréöeasiäki. This isn't like your clan, you can help yourself to anything you need.'

'Don't need to.' He squeezed past her into the glade. 'Anything we'll need, I'll be able to find when we stop. I'm not some soft, southie boy, Íri.'

'I suppose you might even be useful for once.' Her fingers glowed a soft orange as she pressed them to the door. 'Learn-ed trove of countless keys, gateway tied with red string, stranger's hand be warned, beware, of guarding ward's sharp sting.'

'A new spell?' Azaki asked as Itaki wriggled round in his arms and clambered up onto his shoulder. 'What does it do?'

'It keeps you out of my bedroom. If you try to open it without giving the right phrase, you'll feel it.'

Azaki inspected the faint orange glow upon the door. 'And what happens when your trusted, loyal friend who saved you from Kogodakus tries to pay you a visit?'

'He gets to experience the sensation of burnt fingers.' Her tone turned sweet. 'But if there's a sudden stream of other, unsuspecting victims, I'll hold you responsible and put the spell on *your* door.'

He stuck his tongue out. 'Spoilsport. I was going to encourage Toga the Sour to come woo you.'

'Of course you were,' Íri muttered. 'He's not going to be back here for a while, anyway. He's stubborn as a rock.'

'Shall we go, then?'

Soekus waited beside the gate he'd regrown, admiring the knee high grass. 'I thought you'd be straight off. So eager to bear the responsibilities of a Voréöeasiäki, you'd leave your aged father without a farewell.'

'I knew you'd be here,' Íri replied. 'You get all mushy and weepy every time you go off travelling without me. I'm surprised you're not already crying, *aged father*.'

Her father laughed and swept her into his arms. 'I worry about my precious baby girl. Be careful, be safe, don't underestimate these raiders or Anastagus' Companions, and, most importantly, don't talk to any boys.'

'It's going to be a quiet trip,' Azaki remarked as Íri escaped her father's hug.

'You can talk to him.' Soekus' eyes were bright with humour. 'But I want the two of you at least an arm's length apart at all times.'

'So do I,' Azaki said. 'Preferably further, actually. That keeps me safe from whatever blunt objects are going to replace books as the source of my bruises.'

Íri pinched the bridge of her nose, pink-cheeked. 'We've been over this, father. I don't need to get married as young as you did, there're more important things happening, and Azaki's too short and ugly anyway.'

And taken. He glanced north into the endless green, imagining the distant peaks. An odd, hollow feeling gnawed at his gut. *Who knew Otuko wasn't really joking all these years?*

A small, amused grin played on Soekus' lips. 'If you say so, darling.'

Íri growled and jabbed him in the foot with her thiokezöeasiä. 'Is that really what you came here to say?'

Her father's face hardened and the light faded from his eyes. 'No. I fear this scheme Anastagus is hatching upon the lake is just the overture to his plan, something to draw our eye or set the tone. Things may not be what they seem.'

Falaïré laughed and draped her arms over Azaki's shoulders. 'One day, we'll be greater,' she murmured. 'Imagine, the whole world an audience to the truths we spin.'

He hid his smile beneath his hand. *One day.*

'Don't trust anyone you don't know well,' Soekus said. 'Anastagus lured several Voréöeasiäki to his side before he left. He may have persuaded others since.'

Íri cupped the heat-haze of her thiokezöeasiä's sealing spell in her hands. 'If they're defending the Beacon at the Edge of the World, they must still be loyal to the Heart-Tree.'

Azaki offered her a grin. 'At least there'll not be any annoying Greenheart Voréöeasiäki to bother us.'

Soekus laughed. 'Anastagus is technically a Greenheart. He was raised at the Heart-Tree from a very young age, like I was. Íriniel is too, remember?'

Íri blinked. 'Really? I never heard anything about that.'

'Anastagus never advertised it, neither of us did. We both disagreed with their agenda, but they included us in their number. Until Anastagus turned against us, then suddenly he'd never been one of them at all.' He mussed Íri's hair. 'Now, you be very careful. Unless there's a chance I can persuade you not to go?'

Íri's eyes narrowed. 'Goodbye, father. I'll be careful, I promise.'

Soekus' eyes flicked to Azaki and back to his daughter. 'Make sure you keep that promise.'

Two

A wide, brown ribbon of water bent through damp woodland; it swirled past the white stones beyond Azaki's toes, forming a tiny whirlpool where it caught the corner of their small boat. The river gushed in time with the slow drip of the leaves, fading birdsong drifted through the dusk, and deer padded through the bracken a little way from their camp.

'Row, row, row your boat—'

'Shut up, Azaki,' Íri snapped, twisting 'round from where she'd been tying the top of the shelter to the tree trunks. 'We're not even on the river anymore.'

'I've never sailed anywhere before,' he protested. 'I'm allowed to get excited.'

Íri's fingers dug into the small, pale pebbles of the beach, but she tossed her handful of stones into the water beside the boat. 'You've been singing that since we left!'

Azaki poked at the white belly of the nearest and smallest of his five trout. 'So?'

She levelled him with a flat look. 'It's been *two days*.'

'Fine. I'll stop singing.'

'Good.' She lined the shelter's edge with heavy rocks from the top of the beach. 'Any longer and Itaki might've picked the words up, then we'd never hear the end of it.'

'Otuko would've sung with me.' Azaki cleared a small pit in the beach a few metres from their shelter where Itaki was roving. 'You're a bad friend.'

'For two days? I don't believe you.'

Azaki grinned. 'For about ten minutes, then she'd have pushed me over the side.'

'Maybe I'll do that if you start singing again tomorrow, then.' Íri shuffled across beside the hole he'd dug in the beach, sweeping the driftwood and what little dry deadwood they'd found into it with one hand. 'Hurry up, it's getting cold and dark.'

'Not like that,' he said. 'You're meant to light a small bit, then build it up.'

Íri stuck her finger out. A slim line of flame sprang off it and the wood smoked and caught straight away.

'Cheat,' he accused. 'I see you've mastered that spell, though.'

'I have. You should master as many as you can, the incantations slow you down and give away what you're going to do, too.'

'That and you get all embarrassed about your incantations.' Azaki laughed as she turned pink. 'I *knew* that was it.'

Itaki tilted his head at the fire and hopped across to it with all his feathers fluffed up.

Azaki warded him back with a finger. 'Not too close, tiny fiend.'

'Do the fish,' Íri pleaded. 'I'm *so* hungry.'

A good thing these trout are twice the size of the those Otuko and I used to catch, then. Azaki grabbed the first trout and dug a wide, flat stone out of the pebbles. *Ah.*

'Do you have a knife, Íri?'

'No.' She tossed another rock onto the edge of their shelter. 'Damn.'

'All that packing and you didn't bring a knife.'

'What happened to *I can find everything I need*?'

'I can use my falcata.' He reached into the shelter and felt around for the blade.

'I'm not eating anything that's touched that sword.'

'Why not?'

She stared, dropping a rock down on the shelter's far edge. 'You *killed* people with it.'

'I cleaned it afterward.'

'No.' Íri crossed her arms. 'Give me the fish.'

He tossed it at her, laughing as she fumbled it into her stomach. 'What're you going to do?'

The slim blade of fire sprang back to life upon her extended fingers and she poked its tip into the fish's stomach.

It hissed and smoked, bursting into flames. Íri squeaked and tossed it into the river.

'Excellent work.' Azaki watched it sink out of sight. 'Good thing I caught an extra one.'

'Well we can't eat any of them, anyway.'

'*You* can't. I'm happy to eat things my falcata has touched. Starving's really not much fun.'

Íri frowned and turned a bit green. 'Can't we break a rock to get a sharp stone or something?'

'I guess there's a spell I was making we can try and use. It's not finished, though.' He held out his upturned palm and drew the shadows together upon it into a slim, straight, guardless blade a little longer than his hand. 'See?'

Falaïré's soft laughter tickled the back of his neck. 'A spell for bittersweet, red moments…'

Íri studied it. 'Use that, then.'

He poked a finger through the shadows and the blade dispersed. 'I can't make it work, even when I use the incantation. If I make it sharp at the edges, it falls apart. If I get the shape right, it comes out blunt.'

Íri beamed. 'Are you struggling with your spell-crafting?'

'The longer you rub it in, the longer until you get to eat the fish.'

A torn expression flashed across her face. 'It's because you chose a bad thing to make a knife out of. I had the same problem with the Burning Blade. You need to really think about it as two lores, not just focus on shaping it into a blade. The blade shape comes from the shaping part, obviously, but not the sharpness, that's from the intent of the lore of destruction.'

'Hmmm. Two lores.' Azaki turned that over in his head. 'Queen of whispering webs, upon your throne of lies, gift a blade of shadow, and revel in their cries.'

The shadows drew together again and Azaki tested its edge. The blade drew blood with a soft sting, sliding through his skin as easy as freshly shattered obsidian.

'Ow.' He sucked the bead of blood off the ball of his thumb.

'*That's* the incantation you chose?' Íri crossed her arms. 'Really?'

Azaki grinned and weighed the knife on his palm; it wobbled and some bits seemed sharper than others when he inspected it from hilt to tip. 'Do you want to know what I called it?'

She sighed. 'Something similarly awful, no doubt just to wind me up.'

'A little bit that. But mostly because I'd started a theme with my spells and incantations, so I don't want to switch halfway. It's called *the Blessing of the Spider*.'

'Good luck explaining *that* to the other Voréöeasiäki. I can't wait to hear what they'll think.'

Azaki let the knife vanish in a wisp of shadow. 'Queen of whispering webs, upon your throne of lies, gift a blade of shadow and revel in their cries.' He turned this one over and inspected it. 'A bit better.'

'Good enough to do the fish?' Íri's stomach growled. 'Soon?'

He laughed and slipped the tip of the knife into the end of the fish's belly. 'Not too long now.'

Azaki cut the trout open up to the gills, hooking two fingers under the cold, wet entrails and tugging them out. He dropped the handful of offal on a flat rock and stretched to wash his hand in the river's edge.

'Are they slimy?' Íri asked.

'A bit.' He chopped the head and tail off the trout, warding Itaki's curious beak away with a finger. 'Not for you, greedy chicken, you've had your dinner.'

Íri took the fish off him and speared it on a slim piece of willow. 'What about the scales?' She held the fish over the flames. 'Shouldn't you get rid of them?'

'Trout are fine as is.' He did the other fish and dropped the entrail-covered rock into the fire. 'Soon we'll have some dinner and, best of all, none of it's green.'

'You're not going to grow,' Íri warned. 'You'll be short forever.'

'And thus safe from your nymphomania. No need to fear being the boy who steals your virtue and gets turned into some unnaturally-sized vegetable by your father.'

She snorted and stared into the fire below her fish. 'What about Otuko? Does *she* like her men short?'

'She just wants her future children to have grey eyes like she does.'

'Grey eyes, huh.' Íri's trout dipped towards the flames and began to blacken.

Azaki nudged her fish with his. 'Careful.'

She jerked her dinner out of the fire and let out a little growl. 'Now it's burnt. This is so much easier with my father.'

'He has very handy magic. We'll survive, though. It's not all that dangerous down south.'

'I'm going to be cold at night again, too,' Íri moaned.

He chuckled and repeated the incantation to conjure another blade of shadow to poke his fish with. 'Maybe you should make a spell to keep yourself warm, like your reading light, but a whole cocoon?'

She beamed. 'That's an excellent idea.' Her face fell. 'But it'll take a *lot* of practice. Otherwise I'll end up setting fire to myself again.'

Again? Azaki stifled a laugh.

'Well, you've got time,' he said. 'It's what, another day or two downriver to the bridge if the current stays this fast, then five or six to Bluecreek and another over the lake to that grove.'

'True.' She pulled her fish out of the fire to inspect it. 'It looks cooked.'

He released his conjured blade in a small burst of dark mist. 'Not yet. It'll be another few minutes. You've got to let it cook all the way through or you'll get very sick.'

'Who taught you all this?'

'Itaki. My brother, not the parrot. He went raiding from time to time to try and prove himself to the clan. I had to be able to look after myself while he was gone. He taught me to read, to talk, to cook, everything.'

She frowned. 'He died on a raid?'

He nodded and held up his scarred left palm. 'He broke his red oath to me and never came back. At the World's Edge, Estrif and the other Voréoathoki aren't so far away as you might think.'

Íriniel stared at his hand, then reached out and drew it onto her knee. 'You have four?'

'Five.' He turned his other hand over to reveal the thin white line on his right palm. 'They're pretty common in the clans, especially the Webbed Pit. Estrif always keeps his word, so he holds us to oaths taken on his name. They're more or less the only oath that can be completely trusted.'

'What're yours?'

'The first two I swore with my friends.' He poked the two oldest of the white lines. 'Then there's watching your back and never willingly serving the Spider again.'

'And the fifth.'

'Anastagus.' Azaki clenched his fist over the scar. 'I didn't want it with the others, but I needed something to hold him to.'

'I healed that one, too,' she murmured, tracing the scars with the tip of her finger. 'The ones you swore to your friends, are they like the one you swore to help me?'

He sighed under his breath and took his hand back. 'More or less. We swore to look out for one another and stick together. Before, we were all alone against the world. After, we at least had each other's backs.'

'So I've two, really. One to look out for me and one to stay.'

Azaki pulled his trout back from the fire and murmured the Blessing of the Spider spell once more. 'One of those is done, like Anastagus's one. I kept you safe when Kogodakus attacked the Heart-Tree. If I get close enough to the edge of the world, the scars will fade away... Unless Estrif decides otherwise, that is.'

Íri took a small bite out of her fish. 'Hot,' she hissed, swallowing with a wince. 'Very hot.'

He sliced the skin off his piece of fish into the fire with the tip of his blade, then offered the knife to her.

'I'm not using your Spider spell.' She tugged the skin back with her teeth. Grease smeared her chin and dripped onto the beach. 'Not now. Not ever.'

'Because that's much easier and looks so attractive.'

Íri flushed pink. 'Hush, you.' She took another small bite. 'What promise did your brother break?'

He sighed.

'Sorry. If you don't want to say, you don't have to.'

'It's alright,' Azaki said through a mouthful of fish. 'It was a long time ago. I'm used to him being dead.' He shuffled 'round beside her and shooed Itaki away from the other fish. 'He made the blood oath when I was basically a baby. I used to worry he'd get his spider-silk cloak, join the clan and abandon me to be outcast alone. It's far more common than not. He swore that he'd always be there to protect me.'

'And he wasn't.'

'No. When I got to the age he was when our parents died, he stopped looking out for me. I think he wanted me to learn how to grow strong the same way he did.'

'And Estrif killed him?' she whispered.

'Estrif gives as much leeway with his blood promises as he wants, but I've not heard of him *directly* killing someone who breaks the red oath,' Azaki replied. 'Itaki slipped in blood and another warrior's arrow hit him.'

'So it could be a coincidence.'

He gave her a wry smile. 'Only if all the other such unfortunate mishaps that happen to those who break the oath are too.'

'Oh.' Íri nibbled at the last bits of her trout. 'You haven't broken any of yours, have you?'

'Don't think so,' he said. 'Unless you've upset Estrif for other reasons, he usually waits for you to do something you *know* breaks your promise. I still intend to look out for Otuko and Utháki as best I can.'

'Do you,' she murmured.

'And you, blood promise or not.' Azaki gave her shoulder a gentle nudge. 'Friends are worth keeping, if you can.'

'There's nothing we can't do together.' Falaïré sat across the fire from the two of them, her silver eyes shining brighter than the crackling flames. 'This is just the beginning, remember?'

Íri leant against his shoulder and held the next skewered trout over the flames. 'How do we save a town, Azaki? All those poor people, they'll die if we get it wrong, and I don't know what to do.'

Your guess is probably as good as mine. Azaki gnawed the inside of his cheek. *We'll find a way. Somehow.*

He patted her on the head. 'I guess you drive off whoever's attacking it, like at the Heart-Tree, only this time we ought to have a lot more help.'

'Crumbling Cliff Grove will have at least one Voréöeasiäki with an awakened thiokezöeasiä.'

'And the soft-folk hiding in the lighthouse should fight for their lives,' Azaki said. 'The raiders, on the other hand, will probably only have one Companion with them and be keen to go after easier targets before hurling themselves against fortifications. Kill the Companion and they'll retreat for a while.'

'How many of the Companions are there? Are they all like Kogodakus? Erudite Voréöeasiäki?'

'No idea. There aren't loads, though.' He speared his own second fish and dangled it beside the fire. 'Let's wait until we know what's happening, then come up with a plan.'

'Which you'll tell me this time.' Íri's voice sharpened. 'I don't want to find out you've been up to something sneaky while keeping me in the dark again.'

'You won't,' Azaki said. 'I promise.'

'Won't *find out?*' Falaïré's smirk widened beyond the flames. 'That's my Azi.'

He smiled. 'Don't worry about it now, Íri, just eat your fish and get some rest. I'll watch out for the first half of the night.'

Azaki lay on water, an endless, shining stillness. The surface smoked, thin, ash-pale wisps rose into a sky without sun, stars or moon. The vast emptiness drew back the numb, hollow ache of burnt groves, razed green, and Otuko's receding back.

'Falaïré?' he called. 'Are you there?'

Azaki pushed himself to his feet and stared about. *Nobody. And it's quiet.*

He started across the lake, step by step through the mist, gripped by soft melancholy. The gentle curve of the horizon stretched before him, his reflection matching his stride in the water below.

Azaki walked until his legs burnt. He called until his voice failed.

Is she... gone?

'It's an empty place, isn't it?' Falaïré stared up at him in place of his reflection, her dress of shadows curling off her skin like morning fog caught on the breeze. 'Do you like it, my Azi?'

'No.'

'No?' She rose out of the water to stand toe to toe with him. Her nose brushed his, her smirk a finger's width from his lips, silver flame and swirling shadow all he saw as she stared into his eyes. 'I chose it especially for you. It suits you.'

'It's too quiet. There's nothing here but me.'

Falaïré rested her forehead against his. 'And me...'

Azaki tore his eyes from hers and snuck a glance past her dark hair at the lake. *Still nothing.*

'Where's the trick?' he asked.

Her smirk widened and her dimples sprang to life. 'You've got to guess what this place is.'

'I *love* druidic spiritual stuff. Is it a lake? A sea? An ocean? A representation of my mind as come kind of metaphorical astral world?'

'I'm not the little Voréöeasiäki girl, my Azi,' Falaïré murmured, slipping her arms round his neck. 'You're not going to bait anything out of me so easily.'

'It was worth a try.'

'Of course it was.' She slid her fingers up the back of his neck into his hair and tightened her grip close to the point of pain. 'No hints.'

Azaki frowned. 'Is it even important?'

Her silver eyes shone with mirth. 'It might be...'

He stared, studying the humour in those eyes. 'But it's not, is it? There's no deep meaning at all. You're just messing with me.'

Falaïré laughed. 'If you can't find any meaning, then there's no meaning. Still, you were too quick to decide. I was hoping to keep you guessing for a little while. It would've been funny.'

'Damn it,' he muttered. 'Now I'm always going to be wondering if you're just playing tricks.'

She leant her head into the crook of his neck, her breath tickling against his throat. 'They'll all have me in,' she whispered. 'Doesn't that make them important?'

'I suppose. The better I know you, the stronger the bond. That's useful.'

Falaïré slid off him like water. 'Useful?' The silver fire in her eyes froze cold as winter moonlight on mountain ice caps. *'Useful?'*

He grimaced. 'Is that not how it works?'

'Is that how you want us to work? Like those dry old books tell you? Like all the other Voréöeasiäki? A dead piece of wood to wave around like a crutch until you're so old even the slightest magic's beyond your grasp?'

'Are you... upset?'

Falaïré's lips flattened into a thin, wine-red line. 'There is no you,' she murmured. 'No you, no me, no I, not really. There's an us, a we. I thought we both understood that.'

His brow creased deeper. 'I do.'

'Do you?'

The dream faded to darkness.

'If all the green in the world is burnt.' Her soft whisper came right into his ear. 'When the little Voréöeasiäki girl turns her back on you. When your little raider friend leaves you. When the girl that saved you walks away. When the Voréöeasiäki, and the clans, and Anastagus, and everything is gone. If the world fragments are ruined, if the sun, stars, and moons fade, so this dark is all there is left. It will *still* be us.'

'I think we'd be dead.'

'That's better,' Falaïré murmured, threading their fingers together in the dark between them. 'We're one, my Azi. Together, for as long as we live. Remember that and there's nothing we can't do.'

An eerie stillness settled over him and a faint prickle crawled up his spine. Falaïré released his fingers, her slim shoulders tensing and her gaze sharpening.

Azaki opened his eyes in the dark of the shelter.

Íri's breathing came steady and sure beside him and as his eyes adjusted to the faint light of the red moon filtering into the tent, he made out the even rise and fall of her chest. Itaki balled himself up in his feathers between the two of them.

Silence coiled round their shelter from the forest outside.

We're not alone. The hairs on the nape of his neck rose and his heart picked up its beat. *Something's out there.*

He slid a hand across the ground until he found the warm wood of his thiokezöeasiä. 'Deceive, lady of lies,' he whispered.

His magic washed out through the wax-lined leather in a mist as thin and fine as grey silk. Five spirits hung within its snare.

He felt them surrounding their camp in a loose circle, creeping nearer through the night. *Hunted again.*

'They believe we're easy prey,' Falaïré murmured in his ear. 'Let their truth play into our hands, my Azi. One trick and the hunters find themselves the hunted.'

But what trick? Azaki took a shallow breath and slipped his falcata from its sheath, concealing the blade beneath his shirt and arm.

He rolled onto his side, covering Íri's mouth with his hand and shaking her awake.

She tensed and tried to sit up. He leant his weight on her shoulder and kept her down. 'Stay still and be quiet,' Azaki whispered. 'We've company.'

Íri's green eyes narrowed above his hand and he felt her lips curl back, baring the smoothness of her teeth against his skin.

'Sorry, had to make sure you didn't make any noise.' He grinned and pulled his hand away. 'No need for any biting, Íri. I don't think I'd be into that sort of thing, anyway.'

'Who's out there?' she murmured. 'How many?'

'At least five.' Azaki sat upright, holding his breath.

No sound came from outside the tent and the spirits he felt caught within his magic continued their slow approach without pause.

Íri stared up at him and chewed her lip. 'What do we do?'

Azaki wracked his brain. 'I'd guess they're raiders. The ones from Kogodakus's band who couldn't go back to their clans because they'd not proved themselves to Anastagus. I'll go out there looking unarmed and lure them into attacking. I can use the Lady's Veil and I've got my falcata hidden. After they reveal themselves, you can toast them with your thiokezöeasiä. Go for anyone with a bow or a sling first. Don't let them get away, Íri, or they'll terrorise anyone they find in the hope of proving themselves.'

'What about your thiokezöeasiä?' Íri hissed. 'And why does it have to be *me* who—'

'My thiokezöeasiä's too hard to hide.' He grimaced. 'I'm supposed to be a Voréöeasiäki. If I need my thiokezöeasiä to fend off a few tribute-warriors, then I might as well not have it.'

Falaïré huffed against the back of his neck and the wood cooled beneath his fingers.

Íri frowned and dragged her thiokezöeasiä out from under her blankets. 'What if they hurt you?'

Azaki shrugged. 'This is the best plan I have and there's not really any time to come up with a better one. Unseal your thiokezöeasiä and get ready.'

Right. Here goes. He shot her a grin and yawned as loud as he could, standing up and stomping his feet around inside the tent. Itaki cracked open an eye, fluffed up all his feathers, and closed it again.

'Lady of falsehoods, dancing in half-light, whispering softly, of shadows to the right,' Azaki muttered, threading the magic through the minds of the five he felt.

His magic brushed no others.

It's just the five. Good.

'Blaze, beacon of virtuous ire.' Íri folded her blankets aside and scooped Itaki into the corner. 'Be careful, Azaki.'

Azaki offered her half a smile, brushing back the flap of the shelter and stepping out into the night. The faint, fine, grey mist of his magic hung over the quiet swirl of the river and its soft wash against the pebbled shore like a veil of winter fog. He yawned again, picking his way over the stones to the edge of the river and standing over the water as if he meant to piss into it.

The five he felt caught in the web of his magic stopped their approach.

Don't hit me. Don't hit me. Don't hit me. Azaki held his breath. *I hate getting shot.*

An arrow flashed past his left shoulder into the river. A second hissed past his elbow and vanished over the far bank.

Azaki tugged the blade out from under his shirt and dived behind the boat. A wave of heat rolled across the campsite as Íri darted out of the tent. The leaves of the trees above his head smouldered, blackened, and curled. Screams rang from the forest a short way downstream and one of the spirits he'd snared vanished.

He poked his head over the edge of the boat and caught sight of Íri vanishing into the trees, bathed in a bright orange glow, her bare soles flashing in the moonlight.

Azaki felt for the threads of magic of his spell. He sensed two presences beyond Íri in the trees and two lingering at the edge of their campsite. 'Come out, come out, wherever you are,' he called, stepping out from behind the boat.

An arrow whispered through the charred leaves to his left and a shadow slid from the dark of the forest. A second stepped to join it. Uneven squares of flint glinted in the moonlight, sewn onto the upper limbs and torso of a stocky, thick-bearded clansman's shirt. Three upside down vees interlocked in a triangle were daubed across his chest in the same pale green as his eyes.

The Clan of the Three Peaks. He looks a lot stronger than me. Azaki advanced up the pebbles, peering past the raider at the slim shadow behind him.

A dark-haired, grey-eyed woman in black leathers stepped into the light. Blue woad ran across the bridge of her nose and white feathers dangled from her ears.

The Clan of the Whitehawk. She looks like less trouble.

'Tribute warriors.' Azaki stole another step away from the water. 'You must be desperate to attack druids.'

The woman's eyes strayed to the falcata. 'I remember you. You were one of us. From the Webbed Pit.'

'I was.' Azaki crept beyond the prow of the boat into space.

Orange light flickered in the trees past the shelter and another of the spirits he'd snared in the magic of his thiokezöeasiä disappeared.

'You had a thiokezöeasiä when you came back.' The woman exchanged a glance with her companion. 'How'd you get them to let you stay? Could we?'

Could they? Azaki turned it over in his head. *No. I was treated with suspicion and I've a thiokezöeasiä from the Heart-Tree. They've no chance.*

The man grunted. 'Anastagus didn't give us our marks. The Three Peaks won't take me back without good reason now. Whitehawk's the same.'

'The Voréöeasiäki don't know I'm not one of them.' Azaki's spell faded, the magic failing on their wary minds. 'You can't stay down south. Go back.'

'Not without a raiding prize to prove ourselves.' The man pulled a falcata from his hip. 'Your thiokezöeasiä or the girl's will do.' He leapt the gap between them and brought the blade down over his head.

Azaki side-stepped away, stabbing the point of the falcata into the back of the raider's knee, and twisting it. The raider screamed and crumpled to the floor.

That was easy. Like hunting a very clumsy mountain lion.

The woman lunged at him over the cold fire pit. Azaki got the falcata in the way of her knife and shoved her back. She cocked her head at him and span the blade on her palm, darting left. He raised his blade to parry, but she ducked, spun, and slashed low beneath his blade.

A line of fire ripped across his left arm just below the elbow.

Azaki hissed and clapped his hand to the wound, staggering back past the boat into the trees. Hot blood trickled through his fingers and soaked into his sleeve.

She came forward again and Azaki jumped back, letting the knife tip whisper past his chest and kicking her in the hip, sending her sprawling away over the roots. He stepped after the raider, falcata poised, but struck the faint shimmer of a ward and stumbled back.

'Why're you swinging that piece of metal, my Azi?' Falaïré murmured in his ear as the raider jumped to her feet. 'A single trick from us and she'd be helpless.'

Azaki scowled. 'We shouldn't need our best magic against a single tribute warrior.'

'We've other tricks for the unworthy,' she whispered. 'But better to live than risk everything for hubris. If we die, we'll have no fun at all.'

Azaki wrestled with his pride. 'I suppose you're right.'

He pictured himself stepping forward. A shadow of him rose from the mist hanging beneath the trees and advanced over the roots. He slipped off to one side of his echo, prowling along the tops of the roots. The raider turned to track his shade and Azaki drove the falcata through her ribs from behind.

'No,' the raider groaned, stabbing weakly back at him with her knife. 'No. Not like this. Estrif—'

Azaki twisted the blade, tugging it out with a soft, wet noise. The knife thudded into the dirt and the raider sagged over the roots, her gasps turning shallow. Blood pooled beneath her, black as ink in the moonlight.

'See,' Falaïré breathed, standing over the dying tribute warrior as the life faded from her eyes. Her dress of shadows bled into the mist of their magic like ink into water. '*See*. The truth has more power than swords or spells.'

Azaki allowed himself a small smile, but it faded as his eyes fell to the dead raider at his feet. *She's young. No older than Otuko or I.* He sighed and crushed a pang of guilt. *At least it was quick and kind. Better than being shamed and beheaded by her clan, or starving in the mountains.*

Falaïré circled the body, her bare feet tracking the edge of the spreading pool. 'We're not done, my Azi. The other raider still lives.'

'He's no threat.' Azaki pressed his fingertips to the throbbing, burning cut on his forearm. 'His leg's crippled. This is just a scratch.'

'A wounded beast will lash out,' she murmured. 'You know this.'

Azaki grimaced. The long, deep, white lines that ran from Utháki's shoulder to hip flashed through his mind. *True.*

'If you take risks, eventually they'll come back to bite you.' Falaïré reached out and cupped his chin, brushing his cheek with cool, damp crimson-stained fingertips. 'The little Voréöeasiä girl doesn't even know that raider's there...'

Azaki swallowed and glanced through the trees at the flickering orange glow. 'I know.' He wrestled with the stab of pity lodged in his breast. 'It's just—'

'It's the same, my Azi.' Falaïré's lips curved into a smirk, her hair fading auburn and her eyes flashing blue. 'It's always the same. Kill or be killed. Raid or starve. Lie or lose. The chance of having what we want... or the risk of losing it.'

Is it really always the same? He shook away old thoughts before they could seep to the front of his mind. *Only at its root. The rest is different every time.*

Falaïré laughed. 'Different faces. Different names. The same choice.'

Azaki resealed his thiokezöeasiä and she faded with the grey mist of his magic. He cast the Lady's Shroud, dragging the shadows over himself. Under the night sky, they flowed like water, easy as pulling up a blanket, and he crept back toward the camp beneath their veil.

The raider dragged himself along the pebbles toward the boat, leaving a trail of gleaming, wet stones. Azaki strode after him beneath his veil of shadow, placed one foot on the raider's back, and drove the falacta into his heart.

'Done.' He yanked the blade free and took a deep breath, ignoring the sting and throb of the cut on his arm. 'Kill or be killed. It is how it is.'

Over the tops of the trees a faint light began to rise. *Dawn. Good. Best to get moving and not sit around dwelling on things.*

He rolled the corpse of the raider over with a frown and a twist of guilt. 'Sorry. I didn't *want* to kill you, but you'd've killed me or Íri if you could. Even if I left you here injured, you'd've attacked someone else, or the wound would've festered and killed you anyway.'

Íri stepped out of the trees, a deep frown on her face and her thiokezöeasiä clutched in her hands. Thin red scratches peeked through the rips in her tunic over her stomach and side, and slim, crimson lines marred her legs and arms. Azaki glimpsed a hint of rose-pink where a tear ran across the curve of her breasts and dragged his eyes up to the sky.

'They're gone,' Íri's said, her tone bleak as bare scree slopes. 'Dead. I burnt them.'

'You did what you had to,' Azaki said. 'Nobody who knows what they're talking about would say otherwise.'

Íri's steps crunched across the pebbles toward him. 'Then why can't you bring yourself to look at me, Azaki?'

He forced a smile. 'I was trying to be chivalrous. Your tunic's got a few more holes in it than normal.'

A sharp intake of breath echoed across the campsite and Íri squeaked, her footsteps darting away into the shelter.

At least she's distracted. Azaki dragged the body of the raider behind a tree and kicked ash from the fire pit over the blood, stifling a grimace at the throbbing in his arm.

Íri rustled around behind the wax-lined leather, a faint, green glow emanating from the flap.

She came back out with her ruined tunic in one hand and her thiokezöeasiä the other, chewing at her lip. Her cheeks glowed red in the dawn light. 'How much did you see?'

Azaki chuckled and washed his falcata and hands clean in the river. 'Nothing you'd want to hit me over, I promise. I'd only stare at a girl dressed like that if I thought she wanted me to, especially a friend.'

Íri narrowed her eyes. 'I suppose that's probably true. If you were going to look, you'd have made some stupid comment, not pretended otherwise.'

'Exactly.' Azaki waved his left arm at her and winced as the throbbing peaked. 'I don't suppose your Gentle Palm can fix something like this?'

She strode forward and grabbed his wrist. 'I told you to be *careful!*'

'I was pretty careful,' he said. 'It's not too serious.' Íri touched her finger to it and Azaki flinched at the lance of pain that flashed through his arm. 'Hurts a bit, though.'

She scowled. 'I can't fix a cut as big as this with the Gentle Palm. Let me try something.' Íri closed her eyes and began to hum.

A faint green light flickered about her fingers as Íri ran a fingertip along the cut, wavering and dying. She growled. 'Shirt off.'

'What?' Azaki raised an eyebrow at her. 'Just because you ruined *your* tunic doesn't mean you get to steal my clothes. I only have one shirt.'

'Idiot.' Íri huffed. 'I've not finished this spell and I can't get it to work through the leather.'

Azaki pulled the shirt over his head and tossed it over the side of the boat. 'There you go, try not to stare too much.'

She snorted and touched her fingers back to the cut, it tingled like a dead limb and crept closed until smooth pink skin remained. 'I'd feel bad staring at you. It's not nice to make ugly people feel self-conscious about it.'

He laughed. 'Don't worry, I won't.'

Íri leant closer and peered at his upper arm. 'There are so many,' she murmured. 'I can feel them, the magic of my spell's drawn to them.'

'So many what?' Azaki glanced down at his shoulder.

'Scars.' Íri traced a few lines along his bicep.

'You can't even see them.'

'But they're there, aren't they?' Íri drew back. 'How many times have you been hurt?'

24

'They're just scratches.' Azaki grinned. 'Granted some of them came from some pretty large animals, but they weren't ever that nasty and I heal well. Utháki got clawed down the back by a wounded mountain lion once. The scars go all the way from his shoulder to his waist and cause him trouble in the cold. Otuko's got a matching pair of scars that look a bit like a crescent on either side of her right thigh. I'm the luckiest of the three of us.'

Íri let her magic fade away. 'How'd she get that scar?'

Azaki felt a little heat curl around his heart. 'A warrior from the clan took a shot at her as a joke. We laugh about it now, but a tiny bit higher and she'd not be able to have her grey-eyed babies at all. The fever she caught because of it nearly killed her, too.'

'Clearly you didn't look away from *her*, if you've seen a scar *there*.' Íri chewed at her lip. 'What happened to the warrior? Didn't your clan do something?'

'We were outcasts, so no. The clan didn't care and nothing was done.' Azaki shrugged. 'Wouldn't have made much difference, anyway. That warrior, Ulika, she'd really long red hair. Shortly after Otuko was hurt, another warrior came back from hunting and said he'd found a load of her hair caught in a tree. One of the holes the giant spiders lurk in was close nearby and nobody ever saw Ulika again afterward.'

Íri paled and pressed a hand over her mouth. 'That's *awful*,' she whispered. 'I mean, even knowing what she'd done, being *eaten*.'

'Ulika really wasn't a very nice person, though. It wasn't the first time she'd done something to one of us. In fact, I'm pretty sure she killed at least one other outcast.'

'Oh.' Íri scrunched up her face. 'Wait, didn't you say you nearly got in trouble with some red-headed woman you found attractive?'

Azaki grimaced. 'Same woman. Ulika heard about that and broke most of my ribs for daring to think about being with a warrior when I was just an outcast. That was before she hurt Otuko. I hated her after that.'

Íri's face darkened. 'Maybe it was the Spider who got her? If she kept hurting people who were part of your clan, maybe the Spider didn't like it and sent one of those giant spiders.'

'Maybe. I wouldn't bet on it, though. I can't imagine she'd care much.' Azaki pointed a thumb at the growing light over the trees. 'Best get ready for some more paddling, Íri.'

She nodded, tossed him his shirt, then slipped back into the shelter.

'*Maybe.*' Falaïré's soft laughter tickled the back of his neck and her fingertip traced a slick, hot line along his jaw. 'The Spider had nothing to do with it, did she, my Azi? Though I'm sure she watched on with a smile.'

'She hurt Otuko. She was going to hurt Otuko again. She got what she deserved.' Azaki crushed the tiny flicker of guilt. 'Besides, it was Utháki who hit Ulika on the head and threw her in that spider's hole, not me.'

Falaïré's smirk widened. 'True,' she whispered. 'But it wasn't his idea, was it?'

Four

A straight line of stone upon a mound of earth marked the Marsh Road's way south. The bog stretched away into the distance on either side, endless patches of murky water, reeds, moss, and small flitting birds. It thrummed with its own song, of frogs, marsh birds, and the snorting of small-footed, dwarf ponies.

'I miss the boat,' Íriniel moaned.

'How is walking so hard for you?' Azaki asked. 'I'd understand if you were carrying the heavy bag apparently holding all your worldly possessions, but *I am.*'

'I like reading, spell-crafting and napping, not trudging around in the cold.'

Itaki fluttered back on top of the bag. 'No, lazy chicken.' Azaki shook the bag a bit. 'You go fly.'

The bird turned around and rubbed its beak on the leather strap.

Íri laughed and stopped to lean on her thiokezöeasiä. 'He listens about as much as you do, Azaki. Let's take a break, then, just for a few minutes.'

'It's another couple of days to Bluecreek, Íri,' he said. 'If we keep stopping we'll never get there.'

She let out a little huff. 'You walk so fast we're going to get there a day early. We've a couple of minutes to rest. It'll be no good if I'm exhausted when we get there, will it?'

Azaki sighed and slid her bag off his shoulders onto the road. 'Fine, but not for long.'

'For a man from a clan who doesn't take slaves, you sure know how to drive them,' Íri accused.

'You'd make a rubbish slave, Íri. You can't even cook a fish.' He settled himself down at the edge of the road with Íri's bag as a pillow and closed his eyes to listen to her murmuring away.

The wind played across his face and the warmth of the sun soaked into his skin. *I'm going to miss this warm when I find a way back to Otuko and the Webbed Pit. Life's so much easier down south.*

He opened his eyes to find Íri humming to herself. 'Promise born of gentle spring, melodies of summer breeze, ailments and ills forgotten, wounds and aches replaced by ease,' she rhymed.

'Another new spell?' Azaki sat up, trying not to jostle a fluffed up and snoozing Itaki on his knee. 'The one for keeping you warm at night?'

Íri shook her head. 'The Caress of the Hearth, the unfinished one I used to heal your arm. It's for healing things that're more than just small cuts and bruises. I thought it'd be a good thing to be able to do, maybe if I'd known it before, Vogitakus or Tutakus might still be alive.'

'Maybe,' he said. 'It's good you know it now, though. I'm pretty sure Kogodakus shattered my shoulder when we fought and Valia the Creepy won't be about to heal it this time.'

'Don't call her that. She's not creepy.'

'You didn't see her fight Kogodakus.' Azaki shuddered. 'One moment it was all doves and wind chimes, the next it's ravens, shrill eerie whistling and deadly thorns. He was her student for years, in fact, I'm pretty sure he loved her, and she didn't bat an eyelash as he died.'

'Are you scared of her?' Íri laughed. 'You are, aren't you?'

'I think she might actually make me more uncomfortable than Anastagus.'

She scowled. 'Really?'

'You *know* Anastagus is bad news all the time he's there,' he said. 'With Valia, I sometimes forget what she was like fighting Kogodakus. Afterward, I find myself wondering if the heartless thing I saw is peering out through her eyes while she speaks so softly. I'd hate to learn someone I thought I was close to actually felt nothing for me like that.'

'That's just silly,' Íriniel said. 'She's *Valia the Peacemaker*.'

'She's as peaceful as winter cold: numb, heartless and lethal.' He stretched and yawned. 'Are you done with your rest?'

'I thought I'd wait for another minute or two. I want to talk to those people.'

Azaki twisted 'round.

A small huddle of soft-folk trudged towards them on the Marsh Road. They'd baskets and bundles piled upon their backs, crawling toward them even on the wide, flat stone road.

'Refugees from the raiders,' he said.

'They'll be headed to a hillfort, probably the Grey Stair if they're going north,' Íri said. 'They might know something.'

Something twitched in the reeds below. A long, slim, grey-green shape slid into the water.

'They might know what that is,' Azaki said.

'Estrif's Deer,' Íri replied.

'That is *not* a deer. It has scales.'

'*Estrif's.*'

'Should I be worried?' he asked.

The top the creature's head stuck out of the water as it slipped through the reeds. Its slitted eyes tracked them until it vanished into the rushes.

'There are loads of them in the marsh,' Íri replied. 'They're no trouble unless you get too close. I used to watch them with my father when I was younger.'

'They remind me of the giant spiders.'

'I'm still not convinced those are real.'

'Definitely real. I told you about the time Otuko and I nearly got eaten, didn't I? And what happened to Ulika, that red-haired warrior?'

Íriniel folded her arms. 'Yes. Otuko's a really good shot. Otuko hit it loads of times. Otuko's arrows bounced off the shell because it's tough as bronze. You lured it to the cliff edge. Otuko shot the web string off its abdomen so it fell off.'

'Well you didn't really do the bravery of my role justice, but that's more or less right.'

'It wasn't giant.'

'It was a baby, but if a baby's wolf-sized…'

'You've never *seen* a giant one.'

'Not up close. Most're in the Silk Gardens and caves at the base of the Webbed Pit, and you've got to be more than an outcast to go there. The rest dig and stay in those holes in the ground, but they're *big* holes.'

'Is Otuko a warrior?'

'Yes. She's finally a valued part of the clan, just like we always dreamt.'

'So it's like the tribes' rites of passage? She can now get married?'

I'd not thought about that. His stomach squirmed at the memory of the kisses she'd left him with. *Best to keep not thinking about it.*

He frowned. 'We don't really do marriage like you southies do, but yes. She's also free to live inside the clan's holdfast where it's safe and to use the resources of the clan instead of always fending for herself.'

'How can you *not* do marriage?' Íri demanded.

Azaki watched the huddle plod nearer. 'It's just words and promises. We do that, we just don't make such a big fuss over it. Chances are, if you're lucky and live 'til you're forty or fifty, you'll have four or five partners.'

'*Together?*'

'What? No, not at the same time, Íri.' He laughed. 'One after the other. People die, or change, or whatever.'

'So no vows to the Heart-Tree,' she murmured.

Azaki chuckled. 'Do you really think the Spider is going to hold people to their vows? Some make Estrif's blood promise to be loyal while they're together, but not many.' He frowned at his marked palm. 'I'd probably want to.'

Íri scowled and stood up to block the road. 'I doubt you'd find anyone down south who'd do that, so I hope Otuko doesn't mind cutting her hand open.'

He managed a grin over the butterflies swirling in his stomach. 'She stabbed herself through the tongue with a hot fishhook, I don't think that'd be an issue. In fact, she'd probably be pretty keen. She's never really been happy about the prospect of sharing so much as a mushroom with anyone outside of our trio.'

The refugees hastened toward them, stumbling along the road. Children, women, and elders, huddled beneath their cloaks.

No young men. Azaki peered into the group. *Not even one.*

'You going to the Grey Stair, Voréöeasiäki?' A woman in a brown cloak and tunic stepped to the front of their group. 'We'd welcome the company.'

'I'm sorry, but no,' Íri said. 'We're headed to the Beacon at the Edge of the World.'

The lines on the woman's face deepened. 'There're longships all over the lake. If you ain't bound by duty, you'd do better to come to the Grey Stair instead.'

Azaki stood up and set Itaki on his shoulder. 'We're meant to help the lighthouse. Besides, they won't see us.'

The tribeswoman tugged back her hood, revealing hair limed to its dark roots and one blue-dyed lock. 'Voréöeasiä magic... Ain't nobody from our village could cast real spells.'

'You're from the Oudi Tribe,' Íri said. 'Why're you going to the Grey Stair? The Oudi Tribe isn't part of the Neméstakus Confederation.'

'The raiders're going south, Voréöeasiäki,' the woman replied. 'There's big rivers to cross for us that way and I ain't keen to take the risk trying to cross that marsh. My father's family're from the Ithani Tribe, too.'

Azaki leant to Íri's ear. 'Who?'

'The Grey Stair is the refuge of the Neméstakus Confederation,' she whispered. 'The confederation's made up of the three tribes in the northeast, the Gatali, Vunti, and Ithani.'

'Ah,' he murmured. 'Soft-folk clans. One with a sickle sigil borders the Webbed Pit's territory.'

Íri nudged him in the hip with her elbow. 'That's the Vunti.'

The Oudi woman watched with wide eyes and a hopeful face. 'Please, Voréöeasiäki. We ain't got no defence.'

'The Marsh Road is safe,' Íri promised. 'We've seen nobody.'

Azaki nodded. 'The longships will be mostly about the beacon now. They've small crews, so a good number will be needed to lay siege to a big fortress. You've good odds of getting to the Grey Stair unseen if you're careful.'

'I see.' The woman shouldered her burden again. 'Well, I hope they're luckier than us.'

'Wait,' Azaki said. 'Where're the men from your village?'

'Gone.' Tears glistened in the woman's brown eyes. 'The raiders stole or butchered them. All of them.'

'I'm sorry,' Íri murmured.

One of the elders hobbled forward. 'They put them on one ship and it sailed north, Voréöeasiäki. My sons're on it. Where're they taking them? Do you know?'

A sudden din of questions exploded from the huddle.

The lucky ones got butchered. Azaki caught glimmers of hope in their eyes and felt a deep stab of pity. *They'll get no comfort from learning their fate.*

Íri bit her lip. 'I—'

'North, to their lands.' Azaki poked Íri in the back. 'Slaves.'

'They're still alive?' The lines on the woman's face lifted. 'Truly?'

'Yes,' he said. 'The clansmen are warriors, they need others to fish and farm for them. It's a hard life, but not so much worse than down here. They'll find families, have children, there'll just be more snow in winter.'

The elder sighed and squeezed his eyes shut. 'Thank you, Voréöeasiäki. I'm sure I ain't going to see my lads again, but at least I know they're alive.'

Falaïré rose out of the Oudi woman's shadow, her red lips curving into a smirk. 'Well done,' she whispered. 'Well done, my Azi.'

'Luck to you, Voréöeasiäki.' The woman pulled her shawl back up. 'Hope you're able to stop them from getting the lighthouse.'

They shuffled past and trudged on. Falaïré lingered on the road, strolling in a slow circle, her dress of shadow whispering across the stone.

'Slaves?' Íri rounded on him. '*They don't take slaves.*'

'No. Those men are tribute to Estrif, likely as not. There's a great shrine to him in the eastern mountains.'

'You *lied.*'

'They'll never learn differently,' Azaki said. 'Now they'll know their kin are doing well enough, instead of dwelling on the bloody death they'll actually meet.'

Her mouth opened and closed. 'But—'

'It's kinder, Íri. Trust me. Hurt like that festers into hate, and poisons your life.'

She chewed her lip. 'Just don't lie like that to me. I don't care if you think it'd be kinder, I'd prefer the truth.'

Azaki smiled. 'You'll only ever know the truth.'

Falaïré clapped her hands together and laughed. 'One as true as every other truth,' she murmured, her silver eyes shining with glee. 'Oh this little venture will be *such* fun for us.'

Five

Long-legged birds strutted across the mud flats stretching from the grassy road bank to the lake's edge, fluttering between puddles. Charred ruins rose on smoking wooden stilts above the brown ooze and beside a narrow, shallow river stood scorched walkways, burnt huts, and blackened, dangling ropes.

'Bluecreek.' Azaki spied low, curved shapes upon the mud near the water. 'Hopefully a boat survived.'

Íri stared around the ruined homes. 'How many villages like this are gone?'

'Probably a lot, especially as they're not raiding like they normally would.'

She let out a quiet breath. 'I don't understand why they do it. All these people who never hurt them, who *couldn't* ever hurt them.'

He shrugged. 'Same reason people do anything. They want to or they think they've got to.'

'But they don't!'

Azaki put a foot upon the burnt wood of the walkway and tested its strength. 'Most of them do, otherwise they'd be good as dead.'

'That can't be true.'

'Think about me, Íri. If I'd not been chosen by the Heart-Tree, what do you think would've happened to me? The Webbed Pit takes no risks with traitors.'

Itaki stuck his head past Azaki's ear. 'Íri,' he chimed. 'Íri.'

She scowled. 'But if they *all* chose not to?'

'Maybe, but how do they know everyone else will make the same choice? It is what it is. Thinking about how unfair it is will just drive you mad. Come on, let's go see if there's a useable boat.'

A long, straight sword stuck from the mud in the village square, gleaming between the fire-bared bones of building.

A southie blade. Azaki admired the handguard's two diagonal bronze spurs and boar's head pommel. *A nice one.*

Gold chain dangled over the guard and a small terracotta urn rested behind the blade.

He stepped over to the sword. 'Look. At least they took one of the warriors with them.'

Íri stared at the mud-stained blade. 'How do you know?'

'We don't leave good weapons without good reason. Someone died well enough to impress them and they left his blade here to honour it.'

'We?' Falaïré ran her forefinger down the blade's groove. A wet, red trail trickled down the bronze when she took her fingertip away. 'Are we going back to the little raider girl, my Azi?'

Not now. Azaki watched the crimson droplet dribble through the flecks of dirt into the mud. *We can't abandon Íri to fight a Companion and even with our power, the clan would still banish or kill us for our suspicious absence without both Utaki and Otuko's support.*

'But we will, won't we?' Falaïré whispered. 'Because the little raider girl saved a boy from drowning on hate.'

I owe Otuko too much to ever hurt her. Azaki brushed his fingertips over his lips and forced the image of her glistening tears from his mind. *I couldn't do it. Not for anything.*

Íri jumped down onto a scorched plank. 'What about the gold and the wine jar?'

Azaki caught her hand as she reached for the urn. 'I wouldn't.'

'Why not?' She let her wrist hang loose in his grip.

'It's an offering to Estrif. Given we're going to be pretty close to the world's edge, it'd be best not to offend him. I've already got one of the Voréoathoki out to get me thanks to *somebody*.'

Íri clenched her fist. 'The Heart-Tree would protect us, even if Crumbling Cliff Grove is close to the world's edge.'

He pulled her away along the ruin walkway toward the water. 'It's not worth risking it, Íri.'

Two halves of the nearest boat lay on their side in the lake weed and mud at the end of a long scrape mark. A deep white groove ran through the bare rock to the splintered hull.

'Well, that one's not going to float.' Azaki squinted at the broken keel of the next. 'And this one's missing some pretty big pieces too.'

'This must've been a powerful spell,' Íri said. 'The Companion?'

'Spell?' He shook his head and pointed at the deep gouge down the middle of the scrape. 'The longship did that with its keel. They've got soft bronze lining the bottom to stop stuff growing on them and destroying the ship. When the tide was higher, they rammed that fishing boat.'

'Oh.' She turned away to stare at the scrape mark. 'How'd you know that stuff?'

'All the clans know. They're pretty keen to trade stuff for lead to make the soft bronze.' Azaki picked his way round the holes in the walkway to the last boat lying on its side in the mud.

The lake's edge lapped at its barnacle-crusted hull and the mast ran under the smooth brown ooze.

'No obvious holes,' Íri said.

'Just a lot of mud.' He put his thiokezöeasiä down and dropped down onto the edge of the walkway to kick at the boat.

It wobbled and a small orange brown crab scuttled out of the boat.

'And apparently some shy wildlife,' Azaki said.

Itaki fluttered atop a piece of wreckage and watched the crab, tilting his head and craning his neck to track it across the mud.

'Not a toy,' Azaki told him. 'No chewing, it'll bite back.'

'Kick the boat over, then.' Íri dropped her bag down on the walkway with a thud. 'Do you know anything about how to sail?'

'No.' Azaki chuckled and shoved the boat the right way up with both feet.

It settled with a thick squelch. Mud ran down from the mast, dripping from the folded sail into the boat.

'I can navigate us,' he said, 'but we may have to figure the rest out as we go.'

'We're going to have to wait for the tide.' Íri watched Itaki fly to the top of the ship's mast. 'I don't know how long that'll be.'

'It's not that heavy.' He jumped down into the boat and plucked a coil of brown-drenched rope out. 'The mud's pretty smooth, too. I reckon we can drag it a couple of metres to the water.'

Íri watched him loop the rope round the prow and tie it tight. 'What else is in there?'

Azaki scraped around in the mud with his feet, turning up a pair of oars. 'Nothing I want to touch.'

'Can you scoop it out?' She set down her thiokezöeasiä and bag. 'I don't want to sail in all that.'

31

'You come scoop it out, Íri.' He tossed the rope up to her and kicked the mast. 'Everything down here seems sturdy enough. It's only got to get us to that grove, the Voréöeasiäki there must have a spare boat we can borrow.'

She held the rope with a grimace. 'It's… *slimy*.'

'You'll have to wrap it 'round your arm, otherwise it'll be too slippery to pull.'

'I don't want to,' Íri moaned, waving the end about between her thumb and forefinger. 'It smells bad, too.'

Azaki laughed and hauled himself back up onto the walkway. 'Give it here, then.'

She dropped it into his hands. 'You're going to pull it by yourself?'

'I'm going to pull the boat and you're going to push me.' He wrapped the rope round his arm. 'That way, Voréöeasiä Princess Íri doesn't have to get all dirty.'

She snorted. 'Touching you is worse, you're muddier than the rope.'

He grinned. 'But friendlier.'

'Just pull.'

Azaki braced himself and tugged as hard as he could, but the boat lurched forward less than half a metre. 'This is your fault for sitting on it, Itaki. You need to eat less, you chubby chicken.'

Íri wrapped her arms round his waist, put her shoulder into his back, and shoved him forward as he pulled. The boat slid forward over the mud with a dull swoosh and splashed into the water a few steps before they ran out of walkway.

Azaki tossed the rope down into it and collected his thiokezöeasiä. 'Grab your things, Íri.'

'Don't even think of putting me down in all that mud.' Falaïré stood at his side upon the very edge of the charred stubs of the walkway, the shadows of her dress bleeding down through the gaps in the wood, thick and dark as pitch.

He glanced back to where Íri was picking up her bag. 'You're as bad as she is.'

Falaïré laughed and ran a finger down his cheek. 'The only thing the little Voréöeasiä girl and I have in common, is you, my Azi.'

Azaki lowered himself into the boat with his thiokezöeasiä under his arm and released the sail from its ties. A brown, leather triangle with a stone-studded wooden weight at its base unfurled from the mast with a dull thud.

'Catch.' Íri dropped her bag down into his arms and jumped down next to him.

The boat rocked, sending ripples across the lake.

'Careful,' he said. 'I don't fancy swimming.'

'So how do we move?' she asked.

'In theory, the wind gets caught in the sail and pushes us forward.'

'The wind's coming from the wrong way,' Íri said.

'That's why I said *in theory*.' He gathered up the oars and sat himself down. 'Fortunately, this means I get to row again.'

'Row.' Itaki cocked his head down at them from the top of the mast. 'Row.'

'That's right, little monster. Row, row—'

Íri clapped her hand over his mouth. 'One more row out of you and it'll be swim, swim, swim.'

He spat the slimy, slick taste of mud out over the side. 'At least it's cleaner in the water.'

'You can't row all the way, anyway. We'd never get there in time.' She stared up at the sail. 'Where's that rope?'

Azaki tossed it up to her. 'Here. What're you going to do?'

'Tie the sail to one side.' She gestured in the air, then looped the rope through the end of the sail's wooden weight and tied it to the left side of the boat. 'Now the wind will catch it.'

He pointed right. 'But we'll go that way and—' he glanced at the sun '—we want to go toward the bright light in the sky.'

'But at least we're moving,' Íri said as the boat slowly began to drift to the right.

'The wrong way.' A chill crept over Azaki's toes. 'And we're leaking.'

'What?'

'There's water coming in. Very cold water. Though I suppose it'll at least wash the mud out.'

Íri growled and splashed her feet around. 'Excellent.'

'Okay. You bail, I'll hold the oar in the water off the back to steer.'

'Bail with what?'

Azaki grinned and stuck the oar off the back of the boat, leaning his weight on it to keep it in place. 'Voréöeasiä Princess Íri is going to have to get her hands dirty after all.'

The prow angled itself back toward the sun.

'That actually worked,' she said. 'Well done.'

The cold crept up to his ankles. 'Bail, Íri. We'll sink if too much water gets in.'

'Urgh,' she groaned, thrusting her thiokezöeasiä under his arm with his own. 'I wish my father was here, he'd just grow us a boat.' She blinked. 'Maybe I can burn the water off?'

Azaki laughed. 'We're standing in the water, Íri. You really want to boil it?'

'Oh.'

'Yeah. *Oh.*'

'Shut up, Azaki.'

He trapped the oar between the stern and his side and folded his arms. 'I will if you start bailing.'

She scooped a handful of brown water out with a grimace. 'It's *so* cold.'

'That's why we want it outside the boat.' Azaki peered over the side. 'We're speeding up a bit, though.'

'Well, that's good.' Íri raised her voice over the steady rhythm of splashing. 'This is not how I expected this to go.'

He laughed. 'Would you like something to take your mind off things?'

'Please.'

'Ok, then.' Azaki took a deep breath. 'Bail, bail, bail your boat—'

A handful of cold water splashed across his face.

'You know, I actually do feel better now,' Íri said.

He dried his face off on his sleeve. 'Well, the water's still rising…'

'So use the other end of the rope and tie the oar there, then help me.'

Azaki lashed the oar in place, tugging the knot tight, and tied their thiokezöeasiäki to the mast. 'If only we had a bucket.' He groaned at the sting of the cold lake water. 'You'd think whomever owns this nightmare would be used to bailing.'

His hands numbed after a few scoops of reeking water, but the brown line washing back and forth in the bottom of the boat didn't drop. Cold drops spattered across his face and over his shirt, caught on the wind when he threw the water too high.

Itaki fluttered down onto the side of the ship to watch them go, prowling up and down past their eyeline, skittering out the way of the water when they tossed it past him.

'How far's this island?' Azaki asked.

Íri peered over the side. 'If we rowed it'd take a couple of days, but at this speed… Maybe just the one?'

'Damn. That's still a lot of bailing, even if the wind holds.'

'Bail.' Itaki paused between them to preen his chest feathers. 'Bail.'

Íri snorted. 'Not so funny now, is it?'

'We'll roast him when we get to shore. You hear that, tiny fiend? You're going to be a roast chicken for real this time.'

'Bail,' Itaki replied.

'I am bailing,' Azaki muttered.

'Oh, look what I found?' Íri held up a brown lump.

'More mud?'

'No, you idiot. It's a bowl.'

'Handy.'

She grinned at him. Her teeth white as pearls beside the mud spatters. 'We can take turns with this. You first.'

He sighed and washed the mud off the bowl in the bottom of the boat. 'It's a baked clay bowl, so we'd best be careful with it.'

Azaki scooped water out over the side, settling into a rhythm in time with his breathing. The water line dropped until he could feel his toes once more.

When he stuck his head back up over the side, a small low blur rose over the lake in the distance. 'That it?'

'That's the big island behind the grove. Gull's Mound is much smaller. We won't be able to see it for a while yet.'

'Huh.' Azaki stared at the thin grey line. 'If they've raided Bluecreek, they might well've gone for the grove, too.'

She frowned. 'You think?'

'Definitely.' He pointed back over his shoulder. 'That woman said they were going south and there's not much lake left south of here. Not if I remember the map right.'

Íri wiped her hands on her tunic and pulled the map out of the top of her bag. 'You do. There's a few villages south, then the coast comes back up north toward the island the grove's on.'

'We may need your father.'

'You think they'd've managed to burn it?' Íri lowered the map, worry gleaming in her green eyes.

'There're twenty warriors in a longship, more than enough for two or three Voréöeasiäki,' Azaki said. 'Warriors aren't like the raiders we fought at the Heart-Tree. They'll be well-armed, well-fed, armoured, experienced, and they can all cast some spells. Even if Anastagus is saving his best for elsewhere, one of the keorl's leading the raid might be blessed by Estrif. Unless they're one of the Erudite or have a very powerful thiokezöeasiä, then a Voréöeasiä or two and a couple of acolytes stand no chance.'

'Gull's Mound is a long way south,' she murmured. 'All the Erudite are further north where we're expecting trouble.'

'Don't expect there to be anything left. Not unless they've got a Voréöeasiä with a very handy thiokezöeasiä.'

Íri stuffed the map back into her bag. 'I don't know who's there. I guess we check, then carry on.'

Azaki glanced at where he'd tied their thiokezöeasiäki. 'Speaking of thiokezöeasiäki. I don't suppose you've carried on being prodigious and discovered a more powerful ability like Kogodakus had?'

'No. Have you?'

'Also no. Which doesn't bode well should we find ourselves fighting a Companion, because Valia the Creepy isn't going to come save us this time.'

'And we will.' Íri frowned down into the water. 'Still, if one of us is going to get there, it'll be you.'

'Pretty sure it won't. I've no idea how it works. You know I don't understand all the spiritual stuff.'

'Liar,' she accused. 'My father told me how well you must really understand it to have awakened your thiokezöeasiä so fast.'

'I get some bits. Not this bit.'

'What *is* your thiokezöeasiä, Azaki?' Íri chewed her lip, tugging at the fingers of her left hand. 'Mine's my desire to protect and guide this world and its people. It's how I keep the pact the Heart-Tree chose me to uphold.'

Azaki glanced at the prow of the ship.

Falaïré smirked back. 'What're you going to tell her, my Azi? What part of your heart am I?'

He smiled. 'The truth.'

'Good thing you left your clan then,' Íri said. 'I've no idea how that would work, though. Mine and my father's are pretty straight forward. He wants to protect and guide life for the Heart-Tree and I'm not too different.'

Falaïré tipped her head back and laughed, prowling along the side of the boat to slide a hand 'round the back of Azaki's neck. 'The truth is never simple, not for those that understand it, but we don't need any more than we have. Trust the power of our heart and we'll have everything we'd ever want.'

'That doesn't mean there's not more,' he whispered.

'No… it doesn't.' She crouched down close to him and cupped his face in her hands. The mirth faded from her eyes, leaving them bright and cold as the white moon in winter. 'Don't go chasing it, my Azi. You don't need it. You won't want it. Together, we're already more than enough.'

'Azaki?' Íri poked him in the ribs.

'Sorry, lost in thought.' He watched Falaïré fade away. 'I'm not really sure what I'd have to do to get another ability.'

'Bond more.'

'Well yes, but how?'

'My father said it happens when your thiokezöeasiä bonds with another part of your heart. You just have to understand it like you did the first part. If the Heart-Tree allows, it'll develop.'

'More troubles of the heart,' Azaki groaned. 'Fantastic. I still don't even get the first bit.'

'It might not happen. My father only has one ability.'

'So his thiokezöeasiä embodies one part of his heart, but really strongly, and Valia the Creepy's thiokezöeasiä embodies two parts.'

'Yes.'

'Can it be more than two?'

'I don't know. Maybe. How many things can be *that* important to you, though. I—'

'Bail,' Itaki chimed, flapping his wings in the spray.

'You bail… *bird-brain,*' Íri retorted.

Azaki poked the bowl with his toe and watched it float across the boat to bump against her ankles. 'Actually, Íri. The talking chicken has a point and it *is* your turn.'

Six

Smoke drifted across the horizon; a long, faint, grey column before a bright midday sun. Gulls shrieked and circled through it, white specks in the grim sky. The curve of the land rose and fell beneath, creeping closer with every second.

Azaki sniffed. 'Woodsmoke.'

Íri's shoulders sagged. 'The grove's gone, then.'

He ducked the billowing sail and scanned the waters. 'I don't see any longships.'

'They've probably gone already.' She clenched her fists. 'More innocent people dead.'

'Easy, Íri.' He put a hand on her shoulder. 'Let's see what we find. If you get Itaki down from on top of the mast, I'll steer us ashore.'

She stared up at where Itaki sat above the sail bobbing his head in the wind. 'Come down here, chicken!'

The bird poked his head over the edge to inspect her.

Azaki laughed and handed her a small apple. 'Try this. He thinks with his stomach.'

Íri waved the fruit in the air and Itaki fluttered down to land on her shoulder. She snorted and let him gouge a chunk out. 'You weren't kidding, were you?'

'That's how I teach him stuff.' He unlashed the oar and steered the ship towards the small, smoking island. 'Give him food if he does it.'

'Isn't he going to expect food every time he does it?'

'Probably, but he always expects food, the greedy rascal.'

Azaki guided the ship past where the lake foamed over brown rocks and weeds to a shallow beach of pebbles. The hull scraped up beyond the tug of the tide, shuddering over the banks of rocks, and he jumped out onto the stones. Gulls overhead screeched and screamed, and beyond the bank at the beach's end, small flames flickered among blackened bushes and burnt grass.

'Carefully, Íri,' he whispered, drawing his falcata. 'It's still burning.'

She lowered herself over the side and Itaki fluttered from her arm to his shoulder. 'Blaze, beacon of virtuous ire.'

Azaki picked his way across the pebbles, scrambling up the bank, the din of the seagulls drowning out the grating stones under his heels. Warmth crept through the soles of his boots as he stepped onto the grey ground. Small yellow flames licked at the trunks and branches of the charred trees, and smoke curled off the fading white embers lying among the ashes.

'Azaki.' Íriniel pointed her thiokezöeasiä at a lump beneath the grey.

He motioned her back with the blade. 'I'll poke it. If it goes for me, toast it before it gets me, please.'

She nodded and the orange glow of the pyramid at her thiokezöeasiä's crown intensified. Azaki jabbed the tip of his blade into the lump.

It remained still.

He rolled it over with his foot.

A blank, pale face stared up at them. Torn, dark-stained flesh gaped in the hollow of the throat.

'Dead,' Íri murmured, covering her mouth with her hand and turning a little green.

'Very.' He unearthed half a thiokezöeasiä from underneath the corpse with his foot. 'A Voréöeasiä, too.'

'There're no swords?'

Azaki glanced around. Two other lumps loomed on the far side of the clearing and the smoking ash stretched away beneath charred trees.

'No warriors died here.' He strode across and unearthed the other two.

They rolled awkwardly, dragging and flopping, their bones grating and grinding.

'These two weren't killed by blades or arrows,' Azaki said. 'Two many broken bones.'

'Spells?' Íri sidled over, her hand pressed over her mouth. 'It looks like the aftermath of something like Tutakus's spell.'

Azaki nodded. 'But much stronger.' He blew the ash off the dead girl's chest and flicked her hair away. His stomach churned at the unnatural angles her ribs stuck out at. 'Pretty much everything's broken. That red-headed warrior who broke my ribs did it with the blunt edge of my sword, but they didn't look half as bad as this. Something shattered her ribs like you'd break the ice stomping on a frozen puddle.'

'The Companion, then?'

'I think so. No warriors from my clan could cast spells like that, though a keorl or eorl might. You need a thiokezöeasiä or a blessing from one of the Voréoathoki to be powerful enough to break bones like this.'

Íriniel frowned down at the dead girl and chewed her lip. 'We should bury them.'

'With what?'

'We can't just leave them to be eaten by things.'

Azaki scraped a chunk of earth out of the ground with the side of his foot. 'You dig, then. I'll find us a boat. Don't take too long, we need to get to the lighthouse as soon as we can if we want to save it.'

Íri blinked. 'I'll help you look. If we find one, we can put them on our boat and sink it. That'll be quicker.'

'To be eaten by the fish.'

She squirmed and turned a little green. 'Maybe we should bury them.'

'Worms will still eat them,' Azaki said. 'That's what happens to dead things. They get eaten.'

Íriniel huffed and folded her arms. 'Fine. The fish, then. I like fish.'

'Someone will probably eat the fish that eat them.' He laughed as she turned even greener. 'Right then, let's go round to the south side, that's where I'd keep boat.'

'Why?'

'Because the mainland's closest that way.'

A short-masted, blue-painted ship bobbed beyond a narrow pier of planks and dry-stone wall. Above them the gulls swirled and shrieked. Itaki hunched on his shoulder, tracking the large birds drifting across the sky.

Azaki stepped up onto the pier. 'This'll do. We can sail to the beacon in a day or so, depending on the wind.'

'More,' Íri said. 'It's going more against us this time.'

'Look at you, half a sailor already.'

She brandished her fist.

'Alright then.' He jumped off the pier onto the pebbles. 'You grab your stuff, I'll—'

'Beseech, pleas of a gentle tongue,' a girl's voice cried.

A cold fist of fear clamped about his heart, catching the breath in his lungs; it hung over him, coiled and hooded, pinning him in place like a mountain hare beneath the shadow of a hawk. Azaki's heart began to pound and his palms grew slick with cold sweat. The falcata slid from his numb fingers, clattering onto the pebbles, and Itaki fled beneath the pier.

'This is false feeling, my Azi.' Falaïré caught his chin with a soft, warm hand. Crimson stained the fingers of her other hand, dripping from the line of her last knuckle onto the pebbled beach. 'Call for me, we'll show them fear.'

'Deceive, lady of lies,' Azaki gasped, twisting around on the stones as mist rippled from his thiokezöeasiä's crown.

Íri stood frozen on the pier, clenching her fists. Every muscle stood out on her jaw and her eyes were squeezed shut so tight tears slipped from the corner of her eyes.

A girl in a soiled white tunic brandished her thiokezöeasiä at him, its ring-shaped crown glowing red as the second moon. 'You're Voréöeasiäki,' she whispered, crumpling to her knees. 'Oh, thank the Heart-Tree...'

The crimson light faded as her thiokezöeasiä slid from her fingers and rolled onto the pebbles, The fear slipped away and Azaki's breath returned.

The girl clutched at his leg with one hand, shaking from head to toe. Her breath rushed like the wind and beneath the blood-stained tatters of her tunic's right sleeve, he glimpsed a seared, weeping stump.

Azaki clasped the girl's shaking hand and drew her to her feet, resealing his thiokezöeasiä. 'Íri?'

She stumbled to his side, her gold hair sticking to her sweat-beaded forehead like spider thread. 'What was that?'

'Her. She attacked us.' He glanced at his falcata lying on the pebbles. 'Probably thought we were raiders. Can you heal her?'

Íri stared at the seeping stump of the girl's arm. 'I can't heal that. Nobody can.'

The girl whimpered. 'It hurts.'

Íri took her hand between both of hers. 'I can heal it a bit, but your arm…'

'It's gone,' she whispered. 'I know it's gone. He said he was going to keep it when he cut it off.'

'Who?' Azaki asked. 'The Companion?'

Íri glared at him. 'Don't worry about answering that. What's your name?'

'Siade.' She took a shaky breath. 'It wasn't the Companion. One of the raiders did it. He said I'd make a good raiding prize. He was going — he was going to—'

Azaki's stomach churned. *There's always a few who go too far, like Atíko.* He forced the ugly heat of his anger down. *Raiding's about surviving. Even the Voréoathoki don't know how Atíko became an eorl.*

'It's ok,' Azaki said. 'Íri's going to heal your arm as best she can, Siade.'

He stepped back and retrieved his blade as Íri murmured her spell, green light flickering about her fingers. The weeping burn turned to a shiny, ropy scar.

'Better?' Íri asked.

'It doesn't hurt.' Siade touched her fingertips to it and held her breath. Tears leaked down her face. 'How can I be a Voréöeasiä now?' she whispered. 'I'm *useless.*'

'You still have your thiokezöeasiä.' Azaki picked it up off the pebbles. 'The heart the Heart-Tree chose you for is still here. You'll learn to get by.'

Siade's lip trembled as she mopped her tears away. 'At least it was just my arm,' she whispered. 'The raider was going to do worse to me before the other one killed him. All my friends…'

Azaki glanced at Íri, guiding Siade to sit on the edge of the pier with him. 'The other one?'

She took a deep breath. 'I was out here when they attacked. The raider came after me, and — and he cut off my arm. He pinned me down, but the other man killed him.'

'The Companion?' Íri asked.

'No. I didn't see anyone with a thiokezöeasiä. The one that saved me pushed the raider into the water and left me.'

'He just left you?' Azaki craned his neck to look up and down the beach. 'What about the other raider?'

Siade nodded. 'There was a lot of blood from — from where my arm was... taken. I had to burn it closed with a branch from the fire. The other raider never came back out of the water.'

Íri placed her hand on the girl's shoulder. 'Do you want to stay here?'

She shook her head so hard Azaki feared her neck might snap. 'Are you going back to the Heart-Tree? Could I get there in a week?'

He frowned. 'I doubt it. We're headed to help the Beacon at the Edge of the World anyway.'

Siade stared down at the pebbles, pressing her hand against the stump of her right arm. 'I have to come with you.'

You do? Unease gnawed at Azaki. *Why so suddenly sure?*

'You could stay here,' he suggested. 'Soekus the Lifebringer will come to regrow the grove. The raiders aren't likely to return.'

'No,' Siade said. 'I need to come with you.'

'Why do—'

'Okay.' Íri plucked the thiokezöeasiä from his hand and returned it to Siade. 'We'll get our things. You wait here, Siade. Your boat's much better than ours.'

Azaki dropped back onto the pebbles and waved a small apple in the air. 'Itaki!'

The parrot fluttered back to his shoulder from beneath the pier, burying his head in the crook of Azaki's neck and grabbing the apple.

Íri smiled as Itaki nibbled at it, spilling apple bits all over Azaki's shoulder. 'At least someone survived.'

He glanced back at where Siade swung her legs off the side of the pier and stifled a prickle of unease. 'Be careful of her, Íri.'

'She's one of us.'

Azaki rubbed at his chin with the back of his hand. 'Her story doesn't make any sense. I don't think her injury and being here by herself has been good for her.'

'Of course it wasn't *good for her*,' Íri snapped.

He tapped her on the forehead. 'I mean up here. Just be careful around her. She's likely not thinking straight.'

Íri folded her arms. 'Fine. I'm not tying her up or anything, though.'

'I wasn't suggesting it.' Azaki sighed. 'Do you want to go grab our stuff from the ship and keep an eye on Siade? I'll deal with the dead.'

She pursed her lips. 'Try and be respectful about it, Azaki.'

Falaïré leant out of the shadow of a smoking tree as Íri passed it by. 'Don't trust her,' she murmured, her silver eyes shining with mirth.

'Íri won't betray me.'

'The other little Voréöeasiä girl, not your one,' she whispered. 'We saw no sword or marker on that beach. No warrior died here.'

Azaki shrugged. 'If he just drowned somehow, they might've not marked him, but it is *very* unlikely any longship warrior would've drowned in waist-high water a few steps from the shore.'

Falaïré laughed. 'Is that all? Does the rest of her story sound like truth?'

'Shouldn't you know?' He grinned and drew lines in the ash with his toes. 'No. Fire-sealing her own wound with one hand after losing so much blood and not even scorching the rags of her tunic sleeve? A warrior betraying his clan and Anastagus to save an enemy who's already likely bleeding to death? None of it makes sense. She's still scattered, or...'

Falaïré smirked, sliding closer until the tattered shadows of her dress brushed against his legs. 'Or...?'

'Or she's lying,' he muttered. 'But I can't imagine why she'd lie, I think she's just scrambled, like Utháki was after the mountain lion ambushed him.'

'Watch her, my Azi. *Wait.*' Her fingertips drew hot, red lines along the inside of his scarred palm. 'Nobody can hide what they desire forever. When she tries to betray us, we'll strike first. Otherwise...'

Azaki stared down at the three dead bodies in the ashes of the grove and sighed. 'Let's hope whatever it is Anastagus has in mind doesn't work out, Otuko's waiting for me.'

'Be patient, my Azi.' Falaïré slipped a step closer and the sweet scent of red athoëasirki drifted to his nose. 'Trust our heart. They won't ever separate us. They won't ever leave us behind.'

Azaki snorted. 'You know I don't have any idea what that means, Falaïré.'

A sharpness flitted through her eyes and silver light rippled beneath her dress of shadows like lightning amidst the thunderclouds. 'I'll show you. You'll understand.'

Seven

A towering wall of dark-leaved, white-flowered bushes rose over him up toward the twin crescents of the moons, sharp and sweet to his nose. Dark roots sprawled from the ebony trunk, the sapling that'd become his thiokezöeasiä rising from the one before him.

This is the grove I was left in. Azaki stared around. *Before it burnt.*

The first Voréöeasiä he'd fought stepped out beside the sapling. 'The Heart-Tree chose you for a reason, raider.' His eyes blazed in a face as pale and dead as the corpses on Gull's Mound. 'She let us *die* for a reason.'

Others dragged themselves from beneath the dirt. Tutakus and Vogitakus struggled up, their wounds dark and skin pale, and Prasatakus clawed his way out of the ground. Bone glinted in his throat beneath a matted tangle of grey hair and his thin smile showed only the bloody stub of a tongue.

Azaki stepped back, thudding into the hot, smoking timbers of the burning hall. Darkness yawned beneath his feet.

'Azi!' Otuko slipped from the leaves, his spider-silk cloak draped over her arm. 'Come on, Azi. Come home. Come back to me. I *saved* you. You can't leave me. It's not right.'

'You promised, Azaki.' Íri burst through the white flowers. 'You *promised!*'

I did promise. He took a deep breath. *But I owe her everything.* Azaki took a step toward Otuko. *Everything.*

She crushed her lips against his in a tang of salt. 'You're back, Azi,' she whispered, sweeping the spider-silk around his shoulders. 'You're back.'

Otuko slipped from his arms and the cloak slid through his fingers like smoke. The worn, horn hilt of her hunting knife stuck from his ribs, quivering with each beat of his heart.

'Why?' Azaki touched his fingertips to it and stared into her grey eyes, a hot, tight tangle of thorns coiling 'round his heart. 'Why, Otuko?'

'Sorry, Azi,' she murmured, twisting the blade. 'The clan comes first.'

The ground vanished from beneath his feet, pitching him into the black beneath.

He jerked awake as the boat dropped off the crest of a wave, licking the salt spray from his dry lips with a grimace. *Not a fun dream.*

Íri held her thiokezöeasiä off the bow, the crown glowing bright as molten bronze and pushing back a swathe of fog. Siade hunched into a ball by her feet, peering through her fingers into the swirling white. Dark bags hung beneath her eyes and her cheekbones jutted from her face like she'd spent a winter in the mountains with the other outcasts of the Webbed Pit.

'We're nearly there,' Íri called. 'The Refuge ought to be somewhere ahead of us in the mist.'

Azaki staggered to his feet. 'The what?'

'The Refuge. It's the only safe landing place on the island, everywhere else is sheer cliffs and rough waters.'

'The longships' crews will know that.' He gathered his thiokezöeasiä up, straining his eyes into the fog. 'Where's Itaki?'

'Sulking.' Íri shot him a long look and lowered her thiokezöeasiä, letting the glow fade. 'He got covered in spray and now he's sitting at the back of the boat with his feathers all fluffed up.'

Azaki chuckled. 'I'll get him and take the sail down.'

'Why?'

'Because they'll be watching the harbour if it's the only way in or out. We'll have to slowly sneak through.'

He tucked his thiokezöeasiä under his arm and furled the canvas in, lashing it securely to the mast. Itaki prowled the top of a box at the back of the boat, chewing splinters off its corners.

'Hello, little monster.' Azaki held out his hand. 'Come on up.'

Itaki lunged at his fingers, beak agape.

'Oh, so it's going to be like that, is it?' Azaki dug through his pockets for a walnut. 'There, bite that instead. I need my fingers.'

Itaki grabbed the nut in his toes and nibbled at it.

'Azaki!' Íri hissed from the prow. 'I think I saw something.'

He chivied Itaki onto his shoulder and bounded back to the front of the boat. 'Where?'

'It's gone now. The fog moved.'

'Clearly this place was poorly named,' Azaki muttered. 'The whole point of a beacon is that you can see it.'

Íriniel laughed and pointed a finger at the bright white glow shining in the fog above them. 'You can.'

Azaki craned his neck. 'Looks like the sun to me.'

'That's Akrotera's Torch, the light of the beacon.' Íri waved a hand behind the boat. 'The sun's somewhere over there.'

So that's the famous shrine to the Voréoatho of Light. Azaki stared through the fog toward the Lady of Radiance's light. *Eorls of the Webbed Pit have died trying to conquer this place.*

'We're pretty close, then,' he said.

Siade gasped and ducked down. 'There's another boat.'

He twisted 'round.

The shadow of a longship's curved prow reared from the mist off to one side.

'Blaze, beacon of virtuous ire,' Íri muttered.

'No.' Azaki shook his head. 'If the Companion's on there, we'll be in serious trouble. They'll tear this ship apart with that spell he used at Gull's Mound Grove.'

'We're already in serious trouble,' she hissed.

Siade whimpered and snatched for her thiokezöeasiä, tears springing up in her eyes.

'I'll conceal us.' Azaki blew the mist from the crown of his thiokezöeasiä. 'Deceive, lady of lies,' he whispered.

Falaïré draped herself along the edge of the boat, trailing her fingertips through the fine grey mist washing through the fog as their magic ensnared everyone about them. 'What shall we show them, my Azi?'

Íri clenched her fists around her thiokezöeasiä. 'Azaki?'

He grinned. 'Don't worry. They're not going to see us.'

The tar-stained head of the longship's prow loomed from the grey, its deep-carved eyes weeping a stream of red paint down its neck to the bronze ram gliding just beneath the water. Azaki watched it drift past, holding his breath. A score of warriors peered into the fog from over the shields lining the ship's side, bars of red woad marking their faces.

Sworn to Estrif.

Siade moaned. 'Beseech, pleas of a gentle tongue.'

Cold fear crashed down on him like an avalanche, pinning him in place. Íri froze and cries of terror rose from the ship beside them in the fog.

Azaki wrenched his gaze up to Falaïré's silver eyes and ripped himself free of terror's weight. His magic unravelled beneath the fear of the warriors, worn away like woollen thread between rough stones. 'Seal your thiokezöeasiä, Siade,' he hissed. 'You're giving us away!'

She clutched it to her chest and closed her eyes.

He tugged his falcata free and hammered the blunt edge into the side of her head. Siade dropped like a stone.

Íri shuddered and staggered across the deck toward them. 'What did you do?'

'Put her to sleep.' Azaki stared after the shadow of the longship and sheathed his blade. 'She was about to give us away. Her thiokezöeasiä must be something to do with the lore of influence. Both times she's unsealed it she's been scared and we've then both felt it too.'

'We probably should've made her stay at Gull's Mound and wait for my father.' Íri tugged Siade upright against the side of the ship, brushed the dirt off the loaned green tunic and placing her thiokezöeasiä across her lap. 'She's not sleeping or eating much. It's not good for her to be out here.'

Or for us. Azaki studied the still girl out of the corner of his eye, ignoring the dull ache creeping in as the longship approached the edge of his magic's reach. *Something's not right with her.*

'Keep an eye on her,' he said.

'I want to get off this boat,' Íri moaned.

'Me too. I can't even sing row your boat or the longships will hear.'

'Thank the Heart-Tree for small blessings.' She pressed green-lit fingers to Siade's brow. 'There, so she doesn't wake up with a huge lump and a headache after you clobbered her over the head.'

'It was that or get caught in a pitched battle.'

The fog opened up beyond the prow. A spread of wet, dark, stone docks, boats dragged high above the tideline, and short, squat buildings rose out of the grey.

'The Refuge,' Íri whispered. 'Let's find somewhere to stick the boat.'

Azaki nodded and started towards the stern. 'Let me know which way to turn.'

He unlashed the rudder and waved his thiokezöeasiä at Íriniel, grimacing as the ache sharpened.

'Left,' she called.

Azaki shoved the rudder. 'Far enough? Too far?'

'My left, Azaki…'

He shook his head and tugged the rudder back toward him. Íri gave him a thumbs up from the prow and they bumped to a halt against the dock.

'Be careful,' Azaki whispered, releasing his magic. 'We don't know what we're walking into.'

Íri nodded and splashed a handful of water over Siade's face. She awoke with a whimper and a gasp, scrabbling for her thiokezöeasiä.

'It's on your lap,' Azaki said. 'We're at the shore.'

'You hit me.' Siade touched her fingers to her temple and slid back from him.

'You panicked and unsealed your thiokezöeasiä, it was going to give us away...' He shrugged. 'Sorry.'

'We don't know what's up ahead.' Íri jumped over the side of the boat onto the quay. 'We need to be quiet.'

Azaki tapped Itaki on the beak. 'Hush.'

The parrot bobbed his head and buried his face in Azaki's neck.

Siade edged across the gap and onto the dock. 'Where're we going?' she whispered.

Azaki vaulted up and slipped the falcata from its sheath. 'Up. Until we find someone.' He peered up the street from the docks.

A sheer wall of grey rose from the cobbles into the fog.

'That way seems to end with a cliff,' he said.

'There're two parts to the town. Westhil—' she pointed her thiokezöeasiä left '—and Easthil.' She pointed her thiokezöeasiä right. 'The beacon's built on top of the cliff, but while the door's straight ahead from us, you've got to go round the cliff through Westhil to get to it.'

He frowned. 'Left or right, then?'

'Left,' Íri said. 'Crumbling Cliff Grove is part of Westhil, too.'

'Left it is.' He held a finger to his lips and prowled along the cobbles.

Siade stumbled after them, her arm wrapped around her chest and her eyes darting to and fro between every shadow. The street steepened, broken windows and smashed doors gaped in small stone houses lining the smooth cobbles.

'Not a good sign,' Azaki muttered, glimpsing ransacked rooms filled with nesting gulls.

'Halt!' A voice called out of the fog. 'State your names.'

He glanced at Íri. 'Mind providing some light?'

She rolled her eyes and extended her thiokezöeasiä. An orange glow rose from the crown and heat rolled off it, sweeping the mist aside. Azaki shuddered as its warmth soaked into him and released a long breath.

A head height stone wall met the street with a large wooden gate and stone parapet. Rusty helmets and spear tips poked over it.

'Voréöeasiäki!' Another voice called. 'They're Voréöeasiäki!'

'Let them in,' the first commanded.

The gate rumbled and creaked open.

A man armoured in a bronze-banded brown leather cuirass and a bronze helm with a trailing blue crest stepped out from a crowd of grizzled men in leather shirts toting boathooks and cleavers. Three leaping dolphins marked the scarred, crescent-shaped shield on his arm and and the bronze greaves and armguards he wore. 'Our message got through. Thank the Voréoathoki.'

Íri hastened forward.

'Someone's did.' Azaki caught Íri's arm and tugged her back toward him. 'Do you have a name?'

'Omotakus.' The man pulled his helm free of long, dark hair. 'Vil Omotakus. I'm the son of one of the elders.'

'Vil means he's the leader of the warriors,' Íri whispered in his ear. 'It's a title given by the Volōvyf to those who're considered great warriors, like warlords and champions.'

'Azaki.' He gestured to Íri. 'This is Íriniel and our companion is Siade. We found her at Gull's Mound Grove. The longships razed it. She's the only survivor.'

Siade shuffled behind Íri's shoulder.

'I'll take you to your grove,' Omotakus said. 'Getitakus will be pleased to see you. His magic's been very good to us for years, but it's not enough to stop their warriors.'

Íri strode after him, Siade stumbling on her heels. 'We need to send a message, Vil Omotakus.'

'We've birds that'll fly to the Grey Stair, if it's important,' Omotakus said. 'I heard it's now under siege too, though.'

So that's where the other clan's warriors must be.

'If that's the best we can do, we'll do it,' Íri said.

'Then tomorrow, I'll see it's sent,' Omotakus replied.

Azaki stretched his legs to catch them up. 'What's going on here?'

'The Volōeskryf have come.' Omotakus jabbed a thumb back at the gate and his blue eyes turned tired. 'There're twelve longships out there, all with a sword on their sails. I've held Westhil, *just*, with Getitakus' help. Easthil's a ruin. People kept trying to come here in small groups, but the raiders jumped them. Nobody's made it here 'til you.'

Azaki tilted his head to one side. 'So there's about two hundred and forty warriors, plus Anastagus's Companion.'

'Haven't seen much of their commander, if that's who you mean,' Omotakus said. 'They've been patient for the most part, more focused on taking everything we had to leave outside the walls than storming the gate.'

He led them down a maze of smaller streets until the houses ran out before a cluster of trees and brush. The beacon rose over them on their right, tall as the sky, with walls as high as the cliffs and four towers at their corners.

Why are they all out here, when they have walls like that to shelter behind? He frowned. *Whomever's in charge isn't very smart.*

'Crumbling Cliff Grove,' Íri murmured. 'This one's still here.'

'Getitakus,' Omotakus called. 'I've good news.'

A quiet rustle came from the trees and a heavyset man in a dark brown tunic stumbled through the brambles. 'Omotakus, my friend. Who're they? Voréöeasiäki?' A great grin cracked across his face. 'Thank the Heart-Tree, my acolytes and I aren't best suited to fighting.'

Íri folded her arms. 'Defending the world is a Voréöeasiä's duty, fighting or otherwise.'

Getitakus squinted at her. 'You're Soekus the Lifebringer's daughter. What're you doing here?'

'Defending the world, apparently,' Azaki said. 'Or at least this stronghold.'

'The Hands of the Heart-Tree sent us to relieve the siege,' Íri said.

'Can you?' Omotakus asked.

Azaki raised an eyebrow. 'Can we what?'

'Help us.' Omotakus rubbed at his unkempt facial hair. 'You're both half my age.'

'We fought Kogodakus,' Azaki replied.

Falaïré laughed in his ear. 'Fought and *lost.'*

Getitakus' jaw dropped. 'Kogodakus? He's dead?'

'Very.' Azaki fought down a shudder. 'Valia got him in the end.'

'Poor boy. He saved my acolytes for me, you know. A long while back now. Got his face cut open rescuing them from raiders. Anastagus messed his head up.'

Valia the Creepy messed his head up first. Azaki put a hand on Íri's arm as she opened her mouth.

She shot him a sharp look and turned back to the other Voréöeasiä. 'Can you look after Siade?'

Getitakus' eyes strayed to the stump of the girl's arm. 'Of course. You're all welcome to stay with us in the grove, there's just about room. We've not much left, we gave most of what we had to the people of the beacon, but we're happy to share.'

Omotakus spun his helm round on his hand. 'My father and the elders will want to speak with you. If you've come to help us.'

'There's nothing for them to say,' Azaki said. 'They clearly have no idea what they're doing.'

Omatakus fumbled his helmet, catching it by the blue crest a few inches above the ground. 'What?'

'You're defending a lot of easily climbable wall against a smaller and vastly more skilled enemy.' Azaki pointed at the beacon. 'You should all be in there, behind those much bigger walls, with everything of value, starting with the food.'

'And abandon our homes?' Omotakus shook his head. 'Never.'

'You're spread too thin to defend against them.'

Omotakus shouldered his crescent-shaped shield. 'We outnumber them ten to one.'

'The mountain lion doesn't count the rabbits in the burrow,' Azaki quipped. 'Your numbers are spread round the walls, anyway, so they won't count for much.'

Omotakus rubbed at his ragged beard and glanced between the walls of the beacon and the direction of the gate. 'I'll talk to my father and the other kerkam, I hope our elders listen.'

'You probably should.'

Íri stared at Azaki as Omotakus hurried away. 'How do you know that stuff?'

'Because it's obvious stuff,' Azaki replied. 'You saw the warriors on that longship, they're not going to have much trouble fighting scared men armed with boathooks unless the men with boathooks have nowhere to run to and are all in the same place.'

She chewed at her lip. 'I guess.'

Getitakus nodded. 'He's probably right. I should've thought of it myself, but I've never been much of a warrior.'

Azaki's eyes slid to the cluster of wooden bubbles at the crown of the Voréöeasiä's thiokezöeasiä. 'What can you do?'

'Shaping and sealing's my craft, lad,' Getitakus said. 'I've been trying to offer some protection with it, but I've never done much fighting before. The Volōeskryf don't normally bother us here.'

'And your acolytes?' Azaki glanced past him into the trees.

'Manastakus and Nemotakus. Good lads. Like sons to me. They're the only two survivors of the dozen children Kogodakus tried to save for me a decade back. They've a few spells, but like me, they've not done any fighting. I was hoping that other Voréöeasiä would come back after he went north, but we've not seen him. His thiokezöeasiä would've been real handy.'

'What could he do?' Íriniel asked.

'Controlled the water,' Getitakus said. 'Wrapped it all around himself, then directed it wherever.'

Azaki groaned. 'Toga the Sour.'

Íriniel elbowed him in the ribs. 'It's good to hear he's okay. He lost friends when Kogodakus attacked the Heart-Tree and left afterward.'

'He sailed north, toward either White Creek or Grey Sails Grove.' Getitakus's face turned dark. 'I don't know what's happened to him.'

'He's probably sulking somewhere,' Azaki said. 'I can't imagine he couldn't hold his own or at least escape with so much water everywhere. Tomorrow, we'll deal with these elders and get everyone safely inside the lighthouse's walls, then think about some kind of plan.'

'We've some food going.' Getitakus pointed into the trees with his thiokezöeasiä. 'Not loads, but enough to warm you up. Fish stew. The lads and I've got pretty good at making it, if I do say so myself.'

'More fish.' Íri sighed. 'I should've known.'

Azaki chuckled. 'It wasn't exactly going to be rabbit out here, was it?'

'A girl can dream.' She folded her arms. 'I hope the stew's got seaweed in it. I dislike it and it's green, so you ought to hate it.'

'Thanks.' He picked his way along the slippery wooden planks into the trees after Getitakus. 'Come on, Itaki. We'll find you some food, too. Maybe *you'll* like seaweed.'

Eight

Seven wool-robed, leather-capped old men slouched in beaten wooden chairs beneath piles of furs. They sat amidst stacks of parchment, worn tables, and flickering candles, encircled by four small glowing hearths.

'Voréöeasiäki,' the eldest-looking croaked. 'Well met. The kerkam will hear you. My son tells me you think we ought to retreat to the beacon itself?'

'Yes,' Azaki said.

The wind cut through the room, snuffing the candles out around its edges and buffeting at stacks of paper piled across the tables. A pair of bronze scales tables creaked back and forth upon the centre table.

'You can't be serious?' The endmost kerkam clutched at the brown furs on his lap. 'Voréöeasiäki, we can't just *abandon* everything!'

Íriniel pinched the bridge of her nose. 'Stubborn old men, Heart-Tree save us,' she muttered.

'Weaver of fallacies, spinstress of sedition, lull them with your whispers, allay their suspicion,' Azaki whispered, pushing the magic of the Murmuring Spinstress out from him, letting it soak into the elders like blood into dirt.

Íri sent him a sharp look as his magic washed back off her wary mind.

Azaki shot her a grin. 'It's not about abandoning. You've already lost all of it. If you want to die here as well, then stay, but nobody else will be if they've any sense.'

The kerkam gaped.

Omotakus's father leant forward, picking a scab on his cheek with yellow nails. 'What makes you think they're already lost, Voréöeasiä?'

'How long are the walls?' Azaki asked.

'They encircle the whole town, as they're meant to.'

'And how many people who can fight are there to stand on them?'

The elder peeled a piece of scab off his face and chewed on it. 'Enough to watch everywhere. We kerkam are not such novices at this as you think, Voréöeasiä.'

The spell's not going to help. Azaki gnawed the inside of his cheek and let his spell fade. *They're accepting what I'm saying, but it's not making them agree. The magic only stops people connecting dots or picking holes, it doesn't change their minds.*

'Not enough to fight off a proper attack,' he replied. 'You've no warriors, just armed townsfolk. Those warriors' *lives* are bloodshed. They care more for pleasing Estrif than they fear dying.'

'We have you,' one of the kerkam rasped. 'Voréöeasiäki are more than a match for raiders.'

Íri shook her head and stepped forward. 'Their leader's a rogue Voréöeasiä. Azaki and I will have to fight him, and Getitakus and his acolytes can't fight so many warriors alone.'

The yellow-nailed one bobbed his bald, blotchy head. 'Vil Omotakus has warriors of his own. The guardians of Akrotera's beacon.'

'How many?' Azaki demanded.

'Twenty,' Omotakus's father said. 'Enough to hold the gate.'

'Forget about gates and walls.' Azaki pointed out toward the lake. 'You have numbers and you have a couple more Voréöeasiäki, those're the only inherent advantages you have. The rest can be turned against you.'

The bald one coughed into his hand and smeared his palm on his furs. 'How would you use those advantages, then, Voréöeasiäki?'

'We're not fighting them in a gate if we can avoid it, that's for certain,' Azaki said. 'A narrow gap like that takes away our advantage of numbers. No, you take all the food you have and fall back to the lighthouse. Those walls are high, steep, and short, unlike the town walls, which are low and long. We'll have several times as many men waiting at the top as they can send to climb up. If they can't breach the gate, they'll struggle to get in.'

Omotakus's father raised his hand. 'I'm convinced. We saw how many lost their lives holding the gate at Easthil when they first attacked and barely a single enemy fell. A repeat could be an even bigger disaster.'

Three other hands went into the air.

The leftmost coughed. 'When—'

Omotakus burst through the doors. 'They're here!'

'Start moving everyone now. Make sure the food comes or you'll all starve.' Azaki grabbed Omotakus's arm. 'Where?'

'The Westhil gate, the one you entered through,' Omotakus replied. 'We're trying to shoot back, but none of our missiles are hitting their mark.'

'Let's go.' Azaki waded through piles of paper to the door. 'Before it's too late.'

Íri darted to his side. 'Is there a plan?'

'Try not to die and don't let them through the gate.'

'Another gate,' she murmured. 'Siade and Itaki are at the grove with Getitakus and the acolytes. Should someone get them?'

'We'll let them have a break. Siade especially.' Azaki nudged her shoulder with his. 'I'll watch your back, like last time.'

A score of dead townsfolk lay sprawled in the yard inside the gate. Arrows sprouted from their necks and faces, their red-spattered gull feathers fluttering in the breeze. Omotakus let out a low groan and balled his fists, raising his shield over his head.

Azaki jumped up the steps and crouched down behind one of the crenelations. An arrow screeched off the stone above his head, flicking away into the yard. Íri flinched into his lap and a wave of agony and nausea swept over him as her weight landed on his groin.

'Ow,' he hissed. 'Get your elbow out of there. I might want to have children one day.'

She turned pink and scrambled over his legs to sit next to him with her back against the wall. 'Sorry.'

'Otuko's so not going to be happy if you've damaged something important.'

'I thought she was just your friend?' Íri asked.

He twitched and swallowed the knotted tangle of heat curling round his heart before it caught too tight a hold of him. 'She wants grey-eyed babies, I'm an important fall back option for her.'

'Well, she's going to be disappointed. You still squirm at the very mention of babies.'

Azaki chuckled and peeked 'round the rampart, glimpsing a couple score of warriors flitting among the ruined houses. The sun flashed on the bronze squares and bands reinforcing their leather cuirasses.

'This one's on you, Íri,' he said. 'They're out of my range.'

An arrow flashed through the gap in the crenelations and thudded into the wooden shop sign over the yard.

'Blaze, beacon of virtuous ire,' Íri murmured.

A bright orange glow lit the inside of the gate and searing heat washed over him. The hazy ripple rushed from the walls, scorching clansmen from the houses and setting the ruins alight.

Íri's lips twisted. 'I need to be stronger,' she murmured. 'I — I don't want to *burn* them. If they have to die, I want to be able to do it quickly.'

'Maybe when you've bonded more with your thiokezöeasiä.' Azaki watched them stagger out of the smoke, patting flames out on their leathers, casting shimmering ward spells to shield them from the heat. 'For now, we do what we must to survive.'

'And what can *we* do, my Azi?' Falaïré whispered, trailing her finger down his cheek. 'Are we just going to watch?'

'For now,' he muttered below his breath. 'When we're in the beacon and I've a good guess of what they'll do, we'll be sneaky. Until then, we'll keep what we can do secret. It'll be most effective that way.'

'Sneaky.' She raised her right hand, splaying her fingers out and flexing them. Red dripped from their tips onto the stone. 'We do like sneaky.'

It's what we're best at. Azaki rubbed at his cheek. The back of his hand came away smeared crimson.

He glanced at the glowing crown of Íri's thiokezöeasiä. 'Íri?'

'They're coming back,' she said. 'They went in the water.'

'To protect against your heat. Smart.'

Íri scowled. 'It won't help them for long.'

Azaki pulled himself up to look. 'They're going to rush us. The water will give them a few extra seconds to get to the walls before you can toast them.'

Omotakus clambered up the steps, a dolphin-pommelled longsword in hand. 'Did they go?'

'They're coming back,' Azaki replied. 'Get everyone up on this wall or behind the gate. Keep them close together, if everyone's all bunched up, they'll not be able to just cut their way through.'

Yellow light flashed past his shoulder and burst in a cloud of thick, dark smoke above the yard.

'And stay down,' Íri said.

'I'll help them aim,' Azaki said. 'Lady of falsehoods, dancing in half-light, whispering softly, of shadows to the right.'

His illusion threaded through the senses of all save one. A brown-cloaked figure at the back stopped dead and looked straight up at him.

'I think I found the Companion.' Azaki watched the man raise a thiokezöeasiä over his head and whirl it in a circle. 'Yeah, there he is.'

The wind returned, shrieking up the street, driving the smoke up against the wall, throwing arrows and stones aside and fanning the flames of the houses burning either side of the street.

'Damn this wind,' Omotakus growled from behind his shield. 'It's stopping us firing back.'

'That's why he's doing it.' Íri strained her heat haze against the wind. 'His wind's stripping the heat of my magic away before it reaches anything, Azaki. The further from him his magic gets, the stronger it is. Mine's the opposite.'

I know. He stared down at the distant figure of the Companion, who had his thiokezöeasiä balanced upon his shoulder. *He's barely trying, too.*

The warriors howled their battle cry and hurled themselves across the last stretch of cobbles, the hazy shimmer of simple wards flickering in front of them. They hammered into the gate and dust rose up from beneath the parapet.

Azaki frowned. 'Can you keep the Companion busy, Íri?'

'I've got him.' She pushed her heat haze into the wind with bared teeth. The glowing embers of the burning houses brightened and the roof of the nearest crashed down into the flames. 'I'm sure he knows if he gets closer, he loses the advantage.'

'Don't push yourself too far. Just keep him out there so Omotakus and I can make sure the gate holds.' Azaki tossed his thiokezöeasiä to Íri. 'Try not to toast it.'

She gaped. 'Don't you think you might *need* it?!'

A dull crash reverberated through the gatehouse as Azaki dropped off the wall and snatched his falcata from its sheath. The first warriors dragged themselves through the splintered gap between the split doors, forcing the gate open. They cut their way into the yard, spilling out across it in a spray of blood and flashes of yellow and orange spells. Screams and howls rang out.

If they're not stopped here, they'll massacre everyone. Ice crept down Azaki's spine and trickled through his veins. *And if I don't stop them. Nobody else will.* He hardened his heart. *Kill or be killed again.*

Falaïré's laughter drifted to his ears.

Omotakus let out a raw yell and drove his shield into the side of the nearest warrior, hacking at their head. The woman ducked and grabbed his shield, swinging him round and away into the crowd of townsfolk, ripping the crescent shield off his arm.

Azaki circled the nearest warrior on the cobbles. His dented bronze helm loomed above Azaki's head, crimson smears stained the nicked, scratched bronze cheeks like streams of tears, and bronze-studded strips of leather armour covered his broad shoulders, waist and thighs.

'Oh.' The warrior tossed his axe from one hand to the other. 'A druid with one of our blades. Unusual. None of the others had blades.'

'If you ask nicely, maybe I'll let you take it to the Sword Spring,' Azaki quipped.

'That's not how it works.' The warrior lunged.

I know. Azaki cut the axe away and thrust.

The warrior turned it aside off an outstretched palm and a shimmering ward. Green light crackled on his fingers and flashed past Azaki's shoulder into the crowd of fishermen. Hot wet spattered across his back and the stink of burnt meat stung his nose.

He threaded Azaki's Web through the senses of the warriors near him, closing the snare until the phantom cobwebs smothered their noses and mouths, tightening over faces like a noose around their necks.

The warrior in front of him stumbled back, clawing at his face with one hand, and Azaki swung the falcata with all his strength. The warrior tore free of his spell and flinched behind his axe. Their weapons rang together, jarring Azaki's arm, but he clung onto his with numb fingers as the axe skittered away across the cobbles.

A second flash of green light hissed past him to scorch the stones of the wall.

Azaki drove the falcata through the man's eye and ripped the blade free, spattering thick, slimy grey over his hand. 'One for Estrif.'

To give him a reason to stop the Lady of Lies killing me here at the world's edge.

Another warrior stepped over the body as it thudded to the floor. A line of red woad ran down her face over her right eye and loops of bronze chain gleamed round her sword arm. Short lengths of battered links dangled from her leather belt to cover her upper thighs and waist. Battle lust gleamed in her blue eyes.

Azaki stepped aside from her swing and the ground beneath his feet slipped away. *Damn.* He caught hold of the wall and threw himself aside.

Her blade drew a line of sparks where his head had been.

Azaki took a deep breath and stopped the next strike on the falcata's edge, stepping back over a headless fisherman. He checked another blow, then another, trying to twist his wrists over her blade to get the advantage.

She matched every move, turning her wrists to counter his and stepping with him back and forth through the bodies. The tip of her falcata sliced past his ear, etching a line of fire across his cheek. He clenched his teeth and thrust at her stomach.

A hazy ward sprang up on her arm and she trapped his blade between it and the bronze chains covering her thigh, spinning 'round and wrenching it from his grasp.

She's way too good. Azaki ignored the chill knotting in his gut and took a deep breath. *Magic is my best bet.*

He scowled and smeared the blood off his cheek as the woman weighed his brother's blade on her palm. 'Not ideal.'

She laughed. 'I'll take it to the Sword Spring, young warrior. You're brave and you fought just about well enough.'

Azaki swayed away from the first falcata, but the second drew a line of fire down his side.

He clutched at the searing pain with one hand and stumbled back, his breath trembling. 'Queen of whispering webs, upon your throne of lies, gift a blade of shadow, and revel in their cries.' The slim, long blade formed on his palm.

He flicked his wrist forward as she strolled toward him through the corpses. The knife hit her just above the collarbone and sank in halfway to the hilt.

She yanked it out and hurled it back. The hilt bounced off Azaki's hip and burst into shadows as he released his spell.

'Damn,' the warrior hissed. Red sparks guttered on her fingers as she groped at the blood spurting from her wound like wine from a torn skin. 'Estrif... must like you...'

I kept all my promises. Azaki tugged his falcata out of her limp hand, pressed a palm against his ribs. Heat soaked through to his fingers and his shirt clung to his skin. *And I made sacrifices.*

Red pooled across the yard where the fight spread out from the gate. Dozens of dead townsfolk sprawled upon the ground, a handful of blood-spattered, woad-marked, warriors lying among them. Omotakus wrestled with a warrior a few paces away, their blades locked between them, and shouts and cries rang from beyond the splintered gates.

We can't hold them. Azaki's stomach churned. *And we can't outrun them. The townsfolk need time to get out with the food.*

'Which leaves only one choice,' Falaïré murmured. 'Something must make sure these warriors don't pursue us.'

'Íri!' Azaki waved the falcata at the orange glow amidst the smoke streaming over the wall and picked his way through the slippery red pools. 'Back to the beacon!' He drove the falcata through a gap in the bronze plates on the back of Omotakus's assailant and hissed as the cut down his ribs flared with pain. 'We need to go. More're coming.'

Omotakus glanced through the gate and paled, clenching his fist about his red-smeared longsword. 'They'll just follow us.'

We need to delay them.

'Either use our power and reveal it to the Companion, or find another way,' Falaïré whispered in his ear. 'Sometimes, we've no choice but to betray others to reach our goal, my Azi.'

It's not a betrayal, it's a sacrifice. He gnawed the inside of his cheek as Íri darted down the steps from the wall. His ribs burnt and stung and throbbed, harrying his thoughts like a pack of wolves. *We've no choice. Our power's the only thing left up our sleeve.*

Falaïré's laughter drifted from the back of his mind.

'Go, Omotakus.' He cast Azaki's Web over all the warriors nearby and stumbled through the fray toward the beacon. 'Go now.'

'The Companion's coming.' Íri shoved his thiokezöeasiä back into his hand and froze. 'You're hurt,' she whispered, touching her fingertips to his blood-drenched side.

'Good thing you can patch me up, then.' He staggered into the street away from the yard. 'But first you need to collapse these houses and block them off.'

Omotakus gasped. 'But the rest…'

Azaki's stomach churned and he took a deep breath. 'They'll either die fighting alone there, or die fighting with everyone else up here if that Companion catches us before we're back in the lighthouse. We need time to bring some of the food in. We've no choice if we want to save the lives of everyone else here.' He turned to Íri. 'Do you trust me?'

She clenched her fists and closed her eyes, slamming her thiokezöeasiä down on the cobbles.

She does. Azaki sagged.

A wave of heat haze hammered into the houses. Beams glowed and burnt, streaming smoke and crumbling to ash, stone and tile spilt over the road like an avalanche as the houses collapsed. Flames sprang up through the wreckage.

'Of course she trusts us,' Falaïré whispered in his ear. 'You can always trust the truth.'

Omotakus stared into the fires with tears in his eyes as screams rang out from beyond the rubble and smoke.

Íri slipped an arm under Azaki's shoulder and took some of his weight. 'Come on,' she murmured. 'We — we have to go.'

He forced a grin. 'Last time *I* had to carry *you* to bed.'

A hint of a smile passed across her lips. 'I'm not going anywhere near your bed.'

Omotakus stumbled after them. 'Smoke,' he muttered, pointing his longsword across the city. 'That's Crumbling Cliff Grove.'

Íri growled. 'They got in. My father will have to regrow it.'

'This is why you should've retreated to the beacon.' Azaki sheathed his falcata, hissing as the hilt grazed his ribs and a flash of pain seared through him. 'You can't defend everywhere on the town's walls at the same time.'

She sighed. 'I hope Itaki, Siade, and the others at the grove are ok.'

'Itaki'll be alright, he'll just fly away.' He touched the fingers of his cleaner hand to his side, spotting a faint, orange glow upon his fingers. 'Did you do something, Íri?'

'No.' She frowned at the gentle light wrapped about his hand. 'Maybe? Does it hurt?'

He shook his head and watched the glow creep up his arm. 'It's quite pleasant, actually. Warm.'

'Your face has healed.' She sealed her thiokezöeasiä and the orange glow faded away. 'You're still bleeding, though. A lot.'

'Both things to worry about when we're all safely back inside.' Azaki limped toward the gateway into the beacon, casting a glance at Íri's sealed thiokezöeasiä, where slim, hairline cracks now traced the length of the previously smooth wood. 'Probably not even that exciting, just another thing your father helped you do faster than everyone else.'

'If you weren't injured, I'd hit you,' Íri said.

'You hit me all the time.' He staggered through the gate and slumped against the wall, poking at the throbbing cut down his ribs. 'This stings so much, it's so *annoying*.'

Omotakus strode across the short space between the wall and the lighthouse and up the steps into the beacon.

Íri peeled back his shirt and winced. 'I can see your ribs.'

Azaki peered down.

Faint white bone peeked through here and there at the deepest point of the cut.

'Oh, so you can,' he muttered. '*Fantastic*.'

'Is he going to be okay, Íriniel?' A sweat-stained, sooty-faced Getitakus loomed over the two of them, reeking of smoke. 'None of us are any good at healing, I'm afraid. We can only manage bandages and poultices…'

'I'll heal him, it's not *too* deep,' Íri said. 'What happened to the grove?'

'Their Companion has an apprentice of some kind,' Getitakus said. 'He led some warriors around the walls to attack us. We got away, but the grove…'

'How powerful is he?' Azaki poked at where his bared ribs gleamed.

'Stop poking.' Íri slapped his hand away and narrowed her green eyes. 'Promise born of gentle spring, melodies of summer breeze, ailments and ills forgotten, wounds and aches replaced by ease.'

A bright emerald glow suffused her fingers and the flesh knitted itself back together over Azaki's ribs.

The burning, stinging pain faded, and he released a long sigh. 'That's significantly better, Voréöeasiä Princess Íri. Thank you.'

Pink crept up her cheeks. 'Flattery isn't going to make me forget I owe you a punch.'

Getitakus leant on the wall beside them. 'I don't think the apprentice is sane. He stood there in the middle of the fight practically dancing and nearly got hit by half a hundred spells. His thiokezöeasiä's not even crowned.'

'Good,' Azaki muttered. 'One Companion's more than enough. I've a nasty feeling they're all going to be some of the Erudite like Kogodakus turned out to be.'

'All healed.' Íri ran her fingertips over his ribs until he squirmed. 'Are you ticklish?'

'Yes. A bit.' His palms itched and tingled, the white line on his right hand fading from his skin. 'The sacred tree in the grove's gone.'

Ice trickled down his spine. *Which means the Mistress of Whispers can reach me.*

Getitakus blinked. 'How'd you know?'

Íri followed Azaki's gaze to his unmarked right hand. 'He knows. How'd you escape?'

'The grove and the nearby houses caught fire, so they can't get through the street, but it'll spread to the whole town at this rate. I used my thiokezoeasiä to sealed up a bubble of air around us like I do for the pearl divers. We went out through the smoke when it got thick enough to hide in,' Getitakus said. 'Not sure how Siade got out, but she did. She's inside the beacon, up on the north wall away from all the fighting.'

'A mysterious escape.' Falaïré slipped from the shadows of the gate, her silver eyes glowing with mirth. '*Again*.'

Azaki nodded. 'We'll have to check on Siade.'

Íri blinked. 'I'll check on her. You scare her.'

'I'm not scary.'

'You are to her. Leave her be. She needs to be left to heal from her ordeal.'

Falaïré's lips curved into a smirk and she leant in to trace her hot, wet red-stained fingertips along the line of the cut Íri had healed. 'When she betrays us, we need to be ready, my Azi. Strike first... or be first struck.'

Azaki bounced his palm on the points of the eight tines of his thiokezöeasiä's crown and smiled at Íri. 'You go, then, but be careful.'

The wall dropped away in a sheer line, built in white, strong stones set so close Azaki couldn't find the lines where they joined without running his finger along them. As the sun rose toward its zenith, the stones drank in its light, hot beneath his hands and sparkling like the rare opal stones from the Webbed Pit's depths.

Omotakus stared out at the smoke rising from Westhil, his helm soaking in the sun on the crenelations and Getitakus sweated on Azaki's left, mopping his brow with the brown sleeve of his tunic and squinting into the sky. Itaki snoozed in the sun on Azaki's shoulder, watching Getitakus with a lazy eye.

A tall figure bounded from Westhil, waving a white rag on a branch and both his hands in the air. 'Hello! Helloooo! I've just been sent ta chat!'

Omotakus scowled and leant over the parapet, the bronze bands on his cuirass scraping across the stone. 'Is he mocking us?'

Azaki studied the figure with a frown. 'That's the apprentice, isn't it?'

Getitakus nodded. 'I watched him flail about and fall over his own feet for nearly five minutes before we fled the grove. Not sure how he survived. I reckon he might've been blessed by one of the Nerevoréoathoki, sometimes these warriors are.'

Not Estrif. Azaki peered down at the apprentice. *He's not got the glowing red face marks.*

'He's not exactly the stuff of nightmares.' He strolled down the steps to the yard. 'Guess I'll go chat.'

Omotakus hurried after him, one hand on his longsword.

The apprentice swayed back and forth on his feet, tapping a short rhythm against his thigh. He held a twisted branch of pine, worn smooth beneath his fingers, but with bark clinging to its top. Bright blonde, near-white hair dangled over his clear, sky-blue eyes.

Azaki stopped just out of his reach. 'Hi.'

Itaki opened one eye. 'Hi.'

'Hello, birdie.' The apprentice grinned. 'Nice ta meet ya!'

Itaki bobbed his head in time with the man's bouncing, gnawing at his toes.

'Itaki's vocabulary is quite limited,' Azaki said. 'If you're going to offer terms of surrender, he's probably not going to be trusted to make a deal. We'll all be much less keen to surrender for a walnut.'

The apprentice squinted at him and grinned. 'I can probably get ya a lot of walnuts. Ya had ta leave most of the food because of the fire, so ya must be hungry.'

The corner of Azaki's mouth twitched. 'Unfortunately, no number of walnuts is likely to bring about our surrender.'

'Unless I've enough ta fill up the lighthouse, then ya'd have ta surrender... or eat enough of 'em fast enough ta avoid being buried.' The apprentice bounced from one foot to the other. 'Master Duratakus would really like ya ta surrender.'

'We're not going to,' Omotakus gritted. 'We know what happens to our people when they surrender to your sort.'

The apprentice waved his hands in the air. 'Not ya, just him. We only want Azaki Kathal ta surrender.'

Azaki's stomach twisted itself into a tight knot. 'That's mildly concerning. Anastagus mentioned me, then?'

'Couldn't say.' The apprentice beamed. 'Master Duratakus doesn't take me ta see his master. He tells me it's because I'm quite possibly the least intelligent creature on this whole world fragment.'

'Harsh. Does he at least teach you?'

'He showed me how ta dress myself like a proper apprentice.' The man nodded and hopped his weight from one foot to the other. 'I miss all the bright colours I used ta wear, but at least I now look like someone Master Duratakus might be proud of. He said so. Word for word.'

'So apart from my personal surrender, was there anything else?'

'Master Duratakus wanted me ta say something. He made me learn all the words.' The apprentice bounced on the spot, frowned and stuck out his tongue. 'Even the greatest of the Voréöeasiäki's warriors won't be able ta stand against Anastagus, no matter how many innocents they draw inta their war or how much blood they spill for their Voréoatho.'

'Carefully chosen words,' Falaïré murmured, bringing a wash of familiar sweetness with her.

No doubt. Azaki sought for some sign of guile in the apprentice's wide grin and bright blue eyes. *He seems like he's just a mouthpiece.*

'Okay,' he said. 'Well, if that's it...'

'Bye, Azaki Kathal. Bye, nameless, rude man. Bye, birdie. See ya all again soon!' The apprentice waved to each of them and bounded back into Easthil.

Omotakus watched him go. 'What an idiot.'

'I'm sure this Duratakus wouldn't have chosen him for no reason,' Azaki said.

'He's no match for you, surely, Vil Azaki. You slew two warriors in single combat without even using your magic staff.'

Vil. Azaki strained to remember what Íri had said, but drew a blank. *Oh well. It's probably a good thing, so at least something came of me nearly dying.*

He drifted back in through the gate. 'There's more than enough warriors out there, if he's got even a single powerful spell, he could be a real problem.'

Omotakus thumped his fist on the dolphin pommel of his longsword. 'I don't like magic. Don't think I've a drop of it in me. Most of the guardians of the Lady of Radiance's beacon can manage a ward, but not me.'

'I can try and teach you, if you like?'

Omotakus stumbled on the steps back up to the wall. 'You would? But aren't you forbidden from sharing the secrets of the Voréöeasiäki or something?'

'If I am, nobody mentioned it to me,' Azaki said. 'And one spell can be the difference between life and death. It has been for me. A lot. Most of the warriors you're fighting will know at least how to ward themselves and probably how to cast something more dangerous, too.'

'Thank you, Vil Azaki, but I'm afraid I'm just no good at it.'

Íri twisted away from the wall. '*Vil* Azaki?'

Omotakus chewed at his thumbnail. 'I saw him fight, calling him Voréöeasiä like we would if he was Getitakus just doesn't feel right.'

'She's just jealous,' Azaki whispered.

Íri rolled her eyes. 'As if.'

'Where're Getitakus, Siade and the acolytes?' Azaki asked.

'The acolytes are on the Red Moon Tower,' Omotakus said. 'I thought if we were here over the gate and they were there, then Getitakus and the one-armed girl could be in the Star Tower.'

58

'You do know I've no idea which tower is which, don't you?' Azaki asked.

'There're only four,' Íri said.

'Yes.' Azaki pointed at each of them, one after the other. 'That one. That one. That one. And that one.'

'The Red Moon Tower is closest to Easthil, the Star Tower is closest to Westhil,' Omotakus explained. 'The other two, the Sun Tower and the White Moon Tower, are right on the cliff on the north side of the island. I don't think they'll be attacked.'

Azaki glanced round the walls. 'You're probably right.'

Íri nudged him in the ribs with his elbow. 'They're coming. Did you annoy the apprentice?'

'I was relatively nice, actually.' He pointed at Omotakus. 'He was rude, so it's probably his fault.'

Omotakus clenched his jaw. 'Why should I be polite to them?! They came here to slaughter us!'

'Maybe if they like you, they'll change their mind?' Azaki suggested. 'But, more importantly, they might say something interesting if you can get them talking for a bit.'

Íri sighed. 'What do we do?'

'Stop Duratakus,' he replied. 'There're five times as many people up here as there are warriors. With a little help from us, they can be held off. Duratakus is the serious threat. We'll need to kill him before the food runs out. The warriors aren't stupid. They'll fall back with their spoils rather than risk anything they don't need to.'

Omotakus loosened his longsword in its sheath. 'Duratakus may be the serious threat to you, Vil Azaki, but every raider out there is a threat to my people. We can't all be great warriors.'

Íri folded her arms. 'Don't call him that, Omotakus. It's only going to go to his head.'

A group of warriors carried a thick, broad beam out through Westhil's gate. Bits of bronze stuck from one end, gleaming in the sun.

Azaki frowned. 'You should probably tell Getitakus, his acolytes, and Siade to get to the gate, Omotakus – in fact, I'll go.'

Íri caught his arm. 'Be gentle with Siade, Azaki.'

'I'm just going to tell her not to unseal her thiokezöeasiä. She can't seem to control who it affects, so it'll do more harm than good.' He gave her hand a gentle squeeze. 'Try and find a way to upset that Companion, you're the only one with an ability that counters his.'

She narrowed her eyes at him. 'I'm pretty sure your thiokezöeasiä can, whatever *truth* actually does.'

Azaki grinned and jogged away along the wall, keeping one eye on the gathering group of warriors just out of range of slings and bows.

'Azaki.' Getitakus sat on a crooked wooden chair just inside the tower, whittling away with a small knife. 'What is it?'

Siade hunched in the corner, Íri's faded green tunic hanging off her like it was meant for someone twice her age. Her gaunt cheeks and the dark bruises beneath her eyes gave her a ghoulish look.

She looks sick. Very sick.

'We need you two to help hold the gate,' Azaki said. 'They've made themselves a ram.'

'Hold the gate with what?' Getitakus glanced at Siade.

'Whatever you can.' Azaki stepped across in front of Siade and offered his hand. 'You mustn't unseal your thiokezöeasiä, Siade. The townsfolk will panic if they get scared and then the lighthouse will fall.'

She snatched his wrist with bony fingers and tugged herself up. 'What if I've got no choice?'

'Dire circumstances only,' he said. 'Promise me, Siade.'

'I promise,' she whispered, staring at her feet. 'I'll do what I can.'

Getitakus grabbed his thiokezöeasiä and hustled from the tower. Siade stumbled out in his wake.

'Now we'll see.' Falaïré's fingers curled round his forearm. 'We'll see if she's just scared and scrambled... or up to something *sinister*.'

Azaki nodded. 'I'll be watching.'

Her grip tightened. 'Do *not* leave me with your little Voréöeasiä girl, my Azi.'

He winced as her nails dug in. 'I didn't want you to get hurt.'

'Then *use our power*,' she whispered, her silver eyes sharpening. 'Stop swinging around that chunk of bronze and playing with those petty magic tricks. We can reshape their worlds. We've *truth*.'

Azaki placed his hand over hers. 'I'm saving what we can do. I don't want to use it all the time or on warriors who can just be cut down with swords and spells. If everyone knows my tricks, they're useless.'

Falaïré's lips curled into a smirk and silver light flickered beneath her dress of shadows. 'Don't forget what we really want, my Azi. We're not here for these people, the grove, or the beacon, are we?'

'Not *more* heart stuff,' Azaki muttered. 'Besides, I *do* like the groves. They're peaceful, and nice and green.'

She faded away with a soft laugh.

He hurried back onto the wall as the ram crashed against the gate. Spells flashed up at the wall, bursting in showers of sparks against the stone and the wind from Duratakus's thiokezöeasiä howled past the crenelations, screaming over the walls and lashing at Azaki's face. He ducked down and scuttled along through the men hurling rubble and rocks over the edge.

'Azaki!' Íri's irises swirled with orange flame, her thiokezöeasiä glowing bright as the sun. 'The apprentice!'

He stuck his head over the wall.

The apprentice stood a little apart from the warriors carrying the ram, shuffling from one foot to the other in a peculiar rhythm. Stones and arrows hissed down around him, flicking off the ground and bouncing away past his feet. A web of light spread from his feet like roots from a tree, the tendrils latched onto the limbs of the warriors, shrouding them in a bright glow.

'Queen of whispering webs, upon your throne of lies, gift a blade of shadow, and revel in their cries,' Azaki murmured.

He weighed the knife on his palm and closed one eye to line up the apprentice, hurling it. The apprentice slipped on a rock and Azaki's blade hissed over his head.

'Seriously?' He conjured another knife and threw again.

It thudded into the top of the gnarled pine thiokezöeasiä and burst into wisps of shadow. The apprentice looked up at the wall and gave him a wave.

Azaki snorted and waved back, putting his hand on Íri's shoulder. 'He's a weird one, but now we know why Duratakus chose him. That spell looks troublesome.'

The ram thudded into the gate twice as loud as before and the wall shook beneath their feet.

'Augmentation lore,' Íriniel said. 'He's enhancing all their strength together somehow. How did an idiot like that come up with such a spell?'

'Better him than Anastagus,' Azaki said. 'Imagine what he'd do with it.'

Íri scowled and drew herself up. 'I'll destroy the ram. Duratakus is just sitting there, anyway.'

Azaki threw a glance across to the gate into Westhil where Duratakus sat cross-legged upon the ground with his thiokezöeasiä on his lap, draped in a thick brown cloak. 'Don't waste any of your energy. He might decide to get involved.'

She turned to him, eyes blazing with orange flame. 'I'll be fine.' A fierce glow shone from within the hairline cracks down her thiokezöeasiä, settling over Azaki and those around them. 'You just watch.'

A wave of heat haze rippled down the wall.

Flimsy wards shimmered about the arms of the warriors around the ram, but the haze melted through them like they were summer snow, setting leathers and furs aflame, scorching bows, spears, and shields to ash. The heat curled round the ram like fog around a mountain peak and it burst into flames, glowing bright and crumbling to ash.

Íri panted and rested her head on the cool stone of the wall. 'That ought to help a bit.'

Duratakus stood and threw his cloak aside, straightening his smoke-grey, skin-tight tunic. Overlapping circles of obsidian-dark spider carapace swung from his waist as he strode up the slope and smacked his apprentice over the back of the head with his hand. 'Scream, invisible spectre.' He raised his thiokezöeasiä.

The dust and dirt swirled in a circle around his feet, rising up into the air, spiralling higher and higher. The torrent of wind shrieked forward over the heads of the warriors and shattered the gate, spraying splinters across the yard. Screams rose up from the townsfolk beneath.

Azaki exchanged a look with Íri. 'I'll go down to help Siade and Getitakus. You keep them from climbing the wall, Íri. Keep an eye on Duratakus.'

She caught his arm. 'Try not to get hurt this time.'

Azaki shot her a grin. 'As long as I've got you to put me back together, I'll be alright.'

Pink blossomed on her cheeks. 'That's not the point, idiot.'

He leapt down the steps and dragged the falcata free of its sheath.

The warriors threw themselves against a thin bronze line where Omotakus's beacon guard stood at the fore of a dense wall of townsfolk. Manastakus and Nemotakus stood near the centre of the fray with Siade and Getitakus, their brown tunics spattered with blood, soaked in sweat, and plastered in dust and grit. The blood-splattered struggle inched back and forth over a waist high pile of dead townspeople.

If it stays like this, they'll grind their way through hundreds of southie's before they die. He raised his thiokezöeasiä. *I have to—*

'Not yet,' Falaïré whispered in his ear. 'Watch the Voréöeasiä girl, my Azi. This is the chance for betrayal. Her bittersweet, red moment. What are a few more dead faces compared to the damage her deception might do…?'

True. Azaki watched a bronze blade slip through a fisherman's ribs, the press of bodies holding him up as the life faded from his eyes. Azaki's gut thrashed like an eel. *But only if she's really up to something.*

'We have to know, my Azi. The risk's too great. If she lets them in, who knows who will die.' Falaïré tilted his chin up toward where Íri stood on top of the gate with a single finger. 'It could be anyone naïve enough to trust a traitor.'

Azaki swallowed down a thick, hot lump in his throat. It settled round his heart in a barbed knot.

It might not even take long enough for anyone to die. He hardened his heart and took a deep breath, edging 'round the side of the conflict. *And even if they do, better a few now, than many later.*

Falaïré rested her head on his shoulder. 'Sever the ties of our heart, my Azi, or we'll dance from them like strings.'

Siade tucked her thiokezöeasiä behind her back with trembling fingers and the ring of the crown flashed red. Fear crashed down on him like the breaking of a vast wave. He gritted his teeth and tore his way free from under it, swiping the sweat from his brow.

'See,' Falaïré murmured. '*See.*'

The townsfolk hurled their arms to the ground and fled. Getitakus and his acolytes froze, squeezing their eyes shut. The warriors forced their way into the yard, drenched red from head to toe. Azaki hammered the hilt of his falcata into the back of Siade's head and caught her by the folds of her green tunic as she crumpled.

Getitakus's eyes flashed open and he thrust his thiokezöeasiä out, a bubble of white magic swelling up in the gateway. The warriors clawed and shoved at it, but were held fast as if in thick mud. Those in the yard pressed forward, cutting their way toward Getitakus through the few townsfolk brave enough to stand their ground.

If they're not pushed back, we're done for. Azaki placed Siade down on the ground and tallied the dozen trapped warriors with a grimace. *Damn it, Siade. Did Anastagus get to you a long time ago, or did you just not want to die when they came to burn your grove?*

He darted forward, ducking a bronze axe and driving his falcata through the ribs of the nearest warrior. Azaki shoved the body off his blade and parried aside a blade meant for Getitakus's head.

A crackling ball of red flashed past Azaki's shoulder at Getitakus. Manastakus and Nemetakus cast their own spells into it, deflecting it away into the wall where it burst in a shower of crimson sparks.

'Vil Azaki!' Omotakus grappled with a dark-haired woman. 'We must push them back!'

I know.

Azaki drove his falcata through the woman's unarmoured side and cast the Lady's Veil over the rest of the warriors nearby. The warrior twisted on the blade as she fell, ripping it from his hand.

One of the townsfolk hurled himself past Azaki, hacking with his makeshift weapon. Others sprinted to join him, turning the ground behind the bubble into a tight, bloody knot.

Azaki caught his breath and watched as the trapped warriors fell one by one into the heap of dead townspeople in the gate. More than two hundred bodies sprawled in the small gap. The stink of them made his stomach churn and his gorge rise.

Getitakus collapsed to his knees and the bubble burst.

Empty grass stretched beyond the broken gates.

One of the acolytes turned and vomited onto the flagstones, the other collapsed onto his back on a clean patch of ground, gasping for breath.

Azaki sighed and rolled the warrior over with his foot to retrieve his blade. 'Good work, Getitakus.'

'I didn't know I could do that.' Getitakus stared at his thiokezöeasiä with wide eyes. 'I trap air for the pearl divers sometimes, but I've never managed to make a bubble as solid as that before.'

'Well, it's a good thing you can. That was a bit of a close one.'

One of the townsfolk reached a hand out halfway to Getitakus' shoulder, then dropped it and bowed. 'Who'd've thought you were hiding such powerful magic all this time, Voréöeasiä?'

'Vil Azaki.' Omotakus staggered across, blood dripping from inside his elbow. 'I need to rest and get this cut seen too. You've command. My people are in your hands.'

I was kind of already commanding.

'They pulled back.' Íri came across to lean on him, her skin hot as the white stones. 'Duratakus called them away.'

Azaki frowned. 'Odd. If they'd kept coming, they might've won. Getitakus's bubble couldn't have lasted forever.'

Anastagus has been scheming something up again. He sheathed his falcata and closed his eyes. *This attack is no more what it seems than Kogodakus's half-hearted assaults back at the Heart-Tree were.*

Íriniel's gaze flicked to where Siade lay. 'Is she okay?'

'She got caught on the head. She'll be fine.'

'Again?' Íri knelt and pressed a green-wreathed hand to Siade's temple. 'Did you hit her, Azaki?'

'She unsealed her thiokezöeasiä.' Azaki sighed. 'We can't let her near the fighting again, Íri. When she wakes up, try and find a reason to get her as far away as possible. I don't care what it is, just make sure she does what you tell her.'

Falaïré circled the unconscious girl, the shadows pooling from beneath her dress to surround Siade. 'She's only going to try and betray us again, my Azi.' Her hair flashed auburn and her eyes blue. 'She'll only keep going. She'll only get worse. Unless something stops her. And that something...'

Is going to have to be us. Azaki recalled the bitter heat of those words on his tongue, the feel of Ulika's red hair between his fingers, and Utháki's slow, grim nod as they stared into the web-lined pit of the giant spider. *So be it.*

Ten

No heat came from the white flame rippling in the vast bronze bowl. No shadows danced on the slim, pale columns supporting the lighthouse's dome. The edge of the world curved away beyond the pillars; darkness and stars.

Azaki reached into the fire and drew out a handful on his palm.

'Why're we all the way up here?' Íri grabbed his wrist and tipped the flame back into the beacon. 'And *don't* steal from Akrotera's Torch. Wasn't one sacred thing enough for you?'

'So you could experience how I felt being dragged into libraries.' He turned away from the white flame. 'I just wanted to see it. Nobody from the clans has ever gotten this close to it. Some of our eorls have tried to take the beacon for our own, but none of them ever managed.'

'Really?'

'It's a very good place to raid the lake from and the glory of seizing it...' Azaki sighed. 'There're more important things for us to worry about, though. I've got a plan, Íri. Omotakus and I'll persuade his father and the elders, but I need you to tell Siade. I've found everyone else. I think she's avoiding me.'

'Because you scare her!' She folded her arms. 'I told you to be *nice*.'

'I was as nice as I could afford to be without getting us all killed.'

'What's your plan, then?' Íri scowled. 'And why are you telling me *last?*'

Azaki grinned. 'Because I knew you'd hate it? Or maybe I was hoping you'd make that adorable angry face.'

She scowled, flushed pink and tried to keep her face straight.

Azaki laughed. 'Nope. Still adorable.'

Íri growled. 'Just tell me.'

'They'll go for the gate again. It plays to their strengths and Duratakus knows it. We'll need everyone we can to keep them out, so we'll leave the east wall empty. It's the least likely for them to go after. We'll all be by the gate or on the wall above it.'

Íri nodded. 'Makes sense. I'll find Siade. She's probably watching the sea from the north wall. It seems to help her.'

'I've got to talk to the elders, so you've got a short while.'

Azaki watched her disappear down the marble steps of the White Spire.

'Our hook's baited,' Falaïré murmured, prowling the edge of the beacon. 'But why dangle it? We already saw her betray us...'

'It's possible she really thinks she's got no choice or she's doing the right thing. Her head's clearly a mess.' Azaki stared into white fire. 'The fear in her magic isn't a lie. You ought to know.'

'She's still betrayed us, my Azi.' She reached a finger out a hair's breadth from the flame. If we spare her for long...'

'That's a—'

The fire in the bowl flashed bright as the sun.

Azaki flinched behind his arm. Falaïré froze and faded away.

A figure of white flame hovered over the bowl, the air bent and warped around it like Azaki was looking through rippling water and it smelt sharp as a storm. Every shadow fled the tower top and the distant stars brightened.

A deep chill crawled up his spine. 'Akrotera,' he whispered, wiping the sweat off his palms.

The Voréoatho took a step toward him, dimming to a candle's luminance. 'So you are the one of my sister's Volōmotistí followers sent to defend my beacon.'

Azaki swallowed and edged backward, his heart dashing itself against his ribs like a rabid wolf against the bars of its cage. 'Yes? I mean, it's not just me, is it?'

'My siblings and I built this spire for the Volōmothí before our beautiful world was broken.' Her eyes glowed like twin suns, blazing bright as the golden wash of dawn. 'If my brother's followers seize it, they will ruin it to honour him. Preserve this precious relic and you will earn my favour.'

Azaki forced a smile. 'We're already on it. I even have a plan. Kind of needed one, since we don't have very much to eat. I don't suppose you could fix that? Being, you know, a Voréoatho.'

Akrotera reached out and took hold of his thiokezöeasiä. Fire dripped from her fingers like water and trickled all down the dark wood; it pooled on the white stone, shining like liquid starlight.

'Interesting,' she murmured. 'What are you up to, little sister?'

Azaki grit his teeth and clung on as the wood turned searing hot beneath his fingers. 'Er...'

She released his thiokezöeasiä, the bright of her eyes piercing through him like the sun through the shadows. 'Olisolamon okertes ūrrakityál Azaki okertes.'

Magic tugged at his mind and an echo of her words shivered through his thoughts. Azaki squeezed his eyes shut, but behind closed eyelids he found a mountain-studded shadow hung among the stars, drifting forward toward some distant, inevitable horizon. His shadow walked a path of grey sand, footsteps stretching away from his toes toward the same coming brightness. The images spilt together, swirling into a tangle of colours and a strange, grim sense of certainty, whirling through his thoughts until his head spun.

Azaki pinched the bridge of his nose until the lightness faded. *What was that? What does she mean?*

'Olisolamon...?' He poked at a bead of light upon the stave and it burst in a shower of sparks. 'It sounds very serious, but...'

'The waning grace of the Volōmotistí,' Akrotera murmured, her burning eyes piercing through him. 'Olisolamon's fate is entwined with yours.'

As cryptic as Falaïré. Azaki smothered the thrashing knot in his stomach and held his breath until his heart settled. *Why can't she just tell me what she wants?*

'By entwined with...?'

Akrotera's form flickered and the light of her eyes faded like the midday sun dimming to dusk. 'What you do will directly affect what this peaceful world fragment becomes, mortal. Remember that each time this echo of my sister whispers to you of desire. A great shadow looms over Olisolamon; it will swallow this world fragment if it can.' She stepped back over the great bronze bowl and shimmered out of existence.

Azaki released a long sigh. 'Given I'm already defending her beacon, I think I'll just pretend this never happened.' He shivered. 'Better Akrotera than the Spider, at least.'

'We already know what we want.' Falaïré's laughter tickled the back of his neck. 'And we know what we *need* to do, too...'

Azaki's heart sank. 'Siade...'

'Yes, the treacherous little Voréöeasiä girl.' Her lips curved into a smirk. 'Strike first, my Azi,' she whispered. 'Or be first struck.'

He hurried down the steps to the spire's base.

'Vil Azaki.' Omotakus wrung his hands outside the door to the elders' chamber. 'I explained the plan to the kerkam, but they really don't like it.'

'I'll speak to them.' He shoved the door open and strode into the small room.

Omotakus slipped in after him.

'Voréöeasiä,' Omotakus's father croaked. 'We did not summon you.'

'Don't care,' Azaki said. 'What's your problem with my plan? Have you all suddenly gained an understanding of magic that surpasses mine? Or perhaps you've discovered a huge store of food, so we don't need to take risks to avoid starving?'

Several of them shifted and stared at the floor.

One bald kerkam scratched at his scalp with yellow nails. 'It's *too* risky, Voréöeasiä. Letting them in through the gate? Madness.'

Azaki sighed. 'The gate's already breached and their warriors are much better than ours. If we fight them in a narrow space, our numeric advantage means nothing. They'll grind us away to nothing. I told you all this already.'

'We won't agree,' Omotakus's father declared. 'It'll be a bloodbath.'

'I don't care if you don't agree.' Azaki planted his thiokezöeasiä on the floor before him and swallowed a flare of irritation. 'All that's required is Íriniel keeps Duratakus beyond the gate and your people fight for their lives. I'll do the rest.'

'Our people aren't yours to command,' the leftmost kerkam insisted. 'If we don't tell them to follow your plan—'

Azaki's lip curled. *Eorls and keorls lead from the front. They share the risk. Old men who send young men to die for them are not leaders.*

'Unless you're going to fight out there with them, you're not anything.'

'My son,' Omotakus's father gritted. 'You won't give any commands to follow this plan, is that understood.'

'Vil Azaki and the Voréöeasiäki are the only reason we've not already lost, father,' Omotakus said. 'I trust his plans and we simply don't have enough food to try and outlast them behind the walls.'

Azaki gave the half-circle of old men his best imitation of Falaïré's smirk. 'There we go, then.' He swivelled on his heel. 'You'd probably better head to the gate, Omotakus. I think they'll try something sneaky, so I'll be on the east wall. If I'm wrong, I'll return swiftly.'

'Of course, Vil Azaki.' Omotakus tugged his belt a notch tighter as he stumbled after Azaki. 'All the rationing and fighting's making me lose weight.'

Azaki chuckled. 'When I was a child, I went without much food for weeks. You'll be tired, but fine.' He drew Omotakus aside as they reached the yard and took a deep breath. 'There's another detail I left out. The warriors mustn't expect a trap when we lure them in, so some men have to be placed in the gate.'

'But you said…'

'Yes. I did.'

Omotakus swallowed and bowed his head. 'If you think it's necessary, Vil Azaki.'

'The way I see it, either a few men fight in the breach, or a lot do,' Azaki said. 'Whoever fights there is going to die, so better it's fewer.'

'I'll ask for volunteers, but I won't order anyone in there to die.'

'That's fair enough, just don't give anything away. It's likely there're people who'd seek to betray us to save themselves. Tell them it'll be dangerous, so they know what they're volunteering for, but nothing more than that.'

Omotakus spun his helm in his hands, then released a long sigh. 'It's the best we can do, isn't it?'

'It's the best I can manage.' Azaki buried his unease and gave Omotakus a pat on the shoulder, hastening to the east wall. He slipped into the shadows of the Star Tower where a small altar had been carved into the stones at the tower's base.

'To Akrotera.' Falaïré slipped from the darkness around him. 'She defends the untarnished relics of the First World and otherwise rarely opposes her siblings.'

'How do we even know that?'

'It was in the book we used to search for your clan and the Spider.' She traced her red-stained fingertips over the stone-carved image of the sun and the two moons. 'Akrotera. The Lady of Radiance and Flame.'

'She seems okay, as much as any of the virtually all-powerful Voréoathoki are.' He peered round the edge of the steps up to the wall. 'Here comes Siade.'

She stumbled across the yard clutching at the stump of her arm, her thiokezöeasiä tucked beneath her maimed shoulder. Her borrowed green tunic hung off her like it was twice her size and her hair fell thin and lifeless over gaunt cheeks.

Something is very wrong with her. A deep stab of pity pierced through his gut. *She looks as bad as we outcasts did during the worst winters and it's only been days.*

Falaïré's silver eyes turned sharp. 'Don't let her betray us, my Azi. Doing what we must will hurt far less than a knife in the back.'

'I won't,' he muttered.

'If we die here, we'll never see Otuko again, and Íri will die with us,' she whispered in his ear.

'I know, Falaïré.'

Silver light flickered beneath the darkness of her dress like lightning amidst distant storm clouds. 'If you don't, you'll see soon enough.'

He cast the Lady's Shroud and drew the shadows over himself as Siade rushed up the steps onto the wall. Azaki crept after her, watching her wave her thiokezöeasiä over the crenelations.

A warrior in broad, square bronze shoulder plates dragged himself over the wall and rolled to his feet. He looked Siade up and down, and turned to help a second warrior over the wall.

'Now we know, my Azi,' Falaïré murmured into the back of his neck. 'Now we know.'

Now we know. Azaki struggled for some trick or truth, a twist of pity tugging at his heart. *Can't we just tie her up? She looks half-dead already.*

'She'd get free.' Falaïré rested her head on his shoulder. 'And all she has to do to cause disaster is unseal her thiokezöeasiä. She doesn't need to be free to do that, just awake.'

He swallowed and shoved everything as far down as it would go. 'Deceive, lady of lies.'

Grey mist rippled from the crown of his thiokezöeasiä across the lighthouse, ensnaring every soul. Azaki released his spell and let the shadows slip back to the ground. The faint echoes of the warriors formed from the fog and poured down the steps. Siade slumped to her knees on the wall and wrapped her arm around her chest as she watched them go. Azaki forced shadows of townsfolk to rise in the mist along the wall, wrapping them round the warriors clambering onto it like spider-silk cocoons.

They turned on each other. Blades flashed. Red spurted. Spells hissed. Azaki watched them fall one by one. Above the carnage, Akrotera's white flame pierced the veil of Azaki's magic like the sun through clouds.

Why can't she save the beacon herself? Would the Heart-Tree not let her?

'Queen of whispering webs, upon your throne of lies, gift a blade of shadow and revel in their cries.' He stepped forward and thrust the blade into the side of the survivor's throat, shoving him over the wall.

'So much more elegant and deadly than swords or spells,' Falaïré breathed in his ear. 'There's nothing more powerful than the truth.'

Why not just do it yourself, Akrotera? He stared at the warm red trickling down his fingers. *Why do I have to do this?*

'Don't despair, my Azi.' Falaïré cupped his blood-stained hands and pressed them against her breast. 'This is just how the world is. Kill or be killed. If not them now, it might be your little Voréöeasiä girl tomorrow, or the girl who saved us the day after that.'

Better Siade than Íri or Otuko. He hardened his heart. *She's betrayed us, anyway.*

Azaki crouched down before Siade and set her free from his magic. 'Hi.'

She screamed and threw herself back, slipping and sliding in the blood upon the wall. 'Azaki...' She gulped and reached for the thiokezöeasiä she'd dropped.

He flicked it out of her reach with his toe. 'I think there's a few things you ought to say, Siade.'

'I'm sorry,' she whispered. 'I've no choice. Look at me... If he doesn't renew his spell every two weeks, I'll die. I - I don't want to die.'

'One more bittersweet moment,' Falaïré murmured. 'She can't be saved, not even if the spellcaster dies. The spell will still kill her.'

'You killed all of them,' Siade muttered, hunching her knees up and pulling her feet away from the blood. 'Why couldn't you've been at Gull's Mound? You could've saved my friends. You could've saved *me*.'

Azaki's heart sank like a torch into the bottomless dark of the Webbed Pit. 'Technically, they killed each other.'

'Are you going to kill me?' Siade whispered, tears leaking down her pale, gaunt cheeks. 'You are, aren't you? I betrayed the Heart-Tree.' She let out a strangled sob. 'I *am* sorry. I wish—'

'Nobody will know.'

She blinked her tears away. 'What?'

'The truth is you died bravely and quickly, fighting for the world.' Azaki drove the blade of shadow into her heart and twisted. Hot blood poured over his knuckles and soaked the front of the green tunic Íri had loaned the girl. 'That's the best I can do.'

Poor Siade. He stared down into her glassy eyes and swallowed a thick lump in his throat, letting his spell-forged knife dissipate and blinking back hot tears. *She must've felt so alone, so trapped.*

'It's okay, my Azi.' Falaïré slipped her arms over his shoulders. Red dripped from the first knuckles to the fingertips of his right hand. 'We gave her a *beautiful* truth. They would've only killed her when they were done with her. Our way, she dies in defence in the world.'

If they believe it, then it's true. Azaki forced down the raw, sharp knot in his chest. *Her truth ends with a hero's death for everyone but me.*

'It still feels awful,' he murmured.

Azaki gathered up Siade's body in his arms, retrieved her thiokezöeasiä and placed her among the dead by the gate.

A tight knot of townsfolk around Omotakus' blue-crested helm held the gate, stumbling and shoving back and forth over blood-slickened stones and bodies. Red spattered the beacon guards' white cloaks. Shouts and screams rose over the clamour of bronze and the thick stink filled his mouth and nose to the back of his throat.

Azaki gagged and grimaced. *Far worse than raids. And at least winter kills cleanly.* He glanced up to where Íri's thiokezöeasiä shone from the wall and drew his falcata, letting his magic unravel and resealing his thiokezöeasiä.

Azaki shoved his way through to Getitakus.

'I'm spent,' Getitakus gasped, mopping blood off his forehead with his sleeve. 'I kept them out for a bit, but then I tried to block Duratakus's wind. I — he's — there's nothing I can do to stop magic like that, Azaki. I'm sorry.'

It doesn't matter. Siade's dead and they'll soon realise their plan's failed.

Azaki studied the shallow, grit-crusted gash over Getitakus' eyebrow. 'Get some rest. They'll fall back soon, they're not making as much headway as they expected.'

A horn sounded from beyond the walls, a long, high note. The warriors darted from beneath the gate, scattering from the walls.

Duratakus stood before the gate, his thiokezöeasiä raised before a mound of small, smooth pebbles. The wind swirled and twisted behind him, his grey tunic rippled like stormy waters.

Azaki squinted at the pile of stones. *What're those for? Are they slingshot?* Cold terror seized him round the spine.

'Get down!' Azaki dragged Getitakus to the floor.

The wind screamed over his head and something seared through his left shoulder. A hazy white bubble of magic closed over him as he clutched at the burning pain. Stones pinged off the ward and rattled away into the dead. Azaki gasped into the heat soaking into the front of his clothes.

'Heart-Tree preserve us,' Getitakus moaned.

Azaki staggered to his feet, one hand pressed to the burning pain in his shoulder. Bodies sprawled in an arc before the gate, torn to shreds and riddled with holes. Blood sloshed about his ankles, trickling between the corpses and spreading out into the yard. Omotakus's helm glinted beside the splintered edge of the door, a few sparse, blood-soaked strands of blue stuck to the bronze where the proud crest had trailed.

Azaki rammed his falcata back into his sheath, ignoring the flare of agony through his shoulder. 'This is why we don't fight in the gate.'

Getitakus crawled through the bodies hauling them over one by one. 'Manastakus?! Nemotakus?!' He dragged a body in brown tunic out from beneath a pile of the dead and held shaking fingers over its mouth. 'Manastakus, you're alive…'

Azaki sagged against the steps up to the wall. 'Where's Íri when I need her?' He peeled away his shirt and winced at the burning, throbbing, bleeding thumbnail-sized hole beneath his collarbone. 'That's really not ideal.'

Getitakus let out a howl. He rolled the still, pale body of Nemotakus over, cradling his head into his lap.

Siade's in there somewhere, too. Azaki stared into the red lapping against the toes of his boots. A numbness settled over him like deep cold snow. *And Omotakus.*

He reached around with a trembling hand and found another wound upon his back. 'Oh great, two holes. Twice the fun. I suppose this is payback for me laughing at Otuko's scar.'

'Idiot.' Íri's shadow fell over him. 'What did you do?'

Azaki chuckled and hissed as his shoulder flared with pain. 'Duratakus did this. I got off lightly compared to most.'

A green-wreathed hand rested on his shoulder and Íri's legs slid down either side of him. 'I think I'm going to be sick,' she whispered from just above his head.

'It's only blood.'

'Not you, everyone.' She gagged and the green light about her fingers guttered out. 'It stinks.'

'Don't be sick on me, please. I'm already drenched in blood, let's not make it any worse.'

A sudden warmth washed through him and white light flashed in the corner of his eye. The pain in his shoulder vanished.

'Thanks, Íri,' Azaki said. 'You're getting better.'

'That wasn't me,' she murmured. 'It looked - it looked like the fire from the beacon...'

'Oh.' He poked at the unmarked skin where the wound had been. 'Guess She didn't mind me grabbing some of Her fire, then.'

His stomach knotted and churned. *Or killing poor Siade.*

Falaïré's laughter drifted to his ears.

Íri rested her arms on the top of his head. 'She shouldn't've been able to do that. Talking's one thing, but that's different. The Heart-Tree's groves are weakening if one of the Voréoathoki can reach us.'

The Princess of Betrayal can reach me. A fist of ice clenched itself around Azaki's spine. *We need to leave here.*

He forced himself to shrug and smile. 'We're right at the edge of the world and the Crumbling Cliff Grove is long gone.'

'Even still,' she muttered. 'Oh well, at least I get to enjoy looking down on you from here.'

He twisted about and squinted up at her soot-streaked, sweaty face. 'You look awful.'

Íri shuffled back on her seat on the edge of the steps and prodded him in the face. 'Don't be mean. Let's just go get Itaki and go back up to Akrotera's Torch for a bit.'

'So many steps...' Azaki groaned. 'I guess you want some peace and quiet?'

'Yes.'

'And you think bringing Itaki's going to do that? He's pretty vocal at how unhappy he is with being left in that little room all day.'

'Itaki's fine.' She rested her chin and arms atop his head. 'It's you I want to be quiet.'

'Fair enough.' He grinned into the curve of her throat and leant out from under her arms. 'But you'll have to be nice to me up there or Akrotera might smite you.'

A hint of pink blossomed on her cheeks. 'I'll have to stay close, then, to make sure I take you with me.'

'And who would defend the beacon then?'

'Not those stubborn old goats back in the tower.' She scowled. 'They beg for our help, then refuse to listen to us. How did you convince them?'

He shrugged. 'I ignored them. Omotakus trusts us. He's the one actually giving orders, too.'

'Ah, yes. Omotakus would never dare ignore the exalted word of *Vil Azaki*.' She flashed him a smile. 'If only he knew you better...'

Azaki laughed. 'You're such a mean girl, Íri. Always trying to ruin my fun, while doing whatever you fancy. It's like the journey here, I'm not allowed to sing, but you get to give me bruises and make cruel comments about my height.'

Íri snorted. 'Maybe if you were taller, those jokes wouldn't go over your head.'

'So mean...' Azaki wiped the worst of the blood off on his shirt and glanced up at the bright, white glow just beneath the clouds. 'Let's go up, then. It'll be nice to be away from the world for a bit.'

Eleven

The rising sun crept over the edge of the east wall between the White Moon Tower and the Star Tower, bathing them in a warm orange glow. Azaki strode through the two lines of townsfolk on the wall toward where Íri's thiokezöeasiä's crown stuck out over a bald head and a rusted boathook.

'Vil Azaki,' the townsfolk mumbled as he passed them, dipping their heads. Some knelt.

Íri rolled her eyes as he reached her. 'They act like you're some kind of king or warlord.'

'You mean they give me the deference I deserve,' Azaki corrected with a grin. 'Unlike you, you ungrateful urchin.'

'Urchin?' Her tone turned sweet and rose an octave. '*Urchin*?'

'One of those little, spiky, ball-shaped water creatures.'

'I know what it is.' She elbowed him in the hip. 'I was waiting for you to take it back.'

'Not gonna,' Azaki sang.

'Why're you such a child?'

'That's *Vil* child to you, peon Íri.'

She leant on the crenelations and sighed. 'You still think it's a good idea to let them in?'

'Not all of them.' He leant beside her. 'Duratakus has to stay outside, otherwise it won't work.'

Íri chewed her lip. 'This feels like a risky plan.'

'It *is* a risky plan, but we have no food, so there's not much choice. We just need the townsfolk to stick about long enough to lure them all in,' Azaki said. 'Manastakus and Getitakus can deal with the apprentice, you have Duratakus, and I'll do the rest.'

'You're going to fight almost a hundred warriors yourself.' Íri straightened up and folded her arms over her chest. 'I hope you're not being serious.'

'Technically, they're going to fight each other.'

Íri narrowed her eyes. 'And why would they do that?'

Azaki grinned. 'Because it's the truth.'

Falaïré's soft laughter drifted to his ear. 'She's going to ask us, my Azi. She's wanted to know for a while.'

Íri glanced at the mist trailing from the tines of his thiokezöeasiä. 'What does your thiokezöeasiä do, Azaki? You said it was truth…'

He frowned and lowered his voice. 'I believe it grew from the part of my heart that loves tricks.'

'You *lied* to me!'

'No. It's just… complicated.'

She looked across the empty ground to the gate into Easthil. 'We've time.'

Azaki sighed and watched Falaïré prowl up and down in a line behind Íri. 'Trickery's how the clan's survived all this time, it's how *I* survived once my brother was gone. Tricks can be armour for those with nothing else to protect them. A weapon for those with none. The truth's precious.'

72

Íri scowled. 'That doesn't tell me anything and you know it.' She put a hand on his arm. 'It doesn't matter what it is, I won't tell anyone else. I *promise*.'

Falaïré ceased her prowling and stared at him over Íriniel's shoulder with sharp, bright eyes. 'Promises, promises,' she whispered. 'Promises, promises.'

He chuckled. 'It's sneaky. It lets me hide the truth, or change it.'

'Illusions.' She wound a lock of hair around her finger. 'That's how you hid us from the longship. None of the Voréöeasiäki I've heard of had a thiokezöeasiä like that...'

Azaki shrugged. 'If what you told me about thiokezöeasiäki is true, then I think the Heart-Tree wanted someone a bit different. I doubt she recruits her Voréöeasiäki from the Webbed Pit very often.'

Íri shuffled her feet and stared out toward the edge of the world. 'So I *did* see you die. Have you used it on me since?'

He grimaced. 'When Kogodakus got into the Heart-Tree. I let him in to separate him from the raiders so I could stop him. Didn't quite go to plan, though. *Someone* escaped my illusion.'

'Good. Don't use it on me again.' She turned back to him. 'You've no need to hide the truth from me.'

'I don't use it very often,' Azaki said. 'We've got our limits.'

'For now,' Falaïré whispered into the back of his neck. 'For now.'

'Royal plural?' Íri raised her eyebrows. 'Really?'

Azaki patted his thiokezöeasiä. 'We. A child of my heart and me.'

Falaïré rested her head on his shoulder. 'No more sharing the secrets of our heart, my Azi. We don't want her to realise when we leave.'

Íri sighed. 'Sometimes I'm not sure if you're very perceptive or very dense.'

'Sometimes *I* wonder why *you're* so short.'

'I'm not—'

'Would you like to sit on my shoulders, little Íri? You'll be able to see over the top of crenelations then.'

She jabbed him in the foot with her thiokezöeasiä. 'That's enough out of you. Duratakus is coming.'

Azaki glanced up at where Duratakus strolled toward the lighthouse's wall and the warriors spilt from the gate after his apprentice. 'Remember the plan, Íri. You keep Duratakus outside, I'll do the rest.' He nodded down the wall at Getitakus's brown tunic. 'He'll help you.'

'What if I can't?' she murmured.

'You will.' He gave her shoulder a gentle nudge. 'Don't think I've not seen those little glowing cracks all down your thiokezöeasiä. Someone's been sneakily bonding with their thiokezöeasiä while I've been stuck looking after the fiendishly-bitey, talking chicken.'

'I don't like people getting hurt. I don't want to hear any more screams. I - I just want to be able to do it quickly. I thought maybe if I could just make it hot enough...'

Azaki grimaced. 'It'll get easier, like hunting rabbits does. Don't let it get to you too much. It's kill or be killed. They know it, too. You can take my word for that. The clans live and die by the sword.'

Íri chewed her lip. 'But *burning*,' she whispered. 'It's so *cruel*.'

He offered her a small smile. 'The way I see it, it's how and why you use your heart as much as what it does.'

Her green eyes softened and her lips curved. 'You know, if you talked like that more often, people might actually believe you're smart and sensitive.'

'Well, we can't have that.' He watched the warriors approach as the breeze began to pick up and Duratakus stopped in front of the wall. 'For now, just do your best to toast Duratakus. If he gets toasted, great. Otherwise, he'll still be busy trying not to be toasted for long enough to carry out the plan.'

'Blaze, beacon of virtuous ire,' she whispered.

A bright orange glow swelled up beneath the cracks running down her thiokezöeasiä and from its crown; a fainter aura of it settled over them both and all those within a few steps.

'Be safe.' Azaki squeezed her shoulder. 'That's a command, by the way, from Vil Azaki himself.'

Íri snorted. 'Where're you going?'

'To the gate.'

She seized his wrist. 'Not before you unseal your thiokezöeasiä.'

Azaki grinned. 'Nosy.'

'Just do it. Please. I want to see. You can *trust* me.'

'You're not going to like it...' He blew the mist off the top of his thiokezöeasiä. 'Deceive, lady of lies.'

Íri pinched the bridge of her nose. 'Did you choose that just to wind me up?'

He laughed as the fine grey mist settled across the lighthouse. 'It might've occurred to me.'

'Go to the gate, then.' Her grasp tightened on his wrist as he pulled away. 'Don't die, Azaki.'

'I won't.'

'We should've lied to her,' Falaïré murmured in his ear as he descended the steps.

'I like that at least *someone* knows me,' Azaki said. 'If nobody knew any of my truth but me, it'd be like before.'

'It'd still be us. You'd not be that bitter-hearted boy again.' She walked beside him upon thin air as if the steps extended over the heads of the people in the gate. 'It'll always be us, even when everyone else's truths diverge from ours.'

He paused behind the group of townsfolk in the gate. 'I want more, is that so bad?'

The corner of Falaïré's lips curved up. 'Not if what we desire is possible, my Azi.'

'Vil Azaki,' the townsfolk muttered as he passed through them.

Some drew back from him, heads bowed, others reached out to touch him with their fingertips as if to make sure he were real.

The wind rose, shrieking through the gate, ripping splinters and grit from the broken gates and stinging Azaki's face and eyes. The grey mist of his magic hung still and thick as the fog upon the lake.

'They're coming.' A burly fisherman with blood stained bandages around his arm pointed out the gate with a trembling finger. 'What do we do, Vil Azaki?'

Azaki drew his falcata. 'Fight. Every step you take back is a step closer to defeat, and we *must* not be defeated. Akrotera demanded I protect this place. I will.'

Pale flames burst into life upon his bronze blade and white light trickled over his fingers, dripping from the hilt and bursting in bright sparks upon the ground. Duratakus's wind broke against it like water upon rocks and the Volōvyf gaped.

Falaïré laughed in his ear. 'Remember, they hear when we speak their names, my Azi. And the groves are gone...'

'Seems useful.' Azaki poked a finger into the heatless flame. 'Thank you, Akrotera.'

A streak of yellow hissed over his head and spattered against the wall. The warriors charged the gate beneath a glimmering wall of wards.

Here we go.

Arrows flicked off the shimmering wards and pinged off bronze plate and scale. One warrior crumpled beneath his allies feet, a shaft sticking from his neck. Two of his allies paused and stripped the armour from him, portioning it between them as they strapped it onto themselves. The rest crashed into the townsfolk with a roar.

Spells flashed and hissed, swords rang, and screams echoed from the fray. Blood spattered across Azaki's face and the burly fisherman slumped to the floor with a hole the size of a fist through his chest.

Now is the moment. Azaki raised his thiokezöeasiä.

A shadow of himself formed from the fog and strode to the front of the fray. The shades of townsfolk rose from the mist and settled over the warriors like snow.

Azaki watched the gate descend into carnage.

'Perfect,' Falaïré breathed.

The apprentice burst through the middle of the chaos, waving his gnarled pine branch over his head, staggering and slipping in the blood. 'This is so nasty,' he wailed. 'Everyone's dying!'

Manastakus fired spell after spell at him, but the apprentice stumbled over the body of the burly fisherman and they whistled into the warriors fighting each other in the gate.

The apprentice pushed himself up on his gnarled pine branch and stuck a finger at Azaki. 'You're not nice! You tricked us!'

He can see me. Azaki strode forward, but Manastakus hurled himself at the apprentice and they both vanished into the fray. *How did he get free?*

Falaïré stared after Duratakus' student, a sharpness hovering in her silver eyes. 'It's proven hard to weave our truths into a warped mind.'

'Mad?' Azaki recalled the bent, twisted focus of Kogodakus and how it'd bored through his magic. 'Well, at least he's not trying to set everything on fire.'

The struggle tightened around the shrinking group of warriors. Through the knot of fighters, Azaki glimpsed the apprentice smack Manastakus over the head with his staff.

'Damn,' he hissed, darting forward.

He cut two of the last few warriors out of his path. The burning blade passed through bronze, bone, and flesh like a stick through water.

'Master Duratakus!' The apprentice hauled Manastakus over his shoulder by the front of his brown tunic. 'Things have gone a bit wrong!'

Azaki's blade whispered past the apprentice's heels as he sprinted from the gate. 'Damn.'

Getitakus howled with rage, his white bubble closing on empty air just behind the apprentice. Azaki swerved around it. Duratakus thrust his thiokezöeasiä out and the wind hammered into Azaki's chest. He went flying backward across the ground, the falcata slipping from his grasp, and slammed into the wall. Pain seared through his thigh and tears sprang to his eyes.

'Oh *great*.' Azaki clenched his teeth and groaned as he pulled his leg off the blade. Blood spurted into the mud in time with the pounding of his heart. 'Only *I* would end up landing on my own sword.' He took a deep breath and tried to stand, but white-hot agony flared through his thigh and his leg collapsed.

Getitakus strained against the wind, clawing forward a few steps. 'Manastakus!' His teeth were bare and his eyes wild. 'Manastakus!'

'Go to the ship!' Duratakus seized the gnarled piece of pine and thwacked his apprentice in the ribs with it. 'You've ruined Anastagus's plan, you absolute *cretin!*'

75

The apprentice quailed beneath Duratakus' black glare. 'What about this acolyte, master?'

'Bring him, so it's not *total* failure.'

The wind ceased and the pair took off towards Easthil and the longships. Getitakus slumped forward into the mud, slipping and sliding as he struggled to his feet.

Azaki pushed himself upward with his weight on his good leg and his thiokezöeasiä, but pain lanced through his limb and he slid to his knees in the red puddle. 'Voréoathoki damn it.'

'Stop dropping me in the mud and get the little Voréöeasiä girl to heal us,' Falaïré murmured. 'We don't care what happens to that acolyte. Why bleed for him?'

'But Íri will care.' He clutched his fingers around his thigh until the spurting lessened.

'Azaki!' Íri burst round the corner and a gentle orange glow enveloped his leg, the bleeding slowing a little. 'Are you okay?'

Do I look okay? Azaki bit his lip and took a deep breath.

'Go after them,' he said. 'You can patch me up later. Getitakus can't fight Duratakus alone.'

Falaïré hissed and her fingers curled into his shoulder. 'We already *have* what we want, my Azi.'

We probably won't die. We might even leave here before the Mistress of Whispers gets me. Azaki squinted across toward Easthil. *Getitakus is catching up.*

Getitakus's hand reached out for Manastakus's tunic and Duratakus swung his thiokezöeasiä back over his shoulder. The wind knocked Getitakus twenty metres back through the mud, slamming him into the sprawling heap of bodies in the gate and buffeting Íri back into the wall beside Azaki with a low thud. She groaned and pushed herself to her feet.

The last warrior dragged himself over the top of the pile of corpses, gasping for breath. Blood drenched the bronze circles covering his stomach and deep scratches marked the wide, round bronze shield in his hand. He lunged at Íri with his spear, but Getitakus's bubble of magic closed over him and the spear blade stuck fast in the white magic.

Íri turned to Azaki. 'What's hurt?'

'My leg.' Azaki poked his finger into the hole to stifle the slow spurt and winced. 'I landed on something sharp.'

'Don't stick your finger in it, you idiot!' Íri's fingers lit up with green light and she smacked his hand away. 'Why do you always poke things? If I don't heal it now, you'll bleed to death!'

The white flames on his blade burst into liquid light and trickled down his arm. Warmth flooded through him and with a hiss and a wisp of smoke, the wound in his leg vanished.

'Unbelievable.' Íri growled, wiping the back of her hand across her eyes. 'Was Akrotera just waiting for me to start trying to heal it so She could make me look bad?'

'I think that's my reward for driving them away from the beacon.' Azaki squeezed his leg and sighed. 'I get to live... *hooray.*'

'I could've healed it,' Íri muttered.

A stifled gasp from behind her caught Azaki's ear.

The townsfolk crowded round the outside of Getitakus's bubble. The warrior clawed at the white wall of magic with his fingernails until blood smeared the inside, his face turning purple.

'Where're they taking Manastakus?' Getitakus snarled as the bubble's light dimmed.

The warrior sagged, gulping huge breaths of air.

'Stop!' Íri grabbed Getitakus' shoulder, but he shoved her away.

Azaki stumbled to his feet. 'He won't betray his clan for pain or death, let me try something subtler.'

The bubble burst.

'It better work,' Getitakus spat.

Azaki snared the man back within his illusion and waited as he sprinted out the gate. He conjured echoes of Westhil's streets from the mist of his power and forced a shade of the Companion to settle over himself like a second skin. The warrior staggered back to slump upon his knees in front of him. His shield rolled into the mound of corpses.

'Duratakus,' the warrior gasped. 'I got away.'

'Well done,' Azaki said. 'Do you remember where we planned to go after here? My apprentice and I need to have a… *short talk*, so you'll be navigating.'

'To meet Yanastakus. White Creek Grove.'

Getitakus's bubble closed over the warrior's head and crushed it like an egg. Grey and red fluid spattered over the ground and the corpse slumped forward into the mud.

'I wasn't done,' Azaki snapped.

'We know where to go, so let's go,' Getitakus snarled. 'I won't leave Manastakus in their hands again. This time, I'll save him myself!'

Azaki fixed him with a flat stare. 'It would've been more useful to know more about Yanastakus, who's doubtless another of Anastagus's Companions.'

Getitakus glowered and stomped away through the townsfolk who melted out of his path.

'How could he do that?' Íri whispered.

'He's angry,' Azaki replied.

'He's a *Voréöeasiä*.'

'An angry Voréöeasiä.'

Íriniel scowled. 'The Heart-Tree doesn't condone *torture*. At worst, we kill to preserve the peace of the world and the lives of its people. She doesn't choose people who'd do things like he did.'

'Getitakus wasn't thinking about that. He wanted Manastakus back. Voréöeasiäki are just people, Íri. A thiokezöeasiä doesn't make them any better than the rest, it just makes them capable of greater things, good or bad.' Azaki glanced up at the fisherman edging toward them from the crowd. 'We've saved this place, we ought to return to the Heart-Tree.'

And get away from the world's edge before I end up as a spider snack or worse.

She crossed her arms. 'And abandon Manastakus?!'

'He's probably already dead, Íri. Or as good as.'

'Until we know that for sure, we can't just give up.' She sealed her thiokezöeasiä. 'I'm going after him.'

'Well now I have to come, don't I?' Azaki grumbled.

The fisherman managed another step forward and bowed. 'Vil Azaki, Vil Íriniel, please accept our thanks for saving us. If you wish to pursue them, Omotakus and some of us would be happy to help repay the debt we owe by assisting you.'

'Isn't Omotakus unconscious?' Azaki asked.

The fisherman shook his head. 'He woke up last night, Vil Azaki. He's a bit ruffled, but he'll be okay. Should I summon him for you?'

Azaki frowned. 'I guess.'

The fisherman ran back towards the lighthouse and the crowd dispersed.

'He called me Vil too,' Íri said.

Warlord. Azaki grimaced and his stomach knotted itself into a tight ball. *Even the clans banish keorls and eorls who love war too deeply.*

'Something tells me Anastagus's real plan hasn't been ruined at all,' he said. 'Like with Kogodakus, Duratakus has one goal, but Anastagus has another altogether.'

Her eyes widened. 'What do you mean?'

'He wants to destroy the Voréöeasiäki, not Akrotera's lighthouse. You said Vil means something like warlord, right?'

'More or less.'

'People don't love warlords forever,' Azaki murmured. 'When the idea of war turns sour, they cast them out.'

Twelve

The vast wall of dark-leaves and white-flowers rose up to the stars, a flood of sharp, sweet scents. Familiar, dark roots spread from the ebony trunk and a familiar dark sapling stood before him.

Siade sobbed into her hands beyond it. 'I'm sorry.' Her skin clung tight to her skull, her hair white as old bones. 'I'd no choice. I'm so sorry.'

Pale bodies sprawled beneath the twisting, arching roots. The woad and armour of the clans shone beside the simple tunics of southie townsfolk and at the base of the sapling, the blank eyes of the acolyte Duratakus had slain stared up at Azaki through the dirt. The roots throbbed as they fed on the rotting corpses, the grove tree's leaves swelled red, and the sharp, sweet scent of the flowers turned putrid.

Azaki gagged and stepped back, thudding into the hot, smoking timbers of the burning hall at his back.

'Azi!' Otuko stepped from the leaves; his spider-silk cloak in her outstretched hand. 'I found you. Why're you all alone again? I saved you, *remember?*'

'Remember what you promised, Azaki.' Íri stood beneath the red leaves, her thiokezöeasiä's crown glowing as bright as Akrotera's Torch. 'Remember.'

He shifted his weight toward Otuko.

The horn hilt of the hunting knife gleamed in the top of her boot.

Azaki's feet froze. 'I remember.' He stepped past the sapling toward Íri.

The red leaves fluttered and turned green, the putrid stench fading back to sweetness.

'I knew you'd keep your promise,' Íri breathed, offering her hand.

He took her fingers and smiled as the faint orange light and its warmth settled over him.

'But I know you won't protect the world.' Íri thrust her thiokezöeasiä forward.

Heat flashed across his face and he jolted awake.

The sun stabbed at his eyes as the longship rose and fell over the waves.

So much for a nice nap. Azaki pushed himself to his feet and stared out over the lake.

'We should've gone back to the Heart-Tree,' he muttered. 'Knowing my luck I'll find Anastagus, the Spider, and Toga the Sour all having a picnic together at White Creek Grove.'

Falaïré reclined upon the ship's side beside Itaki, trailing her fingers through the spray. 'We're pursuing our desire. What else is there?'

'You make it sound like Anastagus's spiel,' he grumbled. 'All self-interest.'

She smirked. 'We all chase the things we want, but those things don't *have* to be selfish. We wanted to save the Heart-Tree and we did, even though it cost us the little raider girl.'

'Only for a bit.' Azaki touched his fingers to his lips. 'She said she'd forgive me.'

'It won't be easy to have both, my Azi,' Falaïré murmured. 'The little raider girl is far away…'

'Well, we may get a lot closer soon. If the Clan of the Sword Spring is true to form, they will take Manastakus to the Theatre of the Worldbreaker.'

She smirked. 'A dangerous place. A Voréöeasiä might tragically disappear...'

Azaki glanced to where Íri stood at the longships' prow, staring into a rising wall of fog. 'Well, given she knows a little about us, we'll have to be very convincing.'

'The truth can't be stopped,' Falaïré whispered.

They plunged into the fog and she faded away.

'Bail.' Itaki fluffed his feathers up against the cold mist. 'Bail.'

'You can't bail fog, silly bird,' Azaki said.

'Íri.' The parrot scratched at his head with one toe. 'Íri.'

'Do I look like a violent midget?' Azaki waved a walnut at the bird. 'Eat your breakfast.'

'I heard that.' Íri loomed out of the fog. 'Omotakus reckons we're close to White Creek Grove.'

'Somewhat hard to tell in this.' He squinted into the white veil. 'It's even thicker than the stuff about the Refuge.'

'Might be Duratakus or Yanastakus's work,' Íri said.

'Maybe.' Azaki grimaced. 'It's usually pretty foggy around here, though. I heard that's why the Clan of the Grey Sails actually has grey sails, so they can hide in the fog. Besides, our chances of catching the Companion whose thiokezöeasiä controls wind seem a little short to begin with.'

Her eyes flashed. 'We're not going back!'

'I know. I know.' He raised his palms. 'Just don't blame me when we inevitably end up somewhere highly dangerous.'

Or I get killed by a giant spider. Unease twisted in his gut. *What's the Mistress of Whispers waiting for? The rest of the groves to burn? Or just for me to let my guard down?*

Omotakus thudded down the deck, dabbing at the beads of condensation on his bronze armour. 'Vil Íriniel, Vil Azaki, there's another ship.'

'Duratakus?' Íri asked.

'There's no sword on the sail, Vil Íriniel.'

'Fantastic,' Azaki muttered.

'What?' Íri demanded.

He squinted around until he saw the shape ahead in the fog. 'Where there's one…'

'Oh.'

'Maybe we can sneak past,' Azaki said. 'We're in a longship and we're only after the acolyte, not a pitched battle against two Companions and another hundred or so warriors.'

They watched the shape grow nearer through the fog. Omotakus' volunteers clutched their scavenged weapons and held their breath.

'Where's Vil Getitakus?' Omotakus asked.

A chill fell over Azaki. 'Oh *damn.*'

'What?' Íri swivelled.

'Well he's not going to let the ship go by, is he? If he thinks there's a chance his acolyte is on there, or is still angry…'

She pressed her lips into a thin line. 'What's the plan?'

What's the plan, Azi? Otuko's voice welled up in the back of his head, tearing a cold, hollow pit open about his heart.

He plastered a smile on his face. 'Burn their sail first, Íri, then try and sink the ship.'

'I brought down a house…'

'The house wasn't full of warriors who can ward the it and the air's full of water.'

'And me, Vil Azaki?' Omotakus' hand was on the hilt of his longsword. 'My men and I came to fight for you. You saved our home and our lives, the least we can do is save one of you.'

'You just try not to get hit in the head by any rocks this time.'

'Blaze, beacon of virtuous ire,' Íriniel whispered.

A gentle warmth settled over Azaki and a bright orange glow shone from within the thiokezöeasiä. 'Are you really set on that phrase?' he asked.

'*You're* complaining about *my* sealing phrase?'

'Well...'

She scowled. 'Shut up, Azaki.'

He grinned and pointed through the fog at the shape of the ship. 'Don't hold anything back, we don't know how much the fog will stop.'

The heat rippled through the fog, dissipating it like a giant hand had been wafted over the water. The grey sail smouldered, blackened, and curled away into smoke as Íri gritted her teeth.

'Raiders!' Getitakus stumbled from the stern as the first arrows hissed overhead. He took one look at the emblem on the sail. 'Blow, shining, gleaming sphere.'

A glowing white bubble swelled up on the tip of his thiokezöeasiä to twice the height of a man. Spells splashed against it in washes of colour and sparks, and arrows flicked off into the water.

Íriniel forced her heat haze against the side of the enemy longship and a wall of shimmering wards, but only steam rose from the wood. 'It's too wet and there are too many wards. If I want to burn it, I'll end up exhausting myself.'

Getitakus snarled and with a soft whoosh his bubble shrank down to the size of an apple. 'I'll do it, then.'

He launched the bubble of the end of his thiokezöeasiä and sent it sailing across onto the deck of the other longship. It burst, ripping the deck apart and showering nearby warriors with splinters.

That's a new trick. Azaki watched the Getitakus hurl another. *Nasty, too.*

The second one tore open a gaping hole in the ship's side. The longship shuddered and slipped to the side.

Getitakus hurled three more, smashing away half the side of the ship, and sagged to his knees. 'A few less of the savages,' he muttered. 'I hope the others all drown.'

Azaki watched the longship slip beneath the waves and the warriors splash toward the shore. Omotakus' men picked them off one by one with arrows, cheering each time a shaft struck true.

'Best watch out for other ships.' Íri ushered Omotakus toward the prow.

Getitakus dragged himself against the mast and leant his head back.

Good thing he tires fast.

'Expecting trouble?' Falaïré murmured in Azaki's ear. 'What he desires is not what we do...'

'I'm not sure I could do much to stop his magic,' he whispered, retreating back toward the stern. 'Perhaps I should break his thiokezöeasiä like Kogodakus did to Prasatakus? Would that work?'

'Perhaps.' Falaïré leant her chin on his shoulder. 'After all, what good's a broken heart?'

'It's only if he manages to escape our power.'

She laughed. 'You're right to be wary, my Azi. If our perceptions of our desires don't align perfectly with others', their betrayal is inevitable...'

'Strike first,' he murmured, joining dots of water together on the side of the ship with his thumb. 'Or be first struck.'

The red-stained fingertips of Falaïré's right hand slid along his jaw, leaving a hot, wet lines on his skin. 'Being seen fighting alongside this vengeful Voréöeasiä will hinder our return to the little raider girl, but the little Voréöeasiä girl's going to expect nothing less from us.'

'They do have names, Falaïré.'

Silver light rippled beneath the shadows of her dress and a sharpness flickered through her eyes. 'I know.'

'Perhaps I should show them the death of their acolyte. Íri might turn back.'

'Back to the shade of the Heart-Tree,' Falaïré whispered. 'So far from the girl who kissed us. The girl who loves us. The girl who found us. The girl who saved us.'

Otuko... A tangle of thorns coiled around Azaki's heart and he touched his fingertips to his lips. *I can't just abandon her, especially not now I know how she feels. But Íri...*

He sighed. 'You're not helping, Falaïré.'

She laughed. 'We're chasing two things, my Azi, and they're going in opposite directions. It'll tear us apart.'

He frowned down into the frothing wake. 'Only while Anastagus lives. Otuko might leave the clan if I asked her. Her dream's not really tied to the Webbed Pit.'

Falaïré cupped his face between her cool hands and rested her forehead against his. 'We'll see. Either way, it'll still be us.'

Azaki leant back from her and sighed. 'I might need *more* to stop Anastagus. He was a Hand of the Heart-Tree. Íri's thiokezöeasiä's still changing and she's getting stronger.'

Her eyes darkened. 'Don't fear, my Azi. Our heart's still growing stronger, too. Tricks that would've left you breathless before now come easier. Be patient. Together we'll get everything we want.'

'What's so bad about more?'

A shadow flickered in the corner of his eye, deep and dark as the Webbed Pit.

'It's not the same as us,' Falaïré whispered. 'Sometimes it settles over us like silence, others it watches from afar. Don't chase it. Don't let it come any closer. Don't let it in. Our heart is enough. *We're* enough.'

'Azaki!' Íri stomped across.

He twisted about. 'Another ship?'

She shook her head. 'The fog's clearing.'

He sighed. 'Let's hope we're not right in the middle of them, then.'

Íri took a step toward him. 'Are you alright?'

He pulled a grin onto his face. 'I'm fine. Just being wary. I'll come join you at the prow in a moment.'

Falaïré slid her arms round his neck as Íri walked away. 'If our heart changes, so will I,' she whispered. 'It's nice being us, my Azi. Let's not change.'

He smiled as he breathed in the sweet scent of athoëasirki. 'So *that's* what you don't like. You're afraid we won't be us anymore.'

'Promise,' she murmured, tracing her fingers along the scars on his palm. 'Promise it'll always be us.'

Azaki closed his fingers around Falaïré's. 'I promise. We're enough.'

She rested her face against the side of his neck, her smile tickled against the hairs there. 'We'll grow strong together, my Azi, like the little Voréöeasiä girl's father. Eventually, not even he or Anastagus will be able to hinder us.'

He chuckled and started toward the prow. 'For now, I'd settle for being able to match one of the Companions and becoming one of the Erudite so we don't get killed.'

The fog swirled as he joined Íri at the prow, shifting and twisting like a vast swarm of midges.

She peered past the figurehead. 'The wind's picking up.'

'Duratakus?' Azaki watched the fog slide back from them, sucked into a swirling tower of grey. 'This definitely isn't natural.'

Íri pointed to a line of green beyond the spiralling column of mist. 'That's White Creek Grove.'

Azaki watched the swirling vortex of fog touch the water and rip the lake's surface up into the sky. 'Not for long, I suspect.'

The waterspout tore through the line of green and spun back onto the water. Bits of wood pattered down onto the ship and shredded leaves floated down around them.

'Another grove,' Íriniel whispered.

He reached across and plucked the splinters and bits of green from her hair as the vortex faded out. 'Groves can be regrown, Íri.'

Bronze flashed in the corner of his eye. 'There.'

A longship gleamed in the sun as it pulled away from the ruined island.

'The whole thing's bronze,' Omotakus muttered. 'It should be too heavy to float.'

It must be gilded. Azaki squinted at the glimmering ship as it slid away over the waves. *But no warriors would waste bronze on that.*

Íri stared across the water and clenched her fists. 'That must be Yanastakus, the other Companion.'

Azaki's eyes slid to the three bodies dangling by their necks below the shining prow. 'Come on, Íri. Let's check the map and see if we can get to the other grove before they do. Omotakus, please take us east for now, remember every second counts.'

'Of course, Vil Azaki.'

Íri let him pull her away toward the stern. 'How can we fight two of them, Azaki?'

He grinned. 'Sneakily.'

'Be serious,' she murmured.

'There are other Voréöeasiäki there,' Azaki said. 'And that grove's pretty close to danger, so they ought to have been chosen to be able to defend it.'

'I don't want another acolyte or someone like Siade to die.'

He gnawed at the inside of his cheek. 'We'd best beat them, then. I'm sure, with a little time, I can manage something sneaky.'

Íri stared down into the water. 'I just don't understand why they do it.'

'The raiders? Or the Companions?'

'Either. All!' She dug her fingernails into the hairline cracks running the length of her thiokezöeasiä. 'Those Companions were Voréöeasiäki chosen by the Heart-Tree. They were good people with the potential to be great Voréöeasiäki. How could they end up like this? Are they just that selfish they don't care what they're doing?'

'Anastagus is. He used Kogodakus and threw him away. The others, I guess they've got their reasons. Voréöeasiäki are just people, Íri. They're not all good or all bad.' Azaki squeezed her fingers. 'Let's just focus on getting to this grove. Besides, Toga the Sour's probably there, so you can finally rekindle your romance with him out from under the nose of your father.'

'I'll kindle *something* if you're not careful.'

'He's not going to be overjoyed to see me...'

'Togastakus knows defending the groves comes first,' Íri said. 'Grey Sails Grove is the last one left on the lake.'

Azaki frowned. 'We'd better not let it get destroyed, for my sake, if nothing else.'

'*Your* sake?' She folded her arms. 'I thought *groves can be regrown.*'

'They can.' He ran a finger along the third scar on his palm and sighed. 'But in the time they're gone, the Spider might seize her chance to repay my betrayal in kind. I'd hate to die before seeing you and Toga the Sour happily wed.'

Íri chewed her lip. 'I'll find the map.' She darted away toward the stern.

Akrotera could reach us. And Estrif. A shiver of unease swept through Azaki. *The Lady of Betrayal must be able to reach me, too. What's She waiting for?*

Thirteen

The mast creaked and groaned, bent beneath the strain of the second sail lashed above the first. The longship glided through the waves, streaking past small islands and reefs toward the distant cliffs of Grey Sails Grove.

'I'm amazed it's not snapped.' Azaki shielded his face from the cold wind. 'How did you manage to hold it together to put it up?'

'Lore of augmentation,' Íri replied. 'It was still a struggle, though.'

He blinked. 'The thing Kogodakus could use? When did you learn that?'

'Before I met you. You need to have awakened your thiokezöeasiä to be able to use it.'

Azaki scratched the back of his neck. 'I should've practiced after reading that book, it'd probably come in handy.'

'You mean you *didn't?*'

'I had other things on my mind at the time.'

Íri pinched the bridge of her nose. 'Speed or strength?'

'What?'

'Pick one.' She jabbed him in the foot with her thiokezöeasiä. 'You ought to be able to manage one at a time now your thiokezöeasiä's awakened, but we've not got time for you to learn both. We're almost at the grove.'

Azaki turned it over in his head as they raced past a foaming reef toward a shallow pebbled beach. 'Speed.'

Íri nodded. 'Speed it is. Did you actually read the book I got for you?'

'Yes.' He raised his palms when she narrowed her eyes. 'Genuinely.'

'There are two ways the lore of augmentation makes you faster,' Íri said. 'The first is the magic's connected to you like a spell, so you can react quicker, as fast as when you burn your finger. The second requires all the reading, you've got to use it on your muscles.'

'Makes sense.' Azaki grinned. 'Maybe I'll be fast enough to dodge all your violent outbursts.'

'You're not going to be blurring out of sight or anything, Azaki. It just shaves half a second off when you're reacting or moving.'

'That is *incredibly* disappointing.'

She laughed. 'Were you expecting to be so fast you'd just seem to be appearing and disappearing?'

'Well, it would've been nice…'

Íri elbowed him in the ribs. 'Just listen. All you've got to do is shape your magic the right way inside your body for the first part. The second needs a bit more practice to move the magic with your muscles.'

'You make it sound a lot simpler than I suspect it'll be,' Azaki muttered. 'What even *is* the right shape?'

'The same shape as what's there, more or less,' she said. 'Just imagine it kind of wrapping round all your muscles and keep in mind what you want it to do just like any other spell. You'll get the hang of the second part after some practicing and I can probably heal you if you do anything stupid.'

'Why would I need healing if I get it wrong?' he asked. 'Is this payback for me pretending to plan your marriage pledge to Toga the Sour? I was only trying to help…'

'You might tear or rupture something if you only get part of you to move fast.' Íri's tone turned sweet. 'If I wanted to get you back for that *ridiculous* fake pledge, I'd've hit you.'

'You did hit me.' Azaki chuckled. 'I can't wait until it's my turn to teach you something.'

She snorted. 'You are literally the last person on this world fragment I'd get lessons from.'

'What about Anastagus?'

'He was a Hand of the Heart-Tree, so he's probably a pretty competent teacher.'

Azaki folded his magic through his arm, imagining the pictures of muscles he'd seen in the book Íri had found for him. 'This isn't actually that hard—'

'Not *now*.' She stamped on his foot and the magic slipped from his control. 'We're nearly at the grove!'

He shrugged and watched Omotakus's men cut the topsail free into the wind. 'I've not seen any ships, so either we're a fair way ahead, or they are.'

'Or they went round the north of the islands and we went round the south...'

'Or that.'

Íri shook her head. 'You're winding me up again, aren't you?'

'Me?' Azaki grinned. 'What an awful accusation to make, Íri.'

The longship's keel grated against the pebbles as they slid up the beach beyond the tideline toward sharp, steep cliffs.

Azaki waved a small apple in the air. 'Itaki!'

'Where is he?' Íriniel murmured. 'I've not seen him all day.'

'Hiding from the wind under all those boxes.' He waggled the apple in front of the parrot's beak as Itaki fluttered to his shoulder. 'Probably chewing on things he shouldn't be, too.'

Omotakus vaulted over the side of the ship and onto the pebbles. 'Vil Azaki. The Voréöeasiäki were on the track up the hill, but they've gone back into their grove.'

Guess we beat the Companions here, then. Azaki watched Getitakus lower himself off the side of the ship and glare back out over the lake. *Maybe we'll actually manage to get Manastakus back.*

He jumped down onto the beach, wincing as the shock flashed up his legs.

Íri swung herself onto the side of the ship, dangling her feet down. 'Er...'

He cackled. 'Is it a long way?'

'Shut up and help me down, Azaki.'

'Voréöeasiä Princess Íri needs another servant, does she?' Azaki stepped back in front of her small feet. 'Just jump onto me, I'll catch you.'

Íriniel eyed the pebbles. 'Do *not* drop me.'

'I promise not to drop you. I wouldn't here, not with pebbles, maybe if it was sand or water.'

She shuffled to the very edge and grimaced, then pushed herself off.

Azaki caught her round the waist and staggered back a couple of steps with a wince as her knees made contact with his stomach. 'See, didn't drop you.'

Íri wrapped her arms 'round his neck. 'Don't even think about putting me in the water either, Azaki.'

He laughed and strode up the beach. 'The idea hadn't even occurred to me, though you're so light I could probably throw you a long way in.'

'Are you going to put me down?'

Azaki leant his cheek away from her tickling gold hair. 'I'm actually very tempted to carry you all the way, just so Toga the Sour sees his future bride in my arms.'

She growled. 'You're holding me for *that?* Put me down, Azaki. *Now.*'

He set her back on her feet at the top of the stone steps off the beach where the track met the pebbles. 'There you go, Voréöeasiä Princess Íri. Safe and sound.'

Íri crossed her arms and scowled. 'You're *incorrigible.*'

Azaki laughed and set off up the hill between the cliffs. 'The best bit's all the Voréöeasiäki were already watching us land, so if Togastakus *is* here, he's probably already grinding what's left of his teeth away.'

She stomped up the track behind him, muttering under her breath.

Too funny. A smile crept onto Azaki's lips as he watched her fume all the way to the summit. *Íri's reactions are always so great.*

'She wears her heart on her sleeve,' Falaïré murmured. 'Not like us, my Azi.'

'You.' Togastakus sat on a thick root at the entry to the grove, his pristine white tunic standing out against the gnarled, brown trunks and roots like a cloud upon a blue sky. 'Why're *you* here?'

'To visit you, of course,' Azaki said. 'I missed your sullen glares and the smell of half-chewed tobacco leaves.' He waved a hand at the elder Voréöeasiä behind him. 'This is Getitakus. The two of you ought to get along.'

'Stop being such children.' Íri slipped around Azaki's side to stand in front of him. 'Both of Anastagus's Companions are coming here, you'll need our help to defend the grove.'

Togastakus's jaw tightened. 'Your help, maybe, not *his.*'

Azaki chuckled under his breath and stroked the top of Itaki's head. 'Actually, for once, *you're* going to be the most useful.'

Togastakus stared at him and extended a hand with the outline of a heart tattooed onto the back of it in green dye. 'What're we doing?'

Íri glanced between them, narrowing her eyes at Azaki.

'Fine...' Azaki clasped Togastakus' outstretched hand. 'The Companions will turn up with a lot of warriors. We'll encourage them to leave before ruining anything green and peaceful. Fortunately, there's a lot of water here.'

Togastakus grunted and patted the leaping fish upon his thiokezöeasiä's crown. 'I see.'

'Exactly.' Azaki waved a hand out at the lake. 'If you can, let one of the Companions land before you block off the other longships. Given what we saw at White Creek Grove, Yanastakus might come in with just his ship first.'

'You *want* to fight Yanastakus?' Íri scowled at him. 'Why?'

'I'd rather we fight one of them now, than risk fighting both later. Together, Íri, Getitakus, and I can probably take one of the Companions. Stopping the ships and the other Companion before they overwhelm us is on you, Togastakus.'

Togastakus slid off his root and fumbled in his pockets. 'I and my Greenhearts will be more than enough to stop some seagoing savages. Four pure Voréöeasiäki are a match for any number of rogue ones.'

Azaki raised an eyebrow at him. 'If you say so…'

Togastakus folded a tobacco leaf in half and slid it between his lips. 'I do. We're proper Voréöeasiäki. The Heart-Tree will always ensure us victory. Even if it sometimes seems like defeat, it just means she has a greater strategy in mind.'

'Well, we're one grove away from trouble,' Azaki told him. 'So the greatest purpose would be to not to lose this one, too.'

'*Too?*' Togastakus glowered. 'What happened to the others?'

'Burnt, burnt, and destroyed in a very suspicious weather phenomenon,' Azaki said.

'Our task was to free the Beacon at the Edge of the World from siege,' Íri said. 'We came north chasing Duratakus after he fled. He's kidnapped an acolyte from Crumbling Cliff Grove.'

'I suppose Master Soekus can restore the groves.' Togastakus worked his jaw. 'You did well to help the beacon.'

'It wasn't too hard,' Azaki said.

Íriniel rolled her eyes. 'Well, Akrotera's not going to save your life again here, Azaki, so you'd better hope this will be easier.'

'You don't know that,' he said. 'She might. Maybe she'll be nice to me after I did what she asked.'

Togastakus ground his teeth. 'Any other Nerevoréoathoki you've been consorting with?'

Azaki pretended to consider it. 'I think she's the only one so far.'

'You *know* Akrotera's one of the Voréoathoki, Togastakus,' Íri scolded. 'Stop being difficult.'

He chomped on his tobacco leaf. 'If it weren't for Voréöeasiäki like him, the Heart-Tree would be willing to save all our lives.'

'You don't know that, though,' Azaki said. 'Imagine how stupid you'd look if you turned out to be wrong.'

'I'm not wrong—'

'Master Togastakus, there's a sail!' A brown-cloaked Voréöeasiä stumbled through the trees, waving a heart-tattooed hand back toward the beach.

'Here they come,' Azaki muttered as Togastakus hurried away through the trees on the heels of his Greenheart Voréöeasiä.

'Try not to get injured this time,' Íri whispered, nudging his toes with hers.

'I'll do my best. It's not like I enjoy it.'

'I'm starting to think you do. Maybe you've realised it's the only way I'm going to get close enough to touch you.'

Azaki grinned. 'Be careful, Íri. If you're too mean to me, I won't help you climb back into the boat. You'll be stuck here with Toga the Sour…'

She rolled her eyes. 'I hope you finish writing that wedding pledge before you sail off and get killed without me, I'll read it out at your funeral.'

He chuckled as Íriniel set off through the trees, Getitakus trailing after her.

Omotakus took a seat on the root. 'What's our role, Vil Azaki?'

Azaki peered around through the trees. 'As far as I've seen, this track's the only easy way off that beach and the map shows it's the only landing spot on the island. You and your men will hold the narrowest point where the stairs leave the beach. I'd suggest you check for any other ways off the beach, though.'

'Of course.' Omotakus jumped from his seat and ushered his men back down the track.

'What's the full plan, my Azi?' Falaïré slid from the shadows of the woods.

'Well…' He grinned out at where a single grey sail approached from behind one of the smaller islands. 'I don't want Toga the Sour to know how our power works, so we'll make him do all the hard work keeping the warriors busy.'

She laughed and steepled her fingers, pressing red-stained fingertips against pale, clean ones. 'While he's distracted, we could let the Companion kill the old bubble Voréöeasiä. If we go north with him, it'll be all the harder to return to the little raider girl.'

Azaki frowned. 'We can just return his acolyte to him. He'll go back to Crumbling Cliff Grove once he's got Manastakus back and forget all that hate he's got in his heart.'

Falaïré ran her fingers through his hair. 'But we know where they're going, my Azi, and we'd be so close to leaving if we can get there…'

The Theatre of the Worldbreaker. Azaki gnawed the inside of his cheek. *Estrif's blood-soaked shrine.*

'But no further from being exiled on my return,' he said.

'If we wait too long, the little raider girl will grow used to our absence,' she whispered. 'There are others who'd want her. Once she has one of them for her dream, why would she want anyone else?'

A cold pang speared him through the gut. Azaki wrestled it down. *Otuko wouldn't just leave me behind like that. She said she'd never leave me alone.*

He swallowed and tightened his grip on the hot wood of his thiokezöeasiä. 'Technically, she's a little warrior girl now.'

'We're going to have to choose, my Azi.' Falaïré took his face in her cool hands. 'The girl who loves us and the Webbed Pit, or the soft, green world of the south and the little Voréöeasiä girl.'

'Not yet we don't,' he said.

'But soon.'

'Yes.' He sighed and covered her hands with his, staining his palms crimson on her red-dyed fingertips. 'At least it'll still be us.'

Fourteen

A bronze-gilded ship thrust itself out of the haze of rain, its keel scraping through the driftwood and flotsam of the tide line. Warriors jumped out onto the thin stretch of pebbles between Azaki and the ship. The bronze bands and shapes reinforcing their cuirasses glinted over wet, dark, leather, mismatched weapons bristled from their hands, and smeared patterns of woad marked their faces. Crimson tear marks daubed the cheeks of some, others wore red bars across the bridges of their noses or their cheeks.

Azaki squinted through the drizzle at the score of grey sails following Yanastakus's longship through the narrow path between the reefs. 'You're certain this is the only beach?'

Togastakus grunted. 'Yes.'

'Do your thing then, mighty Greenheart.'

Togastakus planted his thiokezöeasiä in the pebbles. 'Surge, Sea of Boundless Purity.'

A shiver rolled out across the lake, like the furthest ripples spreading from a stone cast into a tarn.

Azaki grimaced as the breeze cut through his wet leather shirt like a knife through a fish's belly. 'Can you unseal your thiokezöeasiä, Íri? It's cold in the rain.'

'My thiokezöeasiä's not here to keep you warm.'

'But you're going to have to do it anyway...'

'Fine.' She dragged the heat haze away from the crown with her fingertips. 'Blaze, beacon of virtuous ire.'

The faint orange aura settled over Azaki with the sudden glow of the pyramid and slim cracks upon her thiokezöeasiä. 'That's a lot better,' he said. 'Thanks, Íri.'

Togastakus dug his nails into his thiokezöeasiä and clenched his jaw. 'Will both of you be quiet. I'm trying to focus.'

Tendrils of water reared from the surface of the lake, thick as tree trunks, dripping foam, weed, and small fish back into the waves. Togastakus swung his thiokezöeasiä and they smashed into the first two of the following ships. The two longships crashed together, shattering oars in an explosion of splinters, tangling their masts and sails. The nearer lurched, its prow sinking down until only the snarling, horned figurehead stuck above the waves.

'Perfect.' Azaki drew his falcata and levelled the tip at the bronze-masked Companion standing at the landed longship's prow. 'Now the way to the beach is blocked, you just have to get rid of anyone who comes ashore while we deal with him.'

'What're we doing, Azaki?' Íri whispered as they strode down the beach.

'Well, we've no idea what he can do, so we'll just wing it. Maybe I'll be able to get something out of him before everyone starts throwing dangerous magic around.'

'Blow, shining, gleaming sphere,' Getitakus muttered. A white bubble swelled up on the end of his thiokezöeasiä, then shrank to the size of Azaki's fist.

'What part of *before* the dangerous magic went over your head? You keep that bubble right there until I say,' Azaki ordered. 'If you'd not gone psycho and squished that warrior's head back at the beacon, we'd already know a bit about what Yanastakus's thiokezöeasiä could do.'

Getitakus growled and hurled the bubble into the warriors instead.

It exploded against a hastily raised shieldwall of shimmering wards, tossing men back into the surf and away onto the pebbles.

'Or you can do that,' Azaki said. 'In fact, why don't you go after the warriors, Getitakus. Leave the Companion to Íri and I.'

Íri shot him a sharp look as Getitakus launched another bubble into the wall of wards. 'We might need him.'

'He managed about three bubbles last time before he collapsed,' Azaki said. 'And he's rash when he's angry. He'll just get in the way, or hit one of us. Itaki would be upset if you got torn to pieces by a bubble and I'd have wasted an awful lot of time planning your wedding pledges to tall, dark, and sulky.'

Íri rolled her eyes.

Yanastakus dropped off the side of the ship and stepped back to where the tide foamed out on the brown pebbles. A shining mask of expressionless bronze covered his face below his brazen helm, and bronze greaves, armguards and leaf-shaped scales armoured him from head to toe. 'Azaki Kathal, I presume.'

'Does Anastagus really have nothing better to do than gossip about me? Everyone I meet seems to know my name.'

'He mentioned you were of interest to him.' Yanastakus's mask gave his voice a cold, metallic echo. 'I can't say I understand why.'

Azaki tilted his head to one side and studied the brown eyes behind the eye-slits. 'I can't say I understand why you all follow him. He sent Kogodakus to his death without batting an eyelash.'

'Our goals align for now,' Yanastakus replied. 'For the good of the world.'

'The destruction of the Voréöeasiäki?' Íri cried. 'What *good* does that do?'

Yanastakus glanced across the beach to where his warriors' shieldwall of wards pressed against Togastakus, Getitakus, and the three Greenhearts. 'Before Mūru's theft of their power, our Volōmothí ancestors built wonders. Before the Sundering, even our Volōmotistí ancestors managed to retain some of that splendour. Yet we scrape together mud and twigs to build our halls. Beneath the lake surface at the Anchorstone are ruined spires as tall as the Heart-Tree, but in all the time since the Sundering we've not managed a single step back toward what we once were. Vyfaesiä holds us back.'

'That's a lie,' Íriniel hissed. 'Anastagus has deceived you.'

'I didn't learn this from him, but from the Knotted Stone's vaults, where Sekyrnyr, the Hidden One, has His vast library-shrine of knowledge.' Yanastakus pointed his scroll-shaped thiokezöeasiä crown at them. 'Olisolamon is Vyfaesiä's world fragment, only She could keep it shackled in ignorance for so long.'

Íri's irises spun into orange flame. 'You don't need to destroy the Voréöeasiäki!'

'Vyfaesiä must be forced to let us progress.' Yanastakus jabbed his thiokezöeasiä toward the sky. 'Do you think the other world fragments floating out there among the stars have been so restrained? What happens when they find a way to bridge the void between world fragments and realise how backward and weak we are?'

Azaki narrowed his eyes. 'Anastagus will never give you the chance to change things. He doesn't seem the *greater good* sort.'

Yanastakus fell still. 'When I am strong enough, I will cast him down, but until then I must serve him… and you're in our way.' He tapped a finger upon the crown of his thiokezöeasiä and the whole thing turned to shining metal. 'Gild, lamentation of the brazen world.'

The falcata in Azaki's hand rippled like water. He hurled the bronze blade away to the base of the cliff. *Not good.*

'Queen of whispering webs, upon your throne of lies, gift a blade of shadow, and revel in their cries,' he murmured, forcing the blade of shadow as long as he could.

Íri let loose a searing wave of heat, but Yanastakus's armour sprouted into a curved shield of molten meltal.

Yanastakus stepped out from behind the wall of white-hot bronze. 'Secret flame, wild flame, blue as aconite, liquid fire, were-fire, sate your appetite.'

Bright, blue fire burst into life over his palm, so bright it stung Azaki's eyes. He cast the Lady's Veil and ducked right. The fireball hissed past his shoulder, splashing over the ground like blazing oil. Bronze tendrils lunged like a thousand angry serpents and he threw himself back, rolling across the pebbles. Íri's heat haze surged past him, smothering the blue flames on the beach and spattering the beach in molten bronze.

I really need some better spells. Azaki stumbled back to his feet, watching the grazes on his hands fade away beneath the soft orange glow of Íri's unsealed thiokezöeasiä. *I've nothing to back my tricks up with.*

Ribbons of bronze sliced through the air. Íri forced them back with a grimace. Azaki tried the Lady's Veil and Azaki's web, threading his magic toward Yanastakus's senses, but the magic slid off him like water.

The bronze drew back into a puddle at Yanastakus's feet and flowed from the hull of the longship, rising into the form of man thrice Azaki's height, glowing from the heat of Íri's magic. The golem shuddered, its arms flattening into blades.

'Not ideal.' Azaki glanced at the slim blade of shadow in his hand. 'I think we're back to the same plan as with Kogodakus, Íri.'

'I can't smother bronze like fire!'

'Why risk so much?' Falaïré whispered in his ear. 'Our power is more than enough. Trust our heart, my Azi.'

Yanastakus prowled the beach behind his gleaming golem. 'Coiled shackle, bright shackle, seize your prey tight, curled shackle, swift shackle, captor's delight.' A flail of blue light uncurled from his palm.

Azaki shook his head. 'I am *not* being hit with a whip.'

The golem thundered up the beach toward Íri. Scorching heat crashed into it, melting its legs, and the golem thudded to the ground, dragging itself forward with its arms. Yanastakus's flail hissed toward Azaki. He cut it away with the blade of shadow, but the whip curled round the weapon and ripped it from his grasp.

Azaki cursed and raised his hand to create another, but Yanastakus's weapon snapped round his chest, pinning his arms to his side. A tingling, stinging numbness seized him, as if everything below his neck had fallen asleep.

Not ideal.

Yanastakus's golem split in two. Íri seared one gleaming figure into a thousand droplets of molten metal and scattered it into the tide. The other charged Azaki. He tried to twist away, but his numb limbs refused to respond.

The golem faltered beneath a burning wind and dissolved into a shining puddle among the stones. Blazing orange spread from Íri's pupils to cover all the white of her eyes as she turned her power on Yanastakus. The bronze sprang from the floor like angry eels, absorbing her magic in a rippling gold curtain.

'We tried swords. We tried spells.' Falaïré's murmur tickled the nape of his neck. 'Now it's time for truth.'

Yanastakus growled and drew all the metal back to circle him in rings of liquid bronze. 'Transmute, progression's well-mourned sacrifice.'

Damn. He's an erudite Voréöeasiä, too. Azaki smothered the chill that crept into the pit of his stomach and tensed his muscles until some feeling returned.

Yanastakus's thiokezöeasiä burst into molten metal, the blades and armour of everyone on the beach poured through the air toward him, and the mask flowed from his face, revealing a thin, pale, clean-shaven countenance. He directed great waves of bronze against Íri with his free hand, the rest swirling around him in a stream of glowing globules.

Azaki strained against the glowing whip, but its hold remained. 'Deceive, lady of lies.'

'Finally you call for me,' Falaïré whispered as the mist of their magic washed across the pebbles. 'Why do you always wait so long…?'

Because if they all know what it does, I won't be able to trick them.

He let Yanastakus see him wriggle free of the whip and circle round the beach to flank him. Yanastakus released his spell, directing bronze ribbons across the beach after Azaki's shadow. His echo danced away and the brazen tendrils speared through the warriors in the shieldwall.

Azaki smiled and strode down the beach, concealed within the mist of his power. 'Queen of whispering webs, upon your throne of lies, gift a blade of shadow, and revel in their cries.' He drove the blade of shadow through Yanastakus's chest, grimacing at the hot gush of blood.

'Oh.' Yanastakus's hands dropped and the liquid bronze splashed to the ground, the pain ripping him free from Azaki's illusion like an arrow through a spider's web. 'Now I see. You're just like him.'

'No, I'm not.' Azaki twisted the blade and watched the life fade from Yanastakus's brown eyes. 'I'm nothing like Anastagus.'

I'm not. Azaki ignored Falaïré's soft laughter. *His ugly, single, selfish truth is nothing like our beautiful web of infinite perception. We don't pretend our truth is somehow better than all the others.*

Togastakus stomped across the beach, dripping sweat. 'You killed him.' He clenched his jaw. 'Good.'

The huddle of longships beyond the two sunk between the reefs turned away and set back out onto the lake.

'Well, that's good,' Azaki said. 'I'd've been in trouble if we'd lost this grove.'

Togastakus sneered. 'We'd all have been *in trouble*.'

Íri sighed. 'And we're back to fighting like children.'

Getitakus limped over. Blood streamed from his left knee and shoulder, soaking his brown tunic and the frayed, ragged ends of his brown girdle fluttered in the breeze. 'Let's go! They're getting away!'

Azaki frowned and shook his head. 'We're not sailing out there to get massacred, Getitakus. We'll give chase when we can follow from a safe distance.'

Getitakus kicked a pebble away into the water. 'Fine. I'll tell Omotakus and his men to be ready. At least we got a few of them. They won't be hurting anyone ever again.'

Togastakus' eyes flicked to Íri. 'I'll come with you.'

Azaki groaned. 'Must you?'

'Yes.'

'Then go pack some more green paint for your hand, because we're leaving as soon as those sails are on the horizon.'

Togastakus glowered. 'It's a tattoo, not paint.'

'Less for you to carry, then.'

He turned on his heel and stamped away toward the other white clad Voréöeasiäki. 'I'm going north with Íriniel,' he called. 'You three remain here and defend the grove. If any others come to join our movement, make sure they're worthy. Don't let them stay if they're not.'

Íri poked him in the shoulder with her thiokezöeasiä as she resealed it. 'What is it?'

Azaki sighed. 'I know where they're going.'

Her eyes flashed. 'Where?'

'There's a shrine to Estrif in the mountains across the lake just north of here.' He frowned down at the bronze gilded pebbles and resealed his thiokezöeasiä. 'I can't explain to the others how I know, Íri, but that's where they're headed.'

'Does it have a name?'

'The Theatre of the Worldbreaker.'

Íriniel stared at him, chewing her lip. 'How much have you *still* not told me?'

'I—'

'Don't.' She strode off up the beach.

'You don't tell me every thought *you* have…'

Falaïré rested her head on his shoulder and the sweet scent of athoëasirki washed over him. 'She's angry with us.'

'What did we do?' Azaki murmured. 'We didn't lie.'

'Perhaps the time has come to choose, my Azi,' she whispered.

He glanced to where Íri sat with back against the cliff, his falcata across her thighs. 'How can I? She's my friend. Otuko, too.'

'If we don't choose one, we'll lose both,' Falaïré murmured. 'Follow our heart. What do we want *most?*'

Azaki touched his fingertips to his lips, a lead weight settling in his breast. 'I owe Otuko everything. It's not a choice, really. If she's convinced Utháki to forgive me, I just need some way to return to the clan.' He glanced at where Íri sat.

She caught his look and glared back with blazing orange pupils. 'I don't want to talk to you!'

'The clan…' Falaïré trailed her red-stained fingertips along the scars on his palm, leaving crimson lines along his skin. 'We've sworn no blood oaths to the Webbed Pit, my Azi. Just these three.'

'Utháki will never leave the clan. His mother died just so he'd have a chance to be part of it.'

The corner of her lips curved upwards. 'Would we rather have one friend, or none, my Azi? If this little warrior is going to force the girl who loves us to choose between him and us, then make sure she's ours.'

'I don't know if she'd choose us,' Azaki muttered. 'She thinks we can return to the clan and knows Utháki will never leave.'

'If she's not going to choose us, then she's betrayed us for him,' Falaïré whispered. 'If she's going to choose us anyway, then we should be kind and spare her such an awful choice.'

'How?'

'If the warrior will never leave, then his betrayal's inevitable,' she murmured. 'He *will* choose the Webbed Pit over us eventually.' She touched a crimson-stained fingertip to the scars on Azaki's palm. 'Sever the ties of our heart before we're snared in them.'

The stars gleamed down around a red crescent and its white partner onto pillars of dark rock and slopes of rough, light stones. The distant shadow of mountains loomed beyond the slopes. A patchwork of sharp, grey shapes beneath a dark sky.

Azaki poked at his ribs, his heart weighing heavy beneath them. *The world's edge. Not home, but just the same as it.*

'Akrotera,' he murmured. 'If I still hold any of your favour, don't let the vengeance of Princess of Whispers reach me.'

Omotakus clambered up the hexagonal stone columns beside him. 'Do you know who built this place, Vil Azaki?'

'It's natural, I think.' He patted the column beside him. 'According to the stories my brother used to tell me, it's been this way since the Sundering.'

'It's weird.' Omotakus' hand rested on the dolphin pommel of his longsword. 'When are we moving on? Is it soon?'

'It's not going to get any better,' Azaki said. 'You see the shadows of the mountains? The nearest is where we'll cross the river and cut off Duratakus.'

Íri and Togastakus climbed up after him, wincing at the touch of the cold stone.

'It's freezing,' Íri chattered, wrapping her arms around herself.

'You'll get used to it.' Azaki shielded his eyes from the sky and peered into the night, but saw no watchfires sparkling on the slopes. 'You were the one who wanted to come this far North.'

'You were the one who brought us here,' she said. 'Some shortcut.'

'We can't sail up the rivers without being spotted,' he replied. 'So we land in this inlet, and travel light and fast. The rivers are longer, they wiggle, and they're rowing against the current.'

'How fast?' Togastakus demanded.

'Try and keep up.' Azaki leapt from his pillar to the slope and ran toward the distant outline of the mountains.

'Azaki!' Íri cried.

'She sounds angry still.' Falaïré ran alongside him on nothing but air as he darted up the ridge over the loose gravel. 'I don't think she's going to be able to keep up with us, my Azi.'

'I said *try.*' He reached the top of the slope and glanced back. 'What? How're they so far behind already?'

So soft. Azaki leant on his thiokezöeasiä and stared west toward the distant peaks. *Otuko would've been ahead of me.*

Omotakus staggered over the top, mopping sweat off his face. 'This pace will kill us, Vil Azaki. This weird gravel's too loose to run on in armour, we just sink in.'

'Alright, but too much slower and we won't be fast enough to save anyone without a *lot* of luck.'

Togastakus stumbled over the slope in a whiff of tobacco and dragged himself down the far side. Getitakus followed him, muttering between every gasped breath.

'Keep going,' Azaki told Omotakus as his men jogged past. 'Head for the small mountain nearest us, if I've not caught up by the time you cross the river, wait there.'

'Yes, Vil Azaki.' He paused. 'My men and I, we could carry some of Vil Íriniel's things between us?'

'She should carry her own stuff if she's going to ignore everyone's advice and bring it. Keep running, Omotakus.'

He waited, practising shaping his magic within his muscles until Íri hauled herself over the rise.

'Azaki…' she gasped. 'I can't… run like… this.'

'So I see.' He pointed at the bag on her shoulder. 'Maybe you should've left all your stuff like I suggested?'

She dropped the bag at his feet and doubled over. 'We might… need it.'

'*You* might, though carrying it's probably going to kill a soft, southie girl like you long before anything else does.' He poked the bag with the end of his thiokezöeasiä. 'Have fun.'

Íri straightened up and wiped the back of her hand across her eyes. 'Why're you being actually mean?' she whispered.

'I'm not being mean. Now come on.'

'You *are.*'

'You sound like a child.'

'A child!' She kicked him in the shin. 'I'm not the one who's refused to say more than a handful of words to me since we set sail from Grey Sails Grove!'

Azaki ignored the throbbing in his leg. 'You said you didn't want to talk to me.'

Íri stared. 'I didn't - I didn't mean—'

'You didn't mean what? That I ought to tell you every single thing I know or you'd throw a tantrum? What difference does it make if I know where they're headed in the end, we'd've done the exact same thing as we did!'

She scowled and ground her thiokezöeasiä into the gravel. 'I just wanted you to trust me,' she muttered. 'Friends trust each other.'

He thrust his scarred palm under her nose. 'You think I'm here risking the wrath of the Lady of Betrayal because of some acolyte, do you?'

'No…' Íri stared at her feet. 'But—'

'But what?' Azaki demanded. 'These mountains are the edge of the world. There're no groves here, Íri. If the Princess of Whispers wants me dead, *I'm dead.*'

She blinked. 'She can't get you herself. We'd just have to defeat whatever she sends.'

He laughed. 'Even if that's true, there're plenty of ways. How will you stop a dozen spiders twice the size of horses?'

Íri clutched her thiokezöeasiä. 'I'll turn them to ash.'

'You know *nothing* of the Lady of Lies, Íri. She's just another shadow out beyond the safety of your groves to you.' A twist of fear coiled in his gut at the recollection of how she'd turned on him in his dream and realisation struck like a flash of lightning. 'It won't be spiders She sends. I betrayed Her for *you*, and it'll be you She sends to kill me.'

'I would *never!*'

'Do you think Anastagus the Truthseeker would've ever believed he'd try and destroy the order he devoted his life to?' Azaki snatched her bag off the slope and swung it over his shoulder. 'Come on.'

She stumbled after him down the slope, streaming sweat and gasping for breath, then staggered after him across the gravel banks and dry stream beds.

He paused beside the stream and watched the moonlight gleam upon the rippling water until she'd caught up again. 'Have a drink, Íri, then give me your thiokezöeasiä and strip off anything you're wearing you don't need to be.

She went pink. 'I'm not taking off all my clothes.'

'Obviously. You'll need some of them.' He offered her a grin. 'Although, that's not what I'm going to tell your future husband you said when we catch up.'

Íri glared at him, but her lip trembled and it turned into a smile. 'I'm sorry.' She wrapped her arms round him and buried her face in his chest.

Sweaty Íri. Azaki wrinkled his nose and patted her on the head. *Still, nowhere near as bad as Utháki after hunting.*

'Drink, Íri,' he wheezed. 'And loosen up a bit, or the Lady of Betrayal isn't going to need to do anything after all.'

She drew back and knelt down in the gravel by the stream to gulp water out of her cupped hand, trailing her gold hair in the stream. 'That's a lot better.'

'Good.' Azaki plucked her thiokezöeasiä out of her other hand. 'What're you wearing?'

She narrowed her eyes at him and stood up. 'Clothes.'

He rolled his eyes and tugged her closer. 'Just come here.'

Íri squeaked and turned red. 'What're you—'

He pulled at her sleeves. 'Three tunics? Really?'

'It was cold!'

'I bet it's not cold now you've been running.' He pulled her arms over her head and tugged the top two up. The third came with them, giving him a brief glimpse of her dimpled knees. 'Actually, why don't *you* take those two off.'

Íri dragged the bottom tunic back down over her thighs. 'Turn around. I want to keep the top one, its less sweaty.'

Azaki swivelled to stare up at the red moon. 'Just hurry up.'

Falaïré stepped from the night. 'Not going to turn around?' she whispered. 'The little Voréöeasiä girl won't mind *too* much.'

I think she'd probably murder me. He rummaged through her bag before his imagination provided anything unhelpful. *We don't need any of this.*

'You can turn around now.'

He caught another flash of her knees as she tugged the tunic down. 'You don't need anything in here that much, or those tunics, so leave them.'

Íri glanced at the bag. 'Fine, but if I get cold…'

'You can have my shirt or something.' Azaki grinned at her. 'I'm going to tell Togastakus I've seen what he's spent the last few years dreaming about.'

Colour blossomed across Íri's cheeks. 'You saw nothing!'

'But *he* doesn't know that.'

She snorted, but her forehead wrinkled. 'Are we… okay?'

'We're fine, Íri.' Azaki splashed water on his face and poked her in the hip with her thiokezöeasiä. 'Save your breath for running. We need to get to the Theatre of the Worldbreaker as soon as we can.'

Íriniel eyed her thiokezöeasiä. 'Not the river?'

He tucked their thiokezöeasiäki under his arm and stepped over the stream. 'We won't catch them at the river, but we'll be close enough to see the shrine and have a reason to go look.'

She jumped over the water. 'You could've *told me* that was the plan.'

Azaki sighed and squinted through the night at the cluster of shadows passing over the top of the next ridge. 'Sorry. I'm used to Otuko and Utháki just following my lead for things like this.'

'Well, I'm *not* Otuko.'

'Despite your best efforts to hit me even more than she does, I did actually notice that.'

She groaned and started up the slope. 'You better have.'

Sixteen

The columns of the Theatre of the Worldbreaker rose up to scrape the first rays of a red dawn creeping across the sky, a ring of towering, faceless figures standing side-by-side, hands resting on the pommels of jagged-edged greatswords. Their crimson-daubed eyes wept long, bloody stains over the smooth, uncarved stone beneath the figures' curved horns.

'What is this place, Vil Azaki?' Omotakus muttered.

'Can't say.' Azaki led them round into the shadows of the clawed toe of the nearest column. 'Looks a lot like a shrine to someone, though.'

'*Can't say*,' Falaïré echoed in his ear.

He smothered a small smile at the smirk in her tone.

Omotakus frowned and stared up to where the light of the sunrise fell on the top of toe half a dozen metres above. 'Vil Íriniel? Vil Getitakus? Vil Togastakus?'

Togastakus's jaw clenched so tight his teeth grated. 'This mountain is clearly a shrine to Estrif,' he spat. 'They've carved the whole mountainside away to make those statues.'

'They're at least a thousand metres high… It must've taken a very long time, even with magic.' Getitakus growled. 'What a waste of effort.'

It's older than that. Older than the clans, like the Webbed Pit. Azaki stared up at the statues and recalled the stories his brother had told him. *This place existed to honour Estrif long before the Heart-Tree drove the clans into these mountains.*

'Let's not insult Estrif right at the edge of the world,' he suggested. 'Unless you all want to be smote?' Azaki frowned. 'Smited? Smitten? Íri?'

'Definitely not smitten.' Íri poked at the clawed toe with the butt of her thiokezöeasiä. 'This is the same hard, dark stone as those columns back where we left the ship. It can't have been easy to carve.'

'What now, Vil Azaki?' Omotakus asked.

'Why're you asking him all the time?' Togastakus muttered.

Omotakus glanced between them. 'Is he not the most powerful Voréöeasiä?'

'No,' Íri and Togastakus said.

'Harsh.' Azaki grinned. 'I do have the best plans, though.'

'We need to find where Manastakus is,' Getitakus snapped. 'So we have to get inside.'

Azaki nodded. 'Getitakus is right. I'll scout on ahead.'

'By *yourself?!*' Íri folded her arms and shook her head. 'Not happening.'

'You're too tiny to stop me, Íri. And, more importantly, nobody else is going to be able to sneak in without getting caught.'

'But you can?' Togastakus demanded.

Azaki nodded. 'Omotakus and his men aren't going to be sneaking anywhere in the armour they pinched off the warriors at the beacon, and they're not going to fool anyone into thinking they're actually warriors either. You three all look *very* Voréöeasiä-like.'

Togastakus ground his teeth. 'You've got that raider's blade, I suppose.'

'I have my ways.' Azaki pointed his thiokezöeasiä further into the shadows by the heel of the statue. 'You should all stay out of sight until I return.'

Omotakus ushered his eight men after Getitakus into the thick dark where the statue of Estrif's cloak touched the ground behind his heels.

Togastakus glanced at Íriniel. 'Íri?'

She tightened the fold of her arms and held her ground. 'Don't call me Íri.'

Togastakus glowered at Azaki and stormed after the others.

'I didn't even do anything that time,' Azaki said.

Íri snorted. 'Don't pretend you care.'

He grinned. 'I wasn't, I'm just curious. I don't think he likes that you let me call you Íri and not him.'

'I don't *let* you. You just won't stop.' A hint of pink crept onto her cheeks. 'This isn't the time for your jokes about my *future husband*.'

'No. I've got to go be sneaky.'

She rolled her eyes. 'How're you going to get in without being seen? I didn't even see a way in.'

Azaki shrugged. 'Fortunately, it's still dark, so I've a handy spell.' He weighed his thiokezöeasiä in his hand.

'Don't even think about it,' Falaïré hissed in his ear as the wood turned ice-cold beneath his fingers. 'We're meant to be *together*.'

He hid his smile and poked Íri in the stomach with a finger. 'Shoo, Íri. I'm off.'

She stepped into his way. 'You're coming back, aren't you?'

Azaki blinked. 'Yes. I don't think staying there would be wise just now. I like my head attached to the rest of me.'

'Good.' Íri stared at him with a strange light in her green eyes. 'That's good.'

He cast the Lady's Shroud and pulled the shadows over himself, chuckling at Íri's gasp as he vanished from sight.

Three statues along he found the entrance, a high, arching doorway between the clawed feet of two of Estrif's statues. Four warriors in bronze reinforced leather cuirasses stood around the two oil braziers burning inside the passage.

'Fantastic,' Azaki muttered.

'Tricky for swords or spells, but not for our power, my Azi,' Falaïré whispered. 'There's no shame in using it instead. We do what we must to get what we want.'

Azaki scrunched up his face, but blew the mist from the crown of his thiokezöeasiä. 'I suppose. Deceive, lady of lies.' He shrouded himself within the mist of his magic.

The four guards remained still and quiet as Azaki strolled past their braziers and into the long passage. Dozens of small doors led off into the dark, spiralling stairs rose up into the mountain and plunged down into the ground. He followed the main tunnel toward a distant patch of brightness, resealing his thiokezöeasiä once he'd passed beyond the guards' senses.

This is it. He peeked out into the light.

A great hollow filled the mountain, open to the sky and stars. Concentric circles of stone seats ringed into the shallow slope from the summit down to a wide oval of black sand. An altar fashioned from hundreds of bronze blades stood in the base of a deep marble basin at the oval's centre.

Azaki recognised the two figures standing before it facing him. *Anastagus and Duratakus.* A chill traced through his veins.

'This isn't going to be as easy as I hoped,' he muttered.

Falaïré leant from the shadows. 'We should be careful. Our power couldn't yet snare Anastagus at the Heart-Tree and the Companion's apprentice may be lurking. If we try to catch them, we might be discovered.'

He glanced around for the apprentice and chuckled. 'It seems Duratakus really doesn't want his apprentice around when he's with Anastagus.' Azaki peered down to where the lower rings were filled by small clusters of warriors from almost every clan and a swathe of fighters from the Clan of the Grey Sails. 'We're going to have to get a bit closer. I can't hear and it'd be good to know what's happening.'

This is risky. His heart began to pound against his ribs and sweat gathered on his palms. *But worth it. Soekus did say Anastagus doesn't want me dead, too.*

She smirked. 'Let's hope the warriors of the clans assume we're just one of Anastagus's Companions.'

Act like you're meant to be here and they'll believe you are. Azaki strode out into the light and descended the narrow steps between the seats until he was close enough to hear. *And if they believe it, then it's the truth.*

'Our little warrior girl is here,' Falaïré whispered in his ear.

'Otuko…' He followed the line of Falaïré's red-stained forefinger down to where a small group of warriors in dark leather cuirasses sat beneath the spider and tree banner. Otuko's ash-blonde hair and black leather shirt and trousers stood out from the cluster. She was dwarfed by the figure beside her. 'Utháki too.' He clenched his fists when he caught sight of the eorl in their midst, an ugly, twisted heat flaring up in his chest. 'Atíko.'

Falaïré's soft laughter tickled the back of his neck. 'We don't like him, do we, my Azi?'

'He likes to take the younger warriors as his wives under Estrif's blood oath for a brief time in return for helping them gain recognition in the clan. Not the ones that'd be okay with it, either. Atíko only wants the ones that'll be reluctant. He enjoys watching them give up and letting him have his way. I heard him tell Ulika before she ended up in that giant spider's lair.' Azaki's stomach churned and a thick heat twisted round his heart. 'If he chose Otuko to escort him…'

'We knew this might happen.' Falaïré leant her head on his shoulder. 'If we wait…'

'Even if I return, he'll make Otuko's life as difficult as he can until she accepts,' Azaki hissed.

'Not if he never returns to the Webbed Pit.' Falaïré enclosed Atíko between her forefinger and thumb with a sharpness in her silver eyes. A bead of crimson dripped from the ball of her finger onto her thumb. 'How much do we want to help her, my Azi? How much do we feel we owe her?'

Azaki watched Atíko run his eyes over Otuko and the heat inside curled 'round his heart like flames round a pinecone. He allowed himself a small smile. 'More than enough. I used to hate him more than most.'

He's one of Anastagus' strongest supporters in the clan, too. He studied Otuko's posture and released a long, quiet sigh. *She seems okay for now.*

Anastagus raised his black-gloved hand and silence fell across the theatre. 'Welcome, heirs to Olisolamon. Now, our war begins!'

A great cheer rose from the warriors. They pounded the stone benches with their firsts and stamped their feet.

'We have seized tribute for Estrif's blessing in our conquest and to celebrate the coming liberation of lands that ought to have always been yours.' Anastagus raised his thiokezöeasiä into the air. 'For three days, my Companion, Duratakus, will host you here. Today, now, I will give you a small taste of the entertainment to come!'

A bronze gate on the far side of the theatre to Azaki rattled up and a score of men clutching a mismatched array of weapons staggered out onto the sand. Patterns of white quicklime daubed half, designs of blue woad marked the others.

Bloodsport. Azaki glanced between the captives. *Manastakus is a great prize. They'll save him for the last day.*

Anastagus lowered his thiokezöeasiä and the gate thudded back into place. 'Whoever is victorious will live to dream of freedom. Those that die and soak the sands with their blood will pass knowing Estrif found amusement in their struggle.'

'What if we refuse to fight!' A woad-marked captive hurled his spear at Anastagus. Duratakus stepped in front of his master and knocked it aside with his thiokezöeasiä.

Anastagus smiled. 'If you don't fight, you die. If you fight and you win, and you keep winning for three days, you'll be set free. How dearly do you love these strangers to throw your life away for them?'

'We're—'

One of the quick-limed captives drove his spear through the first captive's throat.

The group of men descended into a knot of hacking and slashing, blood splashed across the dark sands, and screams echoed up to Azaki's seat.

'He's not going set any of them free,' he said. 'Poor fools.'

Falaïré slid onto the bench beside him. 'They're nothing to us.'

Azaki sighed. 'Still, I feel bad for them. This isn't a kind fate. Dying alone.'

'Then free them, my Azi,' she murmured. 'Give them a chance to escape or take their vengeance. Maybe they can even take the blame for the sudden death of an eorl of the Webbed Pit...'

He wrestled with a twist of temptation. 'They'd make a good distraction. And they'd know where Manastakus is. Íri, Toga the Sour, and the others could sneak in and retrieve him.'

'And we could leave,' Falaïré whispered. 'If we wanted...'

'Íri would be suspicious. She knows what we can do.' Azaki swallowed down the lump that rose in his throat. 'Maybe if we showed her a truth where our thiokezöeasiä breaks before we die.'

'As kind a truth as any we could leave her with.' The corner of her lips curved into a smirk. 'Once we've slain the eorl, we can go back to the girl who saved a lost boy from an awful place. Will our debt be paid, then?'

It'll never be paid. Azaki forced old memories away. *Every good moment since she found me is owed to her.*

The struggle on the sands stilled. Two quick-lime daubed, blood spattered captives staggered over wet, black sand. Anastagus and Duratakus climbed the steps up from the altar as the blood trickled down to fill the marble basin.

Azaki's eyes flashed to the speck of red upon the bronze table. 'The seed of the Heart-Tree...'

Falaïré laughed in his ear. 'No risk of exile for us. A hero's welcome, instead.'

'Anastagus shouldn't have it,' he muttered. 'We ought to return it to the Heart-Tree.'

'Or plant it,' she whispered in his ear. 'Plant it in the Webbed Pit and Anastagus can no longer use it.'

'Of course you'd say that.' Azaki shot her a long, flat look. 'Isn't that why I was chosen by the Heart-Tree? Why She let me steal it?'

Falaïré smirked. 'I'm a child of *our* heart, my Azi. I only know what *we* desire.'

He stared down at the seed of the Heart-Tree and touched his fingertips to his lips. 'For them all to be safe. For them to be happy. For me to be happy with them.'

'But while Anastagus lives, he won't stop his war,' she murmured. 'And we've seen what he's prepared to do to his enemies. We've seen how he treats his loyal followers.'

'I know.' Azaki rolled his thiokezöeasiä up and down his thighs, chewing at the inside of his cheek. 'If we take the seed back, then he can't possibly beat all the other Hands of the Heart-Tree, but how can I keep Otuko, Íri and Utháki all safe if I'm back there?'

'We have to choose.' Falaïré slid her unmarred fingers along the scars upon his palm. 'And we know whom we owe more than any other.'

Otuko. Azaki stared down at where she sat, spinning her bronze hunting knife round and round upon her palm. *Íri has her father, her dream is to serve the Heart-Tree. She'll make new friends once I'm gone. Otuko and Utháki have only each other and me.*

'So we take the seed,' he murmured. 'We go back to the Webbed Pit with it. Otuko gets her dream. Utháki gets his. Íri will miss us, then forget us. And we'll survive.'

'Anastagus will seek to use us,' Falaïré whispered.

'We can't defeat him.'

'We don't need to.' Falaïré turned his face back toward where Íri waited in the dark. 'If he sends us south, we might be close enough to keep the little Voréöeasiä girl safe, too. Let him throw us through hardships, we'll surpass him on our way to the stars.'

Seventeen

White-flowered brushes loomed over him; their dark leaves blocked out the starlight. The roots spreading from the ebony trunk of the grove tree little more than shadows beyond the sapling standing before him.

Yanastakus sat cross-legged upon one of the roots, his thiokezöeasiä on his lap. 'Now I understand.' Bright bronze flowed from the wound in his chest. 'You're just like him.'

The shadows of the glade danced and twisted like wind-driven smoke over the roots and beneath them gaped a dark, cold pit and filled with echoes of a lonely, hateful boy's whispered curses.

Azaki stepped back, but the shadows seized his legs with long, thin fingers.

'Azi!' Otuko hung off Eorl Atíko's arm, a glowing red line upon her palm and dark bruises on her face and neck. 'I told you I'd be a famous warrior one day. No matter what it took.'

His stomach churned into a hot storm. *She would never.*

Íri stepped from the swirling shadows and held out her hand. The green outline of a heart marked the back of it.

No. I learn from my mistakes. Azaki swallowed the lump in his throat and dug his fingers into the sapling until it hurt more than the sharp, hot tangle about his heart. *I've had this dream before.*

The wood turned hot beneath his hand and whispers welled up all around him. The shadows fell still, drawing together into a pool at the sapling's base.

'Do you see now?' Falaïré uncoiled from the darkness before his feet. 'If their goals aren't the same as ours, their betrayal's inevitable.'

The grove collapsed into darkness.

'Those were cruel dreams, Falaïré.' He watched the shadows stretch themselves out into an endless tangle of mirrorglass threads through distant stars and drifting mist. 'Why?'

'We're capable of cruelty, my Azi,' she whispered. 'A trick can bring pain to the tricked as easily as a smile to the trickster. And sometimes, a little cruelty can do a greater kindness.'

He clenched his fists. 'You wanted me to see this. I've seen it.'

Falaïré cupped his face in her hands. 'Trusting them so completely is a risk we're taking, my Azi. Is it so hard to imagine the truth we come to see might be something similar? They don't perceive things perfectly the same as we do. They don't want perfectly the same things.'

He wrestled with it as he stared into her silver eyes, his heart sinking within his breast. 'No...'

She smiled and pressed her red lips against his forehead. 'If it comes to pass, we'll still be enough. If they betray us, so long as we're together, we'll never slip back to being that lonely, hate-warped thing, not so long as you remember it'll still be us. We'll be our own one good thing. And that's all we've ever needed...'

He opened his eyes.

Íri's green eyes hovered a short distance from his.

She flinched back, pink blossoming across her cheeks. 'You're awake.'

'I had a rubbish dream.'

Falaïré huffed. 'The truth can't always be convenient, my Azi, not even for us.'

She shuffled her feet. 'I'll wake the others. The sun's up. It's time.'

Azaki watched her shake Togastakus awake. Something hot and ugly coiled around his heart at the sight of the two of them. *Fantastic. This is all your fault, Falaïré.*

Her laughter drifted to his ears.

Oh laugh at me. He stretched the stiffness and the cold from his limbs, and stood up, plucking his thiokezöeasiä from the ground. *It's not funny when it just hurts.*

Omotakus stumbled across, yawning. 'Is it time, Vil Azaki?'

'Íri seems to think so.' He studied the sky. 'We may as well go now, it won't make too much difference.'

He led them past the clawed toes of Estrif's statues toward the entrance, pausing in the shadow of the last of the feet. 'Deceive, lady of lies,' he whispered, blowing the pale mist away from the crown of his thiokezöeasiä.

Fine, grey mist swept out over the Theatre of the Worldbreaker, snaring every soul he sensed within it.

Azaki grinned despite the heaviness that settled over him. *Our bond's definitely grown stronger for me to be able to reach so far.*

'How're we getting in?' Togastakus demanded.

'We're going to walk,' Azaki told him. 'I've magic that'll stop us from being seen. We're going to walk right past them, down the steps, across the sands, then through the bronze gate. Be as quiet as possible and whatever you do, don't touch anyone or anything, or the magic will fail.'

'How'd we know your spell will work at all?' Getitakus growled.

'I've seen him do it before.' Íri shot him a knowing look. 'They won't see us.'

Azaki stepped round the edge of the toe and strode past the guards. The others tiptoed after him with clenched fists and grimaces.

A crowd filled the lowest benches, ringing the empty dark sands around the basin and its altar.

'What savages,' Togastakus muttered. 'They slaughter people here and collect the blood for their awful Nerevoréoatho.'

Azaki jabbed him in the ribs with an elbow. 'Do not insult Estrif when we're in such a precarious situation, you utter idiot.'

Togastakus glanced at Íri's furious glare and flushed. 'I apologise,' he gritted.

Getitakus peered around the ring with narrowed eyes and a dark expression. 'There's Duratakus and his apprentice. Manastakus is here.'

Azaki hurried down the steps and onto the black sand. Beyond the captives' bronze gate, he sensed a single soul caught in the snare of his magic.

'No risks, my Azi,' Falaïré murmured into his ear. 'Even truth may not save us or our companions if we're discovered now.'

No risks, then. Azaki waited for his stomach to twist and thrash, but it remained still and calm. *The guilt will come later.*

'They're nothing to us,' Falaïré whispered. 'Spiders do not mourn flies.'

'Queen of whispering webs, upon your throne of lies, gift a blade of shadow and revel in their cries.' Azaki drove the knife between the bars of the bronze gate and into the neck of the guard.

Hot blood spurted over his fingers and the man sank to the ground, gasping and shuddering.

Sorry. He glanced into the blank eyes with a small twist of regret in his gut. *It's kill or be killed. You'd have done the same to me.*

Falaïré's soft laughter tickled the side of his neck. 'And so all is fair, my Azi.'

Azaki swallowed the small knot of remorse down, stuck his hand through the gate, and pulled the wheel far enough the gate raised to knee height. 'Time to crawl,' he sang.

Íri pinched the bridge of her nose. 'This isn't the time for games, Azaki!'

He chuckled and squirmed under the gate. 'They can't hear and the less obvious things are, the easier it is to keep us hidden.'

'The best deceptions are as close to the truth as you can make them,' Falaïré murmured in his ear.

The rest wriggled under the gate after him as Azaki dragged the guard into the edge of the passage out of sight.

'What now, Vil Azaki?' Omotakus peered into the gloom. 'It's not going to be easy to get back out.'

No, it's not. Azaki met Omotakus' clear blue gaze and hardened his heart. *But I'll do my best to get you out. I promise.*

'You stay here with your men,' he said. 'This might be the only way back, so best not to let anyone else have control of it.'

Togastakus nodded and jammed a tobacco leaf into his mouth. 'And the rest of us search for the acolyte?'

'There are many captives down here.' Azaki closed eyes to try and get an idea of how many there were snared within his thiokezöeasiä's magic. 'They arm them to fight out there, so if we free them and find the weapons room, we'll have some help if things go bad.'

Íri narrowed her eyes and darted to his side as he took off down the passage. 'You're *using* them,' she hissed. 'Like the men you put in the gate at the Beacon.'

He sighed and the small coil of guilt returned to this stomach. 'I'm giving them a chance to escape, too. Would you rather I left them all in chains to die?'

She blanched. 'No, but you don't really care, do you?'

'I care enough to think we should free them.' Azaki frowned and peered into the offshoot passages, cocking his head to listen. 'But how can I really care about someone I don't know? I'll free them and we'll take them with us if we can, but if I have to choose between their lives and yours, I'll kill them myself.'

Colour rose on Íri's cheeks. 'I don't want that!'

'Neither do I, but if that's the choice…'

Chains rattled from further along and Azaki sped up, drawing the falcata from his hip. Almost a hundred soft-folk huddled in shackles against one dirty wall and two warriors leant beside the brazier in the centre of the room.

Azaki held a finger up to his lips and crept forward. He opened the throat of one of them, then drove the blade through the chest of the other.

Togastakus ground his teeth. 'This spell you've made, it's more powerful than anything other than one of the Erudite could wield. You should be exhausted.'

Azaki chuckled and released the captives from his illusion. 'I'll take that and the bitter envy in your tone as a compliment.'

A clamour rose from the shackled soft-folk.

'Hush,' Getitakus growled. 'Do you want them to hear?'

'Free them,' Azaki said. 'Find them some weapons if you can, then head to the gate.'

'What about Manastakus?'

'He's in the next room. Keep freeing everyone you find.' He released the single remaining soul in the next room from his magic. 'I'm going to scout.'

Íri caught his arm as he moved back toward the gate. 'Scout where?'

'Duratakus's apprentice escaped my thiokezöeasiä once before,' Azaki whispered. 'That's how he got Manastakus in the first place. I want to keep an eye on him, or, if he's by himself, remove the problem.'

She chewed her lip. 'Be careful. We don't need to start a fight, just leave.'

'I don't intend to be seen by anyone I don't want to see me. It would kind of ruin things.'

Falaïré laughed, drifting alongside him as he sprinted back through the passage. 'There's a girl who loves us waiting, my Azi...'

Azaki shrouded himself from the sight of Omotakus and his men as he crawled back under the gate, then climbed the nearest set of steps. He scanned the crowd and found the warriors of the Webbed Pit a short distance away round the curve of the theatre's seats. *No Otuko*. His heart seized. *No Atíko...*

'Uh oh,' Falaïré breathed in his ear.

Azaki took a deep breath and sheathed his falcata with trembling hands, striding through the warriors on their benches. He ripped a shadow of Duratakus from the mist and pulled it over himself like a cloak. 'Where's your eorl?' Azaki demanded of one of the Webbed Pit's warriors. 'I wish to speak with him.'

'Duratakus...' The warrior fingered the small obsidian figure of Estrif dangling round his neck. 'He - er - he's just in that passage conferring with one of our warriors.'

Azaki followed the warrior's arm up the steps. 'Thank you.'

He climbed the steps in threes and slipped into the dark hall, letting Duratakus's shade dissolve.

'Is this all you wanted?' Otuko snapped. 'I've already given you an answer. If you ask again, it's going to come in the form of an arrow, eorl or not.'

'I think you'll change your mind when you realise how much easier, or *harder*, I can make things for you, pretty one.' Atíko's voice echoed from a side-room just ahead.

Azaki stuck his head around the corner, his fingers creeping to the hilt of the falcata.

Otuko stood stiff-backed in the centre of the room, her hand on the hunting knife at her waist. Purple-dyed wool replaced the fraying belt he remembered and three thin bronze triangles covered her stomach and chest.

Atíko leered at her from beside the door, one bronze-circlet covered arm across the entrance. 'You're not going anywhere until you've changed your mind.'

A raw, fierce heat flared up beneath Azaki's ribs.

I remember you, Atíko. Azaki tried to swallow the spark of rage, but it refused to fade. The memory of Atíko's sneer as he dropped Itaki's bloodstained blade into Azaki's hands rose from some dark corner of his mind like carrion birds from a corpse. *Watching us starve. Laughing as we froze.*

'When hate was all we had to keep us breathing, how many times did we wish him dead?' Falaïré murmured in his ear. 'For firing the arrow that stole away a brother, for sneering at the child left alone because of it, for laughing...'

More times than I can count. A boy filled with hot and bitter flames peered out through Azaki's eyes. *Do it*, the shade urged. Azaki's youthful tenor twisted into Kogodakus's raw tone. *Do it. Do it. Do it. He deserves it for what he's done. He deserves it for what he'll do. Even the Heart-Tree kills to save lives.*

'Queen of whispering webs, upon your throne of lies, gift a blade of shadow, and revel in their cries.' Azaki curled his fingers round the hilt of the serrated weapon.

Falaïré's crimson lips curved into a smirk. 'This time, we'll do better, my Azi. I *know* we will.'

'I've someone already,' Otuko said as Azaki ducked Atíko's arm and slipped into the room. 'No means no, Atíko.'

'Our arrangement can end the moment he returns.' Atíko licked his lips. 'But he's not here now, is he?'

Azaki slammed the blade into Atíko's throat and wrenched it from ear to ear, driving the knife in so hard its tip grated against bone. Atíko's pain tore him free from the magic.

'I'm here, Atíko.' Azaki released Otuko from his illusion. 'Now it's your turn to die and mine to smile.'

Atíko gurgled and choked, clutching at the blood pouring from his neck. 'Trai – tor!'

Azaki pushed him to the floor with one finger and placed his right boot over Atíko's mouth. 'I see you managed to get yourself in trouble, Otuko. You can't blame me or Utháki this time.'

She stared at him, her fingers still on her hunting blade. 'Azi?'

'Yes?' He wiped the blood off his right hand on Atíko's spider-silk cloak. 'That's me.'

'He was an *eorl*,' Otuko hissed, her knuckles whitening around her bow.'You idiot! They'll never let you return now. I could've handled him myself!'

'I'm not here by myself. They won't ever know it was me.' He let the blade of shadow in his hand burst into wisps of shadow. 'Aren't you happy to see me?'

Otuko twisted her fingers around her bow. 'I'm very happy to see you.' She dropped it and crushed her mouth against his. 'If it were a more convenient time and there wasn't such a risk of having one of those grey-eyed babies a little early, I'd show you just how much.'

Azaki gulped and drew back, his stomach swirling and fluttering like it was full of midges. 'As much as I might like that, I've got some things to do right now.'

'You look nervous, Azi.' Otuko giggled and ran her tongue over her lower lip. 'I don't think I've seen you look that nervous in years. How important are those things?'

Azaki stared at the purple woad marks smudged across her cheeks and the ash-blonde locks he'd mussed. *It's just Otuko.* He tried to imagine kissing her with the same heat she'd kissed him and his stomach squirmed. *It's just a kiss.*

'Very important,' he said. 'Probably a good thing, too. I'm not ready for a baby, not even if it has grey eyes.'

She pouted. 'Well you better get ready soon, because once you're back with the clan, we're making the blood oath and then you're mine forever.'

Marriage. She wants us to be married. Azaki's stomach wound itself into a tight, hot knot. *This is what I get for teasing Íri about wedding pledges.*

'Sounds awful,' he quipped.

Otuko laughed. 'I promise you'll enjoy at least some of it an awful lot.' Her smile faded. 'Now, what're you up to, Azi?'

'I've some friends with me. We're going to let out all the captives, and then I'm going to convince them I've died so I can come with you. I may also steal the seed of the Heart-Tree off the altar just in case Utháki's still mad at me or the clan wants a little extra proof.'

'He's not mad anymore. I beat things through his skull eventually. You know him, he takes a few days to cool off and actually use his rock-brain.' Otuko grabbed hold of his fingers. 'What about Atíko?'

Azaki sighed and hauled the body over his shoulder. 'I'll toss him into the fight when it starts in a few minutes. Nobody will see me.'

Screams and shouts rose up from beyond the end of the passageway and bronze rang from the direction of the sand. Almost every soul he'd snared with his magic ripped themselves free. Fear gnawed at his gut; its icy fingers trailed down his spine.

'I think they've started without you,' Otuko said.

'Someone did,' Azaki muttered. 'Let's go.' He led her from the passage.

The captives fought a desperate battle toward the passage out. Dozens of bodies lay on the blood-soaked sands around the gate and a rippling crimson pool lapped at the bronze altar in its marble basin. Duratakus and his apprentice sat on the first ring of seats, watching the fray.

Not a disaster. Azaki released a quiet sigh. *I can fix this.*

'How on earth did they manage to make such a huge mess of this?' he muttered. 'What idiots.'

Otuko giggled. 'You didn't really think a load of soft southies were going to be much good, did you?'

'I kind of hoped they'd last a bit longer, given they've no choice but to fight.' He strolled down the steps and hurled Atíko's body into those sprawled by the gate. 'Good riddance to Atíko, at least.'

Otuko seized his fingers. 'Where're you going?'

'To sort this mess out.' Azaki pointed his thiokezöeasiä at the tight knot of captives forcing themselves toward the steps against a shimmering wall of wards. 'Some of them need to get away so the Voréöeasiäki believe I'm dead.'

She followed the line of his thiokezöeasiä and narrowed her eyes. 'I recognise that blonde girl with the glowing staff, Azi…'

'Well, you've seen her before, so...'

Otuko glared. 'I remember what you said about her, too. Funny and pretty.'

Azaki laughed. 'Are you jealous?' He grinned at her upturned pout. 'You are, aren't you? You're adorable.'

She wrung her hands around her bow. 'If I learn you and her have been up to anything…'

'Later, Otuko. I promise you'll have time to play at being the jealous wife. Get Utháki and I'll come find you both as soon as I can.'

Azaki darted over the bodies, releasing everyone from his magic.

He shoved his way through the captives to the front, where Íri forced the line of wards back with a stream of scorching wind. 'What the hell did you do? I said be quiet as you can!'

Getitakus turned to him a dark glint lurked in his eyes. 'Manastakus betrayed us. That apprentice got to him. Convinced him Kogodakus was still trying to save people somehow, just like he once did them.'

'Fantastic,' Azaki muttered. 'I came all this way, risked so much, and he just goes and swaps sides.'

I bet the Lady of Betrayal is laughing Her head off at me. Maybe this is what She was waiting for.

'He's dead.' Getitakus' hands shook and the gleam in his eyes darkened further. 'He tried to raise the alarm. I killed him myself.'

Serves him right. Azaki spotted Togastakus hurling spells into the wards on the other side of Íri. *At least Duratakus isn't getting involved.*

Azaki craned his neck over the warriors and their wards at the seed of the Heart-Tree resting on the bronze altar. 'Keep going forward. I'll try and get rid of some.'

Falaïré's fingers ghosted through his hair and down his cheek, leaving a hot, wet smear on his skin. 'Promises, promises,' she murmured.

Azaki glanced at the crimson dripping from her fingers. 'Deceive, lady of lies,' he whispered, stifling a groan as the ache bit deep into him.

He forced the shadows to rise from the fog, bending the echoes of captives over each warrior. Shrouding himself from their eyes, Azaki cut his way through the fray toward the altar with leaden, trembling limbs.

'Oh no you don't!' Duratakus's apprentice leapt from the sands into the knee-deep blood and flailed his way to the altar. 'You're not making off with this special fruit, nasty sneaky druid!'

Azaki paused on the steps. 'I definitely am.'

'Master Duratakus would be very angry.' The apprentice waved his heavily glued pine branch over his head. 'I only just fixed my staff after the last time!'

'How about you let me take the seed and I kill Duratakus so he can't break your... staff.'

The apprentice cocked his head and frowned, snatching the seed off the altar. 'I'm a good apprentice. Master Duratakus will be proud of me for saving his seed. He might even let me learn some magic now!'

Azaki lunged, but the apprentice stumbled out of his tired grasp and scrambled up the steps toward Duratakus.

Falaïré stepped from the shadows of the altar onto the pool of blood. 'He's run off with what we want, my Azi...'

'I noticed.'

Íri staggered to his side. 'We need to go.' A thin red scratch ran across her torn, blood-drenched tunic from one hip to just below her breasts and her eyes brimmed with orange flame.

'It's fine.' Azaki waved a hand at the carnage behind and tottered on the steps. 'They're fighting each other, see?'

She slipped under his arm to catch his weight, frowning and touching a finger to his cheek. 'You've got purple on you.'

'Do I?' He grinned and let her take some of the weight off his legs. 'Well, *you've* got red on you.'

She scrunched her nose up and resealed her thiokezöeasiä. 'Let's go.'

Azaki weighed up his options, setting everyone free from his magic and resealing his thiokezöeasiä. 'Duratakus and his apprentice have the seed of the Heart-Tree.'

Íri gasped and swivelled to stare over the retreating warriors at Duratakus upon the steps. 'It's here?'

'We can't leave.' His gaze slipped to where Otuko helped Utháki up the steps and into one of the passages. 'Not yet.'

'You're right.' She took a step toward the sands, dragging his weight with her. 'Come on.'

Azaki staggered up the stairs after her. 'I'm *very* tired, Íri.'

She blinked. 'Your thiokezöeasiä?'

'I've never used it so much or on so many people.' He groaned and stumbled through the sprawled corpses on numb, dead legs. 'It's really a miracle I'm still conscious.'

Íri's expression softened. 'Rest for a bit, then. We'll chase after them once you're feeling better.'

A hot, wet drop landed on Azaki's cheek.

His fingers came away red. Blood?

The red liquid lapping at the altar shivered and rose into a towering horned figure ten times the height of a man. It strode onto the sands in a single step, a trail of crimson spattering the dark sand in its wake.

'Little mortals,' a deep voice rasped. 'What a delightful show you've put on for me, so much more *exciting* than the slaughter of unskilled peasants.'

Estrif. Azaki's blood turned to ice and he stole a shaky breath through a fist of panic. *Why does this always happen to me?*

The colour drained from Íri's face as she backed away, groping for Azaki's arm. Togastakus edged forward and seized her shoulder, dragging her back behind Omotakus and his men.

Estrif's faceless, bloody avatar swept its eyeless gaze over them. 'What boon would you have of the Prince of Bloodshed, Getitakus? I wish to reward you for how you slew your treacherous apprentice with such *zeal.*'

Getitakus licked his lips and stared around him at the dead. 'Power. So I can destroy the savages that plague our world and men like Anastagus. No more good lads like Neméstakus getting killed because of them. No more decent boys having their heads messed with.'

Azaki shook his head. *Idiot.*

A red tendril sprouted from Estrif's arm and wrapped about Getitakus and his thiokezöeasiä. 'Power it is.'

The thiokezöeasiä turned to shining silver, its crown broadening into a leaf-bladed spearhead, and the brown tunic shivered and thickened into stiff, black leather. The crimson tentacle splattered onto the black sand.

'Thank you,' Getitakus muttered, clutching his new thiokezöeasiä to his chest.

Estrif's gifts come at a price. Azaki felt Estrif's smile behind the featureless red face, a terrible, bright, savagery, hot and hungry as the bared bloodstained teeth of a rabid wolf.

Estrif laughed, a rasping, hoarse whistle. *'Everything* has a price. Come, Azaki Kathal. Red oaths you've taken and red oaths you've kept. What would you have to reward your sacrifices?'

Íri shook her head at him in the corner of his eye and struggled free of Togastakus's grip.

Don't worry, Íri. I know the price of Estrif's blessings.

'Without seriously harming anyone, let nobody be able to leave the Theatre of the Worldbreaker for the next three days,' he said. 'Swear an oath you'll do it.'

Estrif bent and seized hold of him, wrapping long, hot fingers around his waist and lifting him up. 'Are you *sure* that's all you'd ask of the Worldbreaker, little mortal?'

Azaki strained every muscle, but the Voréoatho's grip didn't loosen. 'I am.'

'Very well. I swear. *A promise. One that's more than just words.* I'll cage you all together and watch you devour each other.' Estrif thrust his horned, faceless head close to Azaki's face and sniffed. 'Ah, you reek of my littlest sister, mortal.'

He buried a flash of panic. 'Well, in my defence, it's been a while since I bathed. We were kind of busy…'

'I saw. Olisolamon okertes ūrrakityál Azaki okertes.'

Magic tugged at his mind and the words echoed through his thoughts. In the eye of his mind, his shadow followed a path of grey footsteps into the stars and in its wake, Olisalamon drifted into the dark. The impressions spilt together, swirling into a cacophony of colours, flashing faster and faster toward distant, dizzying light.

'Not Volōmothí.' Azaki shook his head clear. 'Can't understand.'

'You will.' Estrif tossed him away onto the sand. 'Promises, promises, little mortal. *Promises, promises.*'

Heat flared up on Azaki's scarred palm as he rolled to his knees and the Voréoatho's form burst into a shower of hot, red rain, spattering onto the dark sand.

Eighteen

Azaki clenched his left fist and stared across the black sand and bodies. Crows hopped among the dead, croaking and squabbling as dusk fell, plucking at open wounds and gore. Omotakus sat a little way along the stone bench, rubbing the nicks from the edge of his longsword with a thin, flat stone in slow, steely scrape.

'Show me?' Íri slid onto the bench beside him.

He tightened his fist. 'It doesn't matter.'

She wriggled her fingers into his fist and tugged his hand into her lap. 'They're gone.'

Azaki glanced at the smooth, unmarked skin on his palm and took his hand back. 'He released me from them.'

'Why?' Íri whispered.

'Usually, it's because He doesn't wish to punish the one who took the oath,' he said. 'Sometimes, when Estrif knows the promises can't be kept and it's no fault of the one who took the oath, He'll remove the mark.'

She hunched her shoulders. 'Do you think — do you want — are you going to have to serve the Spider again?'

'It's Otuko and Utháki I'm worried about. We swore we'd never be separated or left behind and that we'd always look out for Otuko.'

Íri released a long sigh and shuffled across until their legs touched. 'I'm worried about Getitakus. That thiokezöeasiä…'

'He's an idiot. Estrif's blessings have a price. He's the Lord of Sacrifice and every gift he gives requires something dear in return. Why'd you think I asked for something that affected us all equally?'

'A rare moment of intelligence from you,' Íri said. 'Still, I doubt he'll be able to do much. This is the Heart-Tree's world.'

The Theatre of the Worldbreaker rumbled and the ground shook. Fine, black dust trickled down from the rings of seats above.

Azaki shot her a wry smile. 'You were saying?'

'Shut up, Azaki.' She pushed herself up off his shoulder. 'Let's get back to the others before anything happens.'

Omotakus hurried after them.

Azaki stepped onto the arena and the ground vanished under his feet. They plunged into the dark on a cascade of black sand.

He held his breath and closed his eyes as he fell, letting the wind rush past as he wrestled with the churning in his gut. *We'll be fine. Estrif doesn't break oaths.* He thudded into something solid, the wind burst from his lungs and he went sprawling across cold stone.

Íri moaned from somewhere in the dark behind him. 'Are you okay, Azaki?'

'Winded,' he gasped as the pain faded. 'Omotakus?'

A low groan came from the gloom. 'Been better, Vil Azaki.'

Orange light and gentle heat washed over them and Íri's reading light rose from her fingers.

Azaki glimpsed red on Omotakus' longsword and under the fingers pressed to his side. 'Fell on it?'

'Right on it. Lost my helmet, too.' Omotakus drew his hand away to show a long, shallow cut between two of the bronze bands upon his leather cuirass. 'I'll be alright. I can still fight.'

Íriniel touched a green-wreathed hand to the bronze scales above the wound and Omotakus released a long sigh. 'Where's everyone else?' she asked.

Azaki glanced round at the dark stone walls and peered into the shadows. 'Not here.'

'This is all your fault, Azaki,' Íri accused. 'What were you thinking?'

'It gives us a chance to get the seed back,' he said.

'What's going on, Vil Azaki?' Omotakus asked.

'Estrif has trapped everyone inside the Theatre of the Worldbreaker. I suspect we're providing more entertainment for him, too.'

Movement flashed in the corner of Azaki's eye. An arrow hissed past his face and shattered against the stone wall, pieces of white feather floating down onto Íri's chest. Omotakus dived to the ground and Azaki pressed himself flat against the wall.

A faint breeze washed past and soft footsteps shuffled in the passage.

'Blaze, beacon of virtuous ire,' Íri hissed, sending a roiling wave of searing heat into the dark.

A single figure burst into flames and writhed upon the ground, their screams echoed down the passage until they fell still.

'No more light, Íri,' Azaki said.

She resealed her thiokezöeasiä and let her spell fade.

The darkness swallowed them, heavy, still, and silent.

'What now?' Íri whispered.

'We creep around in the dark until we find Duratakus and his apprentice.' He blinked until his eyes adjusted a little. 'We've three days.'

Omotakus muttered a few choice words under his breath. 'I already hate this, Vil Azaki.'

'Have you done any hunting?' Azaki asked.

'No.' Omotakus clenched and unclenched his fingers on the hilt of his blade. 'Never.'

'Well, there's a first time for everything, then.'

'Be nice, Azaki,' Íri chided.

'Just follow my lead,' he said. 'You too, Voréöeasiä Princess Íri. Estrif is the patron of hunters and this is his game.'

'Fantastic,' she muttered, grabbing hold of the back of his shirt.

Azaki chuckled, prowling along the passage on the balls of his feet, head cocked. He splashed into something as they turned the corner and found himself looking down on a trio of corpses.

Azaki studied them. *Some of the captives.* He tugged an arrow out of the ribs of one and ran his fingers along the shaft until he found the fletching. *Otuko...*

'What is it, Azaki?' Íri whispered.

He dropped the arrow and dipped a finger into the cooling blood. 'Some of the captives we freed didn't last long. The blood's still slightly warm.'

They picked their way through the bodies, following the dark passage up a gentle slope. Azaki ran his fingers along the smooth, cold walls, straining his ears into the black, his heart hammering. Íri's hot fist pulled his shirt tight around his ribs and her breath washed fast and hot against his back.

'Ow,' Azaki muttered, reaching back and loosening her fingers. 'You're making it chafe.'

A soft slither came from ahead and a bow creaked. He shoved Íri back between him and the wall and tensed. Something hissed past his legs and skittered away into the dark.

Azaki glimpsed a shadow moving along the wall. 'Queen of whispering webs, upon your throne of lies, gift a blade of shadow and revel in their cries,' he murmured.

Another missile hissed down the passage; it rang off Omotakus' armguard and dropped to their feet.

Azaki bent and felt for the fletching. *Not Otuko.*

He weighed the small blade in his hand and hurled it toward the flicker of movement, but it clattered off the wall and onto the ground.

Azaki pried Íri's fingers loose from his shirt and cast the Lady's Shroud, dragging the shadows over himself. 'Queen of whispering webs, upon your throne of lies, gift a blade of shadow and revel in their cries.'

Beneath the veil of his illusion, he crept up the slope, back pressed to the wall. A single warrior crouched behind the corner, an arrow nocked to his bow. Azaki wrapped his hand over the warrior's mouth and thrust the blade of shadow into the side of his neck.

He grimaced at the hot gush of blood, watching it soak into the white tree and spider marking his chest.

'Hello, clan-kin.' Azaki patted down the warrior's pockets and helped himself to the bow and the three arrows still in his quiver. 'Sorry about this, but you know how it is.'

A hand clasped his shoulder.

Azaki's blood froze and he twisted round, arm raised.

Falaïré smirked back at him. 'Boo,' she whispered.

He released a long breath as the ice thawed from his veins. 'You are the absolute worst.'

'I am like I am, because you are like you are,' she sang.

'Yeah, yeah, it's my own fault,' Azaki muttered.

She laughed and ruffled his hair. 'If you use our power, we'll be able to sense everyone you ensnare.'

'It'll exhaust me. We're going to be down here for three days.'

Falaïré's silver eyes sharpened. 'We get stronger every time we push ourselves, my Azi.' She ran her red-stained fingers along the curve of the bow, leaving a long crimson smear. 'Besides, once we've hunted most of them down, the little Voréöeasiä girl will believe we're too exhausted to have changed her truth.'

'We need to find Duratakus.'

'Well… we've got bait,' she whispered.

He swallowed and strode back to where Íri and Omotakus waited. 'It's me.'

She poked him in the stomach with her thiokezöeasiä. 'What is that spell called?'

'The Lady's Shroud.' Azaki grinned at her curious stare. 'Do you want to hear the incantation?'

Íri rolled her eyes. 'Something tells me I don't.'

He chuckled and reached for her arm, his fingers brushed through her hair onto warm, soft skin.

She squeaked and shoved his hand away. 'What're you doing?'

'Sorry,' he whispered. 'I've had an idea.'

'What…? And why do I feel like I'm not going to like it?'

'Because you're probably not.' Azaki frowned. 'I want you to unseal your thiokezöeasiä.'

'There'll be light.'

115

'That's the point. Hopefully, Duratakus will come and investigate.'

'So will many others, Vil Azaki,' Omotakus warned.

'In small groups, I hope,' Azaki said. 'There's method behind the madness, I promise.'

'Blaze, beacon of virtuous ire,' Íri whispered.

Orange light washed down the passage, stabbing at Azaki's eyes. Íri's face appeared a hand's length from his.

'Were you trying to sneakily steal a hug and blame Omotakus?' Azaki murmured.

'A hug? From you?' She elbowed him in the hip. 'You only look nice in the dark.'

He chuckled. 'You're just upset you weren't trapped in the dark with your future husband instead of me. Think of all the tobacco flavoured kisses you could've been sharing.'

A loud rumble rippled through the stone and the ground shook. The walls shifted and twisted, smooth obsidian rippling and flowing like water, and their passage bent around in the opposite direction.

'What was that?' Omotakus tensed behind his longsword. 'Gods I hate this. My nerves feel like they're about to snap.'

'Estrif.' Azaki tested the string on the bow. 'I suppose it'll be no fun for him to watch us unless we're all close to each other.'

Thunder echoed down the passage from the faint glimmer of light. Dust poured from the ceiling with each crash and small stones skittered down the steep slope past them into the dark.

Azaki spat some of the dust from his mouth. 'Why is it always up? I never should've let you choose the way, Íri.'

'Why're you always talking?' She shook a small cloud of grey out of her golden hair. 'And it's your entire fault we're doing this to begin with.'

He grinned. 'That is completely true, but I deny it anyway.'

She glared at him, her irises swirling with orange flame. 'When we get back to the Heart-Tree, I'm going to shackle you in one of the libraries with nothing to eat but kale.'

Azaki laughed, but his smile wilted as she turned away. *I'm afraid I'm not coming back, Íri.*

Omotakus staggered after them, dragging himself along the wall of the passage and dripping sweat. 'I need another rest, Vil Azaki,' he wheezed.

Azaki winced at another series of crashes. 'Whatever's making all that noise is pretty close, so take it now before we get sucked into another fight.'

'You should've taken off some of that heavy armour, Omotakus.' Íri wrinkled her nose at the bronze-banded leather cuirass. 'It weighs more than I do.'

Azaki raised an eyebrow at her. 'You're black, said the raven to the crow.'

Pink rose on her cheeks. 'You shut up, Azaki.'

'Make me, midget.'

She snorted. 'Maybe I will.'

'Nah.' Azaki grinned. 'You don't scare me, you're too tiny and you can't go running to your future husband, because we've fortunately misplaced him.'

Íriniel folded her arms. 'Do you actually think I'm going to marry that stubborn idiot?'

He pictured the two of them together like the pairs he'd seen in the clan and frowned. 'Probably not. Even he's not stubborn enough to put up with all that violence and meanness.'

'I'll give you violence and meanness,' Íri muttered, raising a fist at him.

'Oh no.' Azaki shook his head. 'I'm not getting suckered into being the boy Soekus the Lifebringer turns into a giant turnip for getting cosy with his Voréöeasiä princess daughter. I'd rather marry Toga the Sour myself.'

She turned away as another peal of thunder echoed down to them. 'I wouldn't marry you even if you were a turnip. Otuko's welcome to you.'

Azaki laughed. 'I'd imagine she'd expect to get first call on that anyway, given she's known me longer, but if I happen to bump into her, I'll pass the message along. Íri's so besotted with her Greenheart lover's goatee that I'm fair game for making grey-eyed babies with.'

She narrowed her eyes and kicked gravel back past them into the darkness. 'You're very annoying.'

'It's a point of pride for me.'

'I'm good, Vil Azaki.' Omotakus pulled his longsword from its sheath. 'Let's go see what's happening up here. I want to leave this cursed place.'

'Don't offend Estrif, Omotakus,' Azaki chided. 'Not unless you want to be stuck here for the rest of your days.'

'Even so,' Íri murmured. 'It's about time we found Duratakus and his apprentice. We've run into plenty of their warriors.'

Falaïré laughed in his ear. 'If Duratakus and his apprentice are up ahead, we'll need our power.'

Azaki tightened his grip on his thiokezöeasiä as the wood turned hot beneath his hand. 'Deceive, lady of lies,' he whispered. The grey mist burst from within the tines of his thiokezöeasiä and his magic snared a scatter of souls still left in the arena.

More than there ought to be. Azaki cursed. *Estrif's oath doesn't stop him letting more in. I wasn't clever enough.*

'Let's go, then.' Íri started up the slope toward the square of bright light.

Another crash thundered past them as they hastened toward the light, leaving Azaki's ears ringing.

He stumbled out into piercing brightness and a freezing wind. *They're all here.*

Togastakus stood within an orb of water, fending off the howling wind from Duratakus' thiokezöeasiä. The apprentice bounced on his feet in his master's shadow, watching Getitakus thrust his thiokezöeasiä at a scatter of struggling warriors and their former captives.

Heat seeped into the soles of Azaki's feet.

He glanced down.

Ragged scraps of flesh and splintered bone scattered a wash of crimson and a few patches of dark stone.

'Voréoathoki preserve us,' Omotakus muttered, edging toward the fight with both hands on the hilt of his longsword.

Azaki stared at the vast horns rising from the ground on either side of them. *We're atop one of the statues of Estrif's head.*

'What on earth did this?' Íri lingered on the step of the passage, clinging to the wall against the wind.

'Getitakus.' He pointed a finger at the shining silver thiokezöeasiä wielded by the figure furthest from them. 'Estrif's blessings aren't bestowed for free. He is entertaining the Prince of Bloodshed.'

'But he's supposed to be a *Voréöeasiä*.'

Azaki shrugged. 'Just because the Heart-Tree gave you a fragment of her power doesn't mean you're any less capable of awful things than anyone else. Only greenhearts believe that nonsense.'

A flash of white screeched from the spear-bladed tip of Getitakus's thiokezöeasiä; it struck a wrestling pair and tore them apart in a thunderclap so loud Azaki's head span, spraying gore and broken bones across the ground. A former captive crawled away sobbing, missing a leg and drenched in gore. Getitakus speared him through the back with his thiokezöeasiä's crown.

Azaki clenched his fists. *The red mist's come down so far he doesn't recognise friend from foe.*

Íri gaped, the orange flame swirling in her eyes fading a little.

'Come on, Íri. Let's end this.' He drew the falcata from his hip. 'Watch out for Getitakus, he's clearly not in his right mind.'

'What do we do?' she whispered.

'I don't know. We're more recognisable than the rest to him, but…'

She screwed her eyes shut and stepped into the blood. 'Streaming, red, righteous rage, wrathful ruin returned, repaid, wretches routed, or razed, found wanting, on being appraised.'

A spark of orange fire sprang up upon on her right palm, spreading into a glove covering her arm to the elbow. A glowing whip sprouted from her clenched fist, hissing and steaming in the wind, white-hot at its tip.

'Yanastakus?' Azaki glanced at where Togastakus's orb of water bent beneath the pressure of Duratakus's wind.

'He gave me the idea to add the whip bit,' Íri said. 'I thought it would be better than a sword or something like that.'

'You *are* a bit small for a sword fight.' He eyed the whip. 'Let's go rescue your future husband from his bubble, then. Please try not to hit me with the whip of fire.'

'We need the seed,' Falaïré whispered in his ear. 'Nothing else.'

We'll get it. Azaki smiled as he slipped round the edge of the struggle. *And we'll get everything else, too.*

Íri's whip snapped out at Duratakus. His apprentice stuck his pine branch in the way. The white-hot flame curled round it and burst apart, singing the gnarled branch.

'What a nasty spell!' the apprentice wailed. 'It's almost as nasty as the angry druid who keeps making everyone explode!'

Duratakus shoved his apprentice away with one hand and redirected his wind at Íri. Azaki watched the heat haze and wind clash over Togastakus's bubble, setting it to steaming and swirling as Togastakus endured the brunt of both pieces of magic.

'While they're busy, we may as well rid ourselves of the apprentice,' Falaïré murmured. 'His warped mind is dangerous.'

Azaki nodded, pulling the mist of his magic about him and concealing himself from the sight of everyone but Duratakus' apprentice. 'You know what I want,' he said, circling the clash of magic.

The apprentice clutched his burnt pine branch to his breast. 'You can't have it! It's my staff!'

'Not what I'm after…'

'I know what you want, nasty, sneaky druid! You can't have the seed. Master Duratakus gave me the most important task of holding onto it and not getting in his way!'

Azaki sighed and circled a little closer. 'I'm beginning to feel slightly sorry for Master Duratakus.'

The apprentice raised his pine branch. 'I feel sorry for the Tree Voréoatho. All her druids are so horrible beneath their lies! She must be so sad!'

Azaki lunged. The apprentice scrambled back, tripped upon a fallen warrior and rolled away. Duratakus stepped over his apprentice with a clenched jaw and extended his thiokezöeasiä out in a horizontal line.

The wind swirled and rose, spattering them with flecks of red foam and hot chunks of flesh. It tugged at Azaki, shoving him back across the ground toward the passage, and swept a warrior at the edge into the sky with a fading scream.

Duratakus put one foot on the back of his apprentice and gritted his teeth. The wind kept rising, dragging others off the edge one by one.

Omotakus crawled into the safety of Togastakus's orb of water, clutching the broken hilt of his longsword. The wind ripped the heat haze away from Íri's thiokezöeasiä and she teetered on her feet, her gold hair flying.

'Íri,' Azaki shouted into the howling gale, straining every sinew into the wind.

Togastakus seized her arm and dragged her inside his bubble, crouching down behind his shield. The orb of water bent beneath the wind, pressed near flat to the ground.

119

Red flashed in the corner of Azaki's eye. A dark figure hurled itself into its path and crumpled to the floor.

Getitakus?

'Strange.' Falaïré's whisper came through the wind like a hot knife through ice. 'Perhaps he took what Estrif said about his sister's scent to heart? It'd take something strong to pierce the bloodlust of Estrif's gift.'

Azaki clenched his jaw as his feet began to slide back across the ground and stabbed the falcata's tip into the stone. The blade scored a shallow line in the stone, spurting sparks until his heels hit the step.

Above him, the clouds drew together into a spiral, churning into a dark, thick maelstrom. Gravel-sized hailstones hammered down around him, stinging his skin and bouncing off the stone.

This is mad. He squinted at Togastakus's shrinking orb. *How long can Duratakus keep this up for?*

A bright flash rippled across the sky and thunder crashed over them.

'Run,' Falaïré hissed, her fingers tightening on his shoulder. 'We're too *high.*'

The world burst into white. A deafening crack tore at his ears as the lightning struck the horn of Estrif's statue to his left.

Thunder crashed overhead.

He held his breath, squinting through the storm at Duratakus's blurry brown figure. *We can't run, we need the seed.*

The lightning flashed, searing his eyes. Azaki squeezed them shut and blinked until the green spots faded. Togastakus, Omotakus, and Íri huddled inside the bubble of water as the dark clouds burst apart and the hail thinned.

Getitakus struggled to his feet, groping for his thiokezöeasiä among the bodies and weapons piled up against the wall. Flecks of red swirled in his eyes like tiny embers in the draft of a campfire. 'The Companion killed himself.'

Azaki staggered forward as the wind slackened. 'The apprentice?'

'Nooooooo!' A slim figure sank to its knees at the edge. 'Master Duratakus!'

'Inexplicably still alive,' Falaïré murmured. 'Be wary.'

'He must've been blessed by one of the Voréoathoki,' Azaki muttered. 'No way he survived that otherwise.'

Getitakus pulled open one of the tears in his black leather cuirass and grimaced. 'Nasty bruises. Better than it hitting you, though, Azaki.'

'Not for you, surely.' He strode toward the bubble, keeping one eye on the sobbing apprentice. 'Why did you throw yourself into a spell for me?'

'I'm just another Voréöeasiä. You're meant for bigger things, Estrif all but said so.'

Togastakus let down his orb and collapsed to his knees. 'Don't listen to the words of—'

Azaki kicked Togastakus over. 'What did I say about offending Estrif in his own shrine?'

'Are you okay, Azaki?' Íri staggered to her feet. 'Where's the seed?'

He patted himself down. 'I actually didn't get injured by anything this time.'

'What about me?' Togastakus muttered, dusting himself off. 'I saved you, not *him.*' He ground his teeth and stood up. 'Meant for bigger things. As if the Heart-Tree would allow it.'

Íriniel sealed her thiokezöeasiä with a sigh. 'The aspect of Azaki's thiokezöeasiä is well suited to opposing the champion of the Spider and it crowned faster than any other thiokezöeasiä, Togastakus. Getitakus might well be right.'

Falaïré's quiet laugh brushed his ear. 'And we *will* oppose him, my Azi. Even without the manipulations of Voréoathoki, he's keeping us from what we want.'

Íri pushed his falcata to one side and tugged open his shirt.

'Er… it's a bit cold up here for that, Íri, and we've got an audience…'

Her wind-reddened cheeks brightened. 'Idiot. I'm checking you're actually uninjured. We both know you'd pretend you were fine to try and look tough.'

An arrow hissed passed her ear and thudded into the apprentice's pine branch.

Purple feathers. Azaki swivelled about. *Really, Otuko?*

'I will avenge you, Master Duratakus!' The apprentice rose from the edge of the drop, tripped over his own feet and sprawled headfirst to the ground.

The red flecks in Getitakus' eyes glowed bright as night watchfires and he launched a bubble from his thiokezöeasiä. It curved just past the apprentice's side and sailed away into the sky.

A flicker of movement caught Azaki's eye.

Here we go again. He held his breath and stepped in front of Íri. Pain lanced through his shoulder, driving the breath from his lungs. *I really hate getting shot.*

'Azaki!' Íriniel's fingers rippled with green light.

He wrenched the arrow out with a hiss and glowered at the purple feathers. 'I hate getting shot!'

But if she's not worried about me getting in the way, she's not going to stop.

She pressed her fingers to the bleeding hole and the flesh knitted itself back together. 'Idiot,' she murmured. 'I can heal myself. I don't need you jumping in front of arrows.'

'Don't worry, it won't happen again. I'm going—'

A loud rumble rose from the ground and Íri plummeted away in a rush of black sand. The whole flat circle of stone between the horns of the stature dissolved beyond his feet.

'Not at all ideal,' Azaki muttered, peering into the gloom.

'No.' Falaïré stood on the air beside him. 'Estrif must not want the fun to stop yet. Still, with Duratakus gone, there seems to be nobody powerful enough left to worry us or your little Voréoeasiä girl.'

'True.' He turned back toward the passage and waved the bloody arrow. 'And this gives you a chance to say sorry for shooting me again, Otuko!'

'You asked for that, Azi! Letting her run her hands all over you!'

Azaki laughed and tossed the arrow away. 'She was trying to heal me, possessive girl.'

Otuko prowled from the dark, wearing smudged purple woad and a huge pout. A thin, bright scratch marred the three overlapping triangles of bronze protecting her torso. 'You're *mine*. It's taken years to even get you to realise. I'm not having some blonde southie harlot steal you away now.'

He stepped back from the drop and mussed her hair. 'Well, once we've got the seed, it'll be just us.'

She shoved him against the wall and crushed her lips against his. 'It's *already* just us, Azi. Utháki fell down as well.'

Azaki swallowed down a stomach full of fluttering. 'It actually *is* too cold up here.'

She giggled and curled her fingers into the front of his shirt. 'I know. I'd probably end up pregnant, too, and that'd be troublesome right now.'

'More like terrifying,' Azaki muttered. 'You're bad enough now, shooting me again for no real reason. If you were all cranky and pregnant, you might've actually killed me.'

She grinned and tightened her grip on him. 'If I catch some blonde girl who's not me all over you while I'm carrying our child, you can be pretty sure of that.'

'Ah well.' He let her stretch up and press her lips to his. 'I already owe you everything. You don't need to worry. If I'm what you want, I'm yours.'

Otuko rested her head on his chest. 'All I did was make you stick about with me instead of sulking by yourself in that little cave.' She took a deep breath and smiled. 'But I do want you, so I'm not going to tell you you're being stupid anymore.'

Twenty

A firm grip shook him awake by the shoulder.

Azaki opened his eyes.

A warm thigh pressed into his cheek, her forearm cradling his head against her stomach. He breathed in a tang of leather, sweat, woad, and a soft musk with a faint smile.

Otuko. He twisted round and glanced up.

The pale curve of her breasts swelled beneath a web of leather strings.

Oops. He grimaced and squashed the knot in his stomach. *Don't look away. You need to get used to it. This is what she wants.*

'Stare as much as you like.' A wicked glint appeared in Otuko's eyes and she tugged the hem of her shirt up to her neck. 'There, I'm all yours anyway.'

Otuko's breasts hung beneath the bunching of her shirt, near as pale as snow, her nipples pink as the tip of her tongue and small as rosebuds. She slipped her fingers through his and drew his hand up the smooth skin of her stomach to cup her left breast. Her skin felt soft as spider-silk and hot beneath his rough hand. Heat flooded Azaki's veins and rushed to his face. A trembling, shaking warm pooled in his belly like liquid flame.

This is a bad idea. Azaki met Otuko's smouldering eyes and his pulse quickened. But it's what she wants.

Otuko bit her lip and shuddered as her nipple brushed against the centre of his palm, swooping to press her mouth against his, slipping her tongue past his lips with a quiet moan. Azaki cupped the weight of her breast in his hand and gave it a gentle squeeze.

She gasped and blushed. 'We better stop now,' she whispered. 'Or I'm not going to be able to.'

Azaki swallowed and dropped his hand. 'Stopping.'

That wasn't as weird as I was afraid of. He smothered the faint fluttering of unease, letting the bright heat of the thrill burn it away. I can do this.

Otuko pulled her shirt back down and grinned. 'How was that, Azi? You like getting to see some more of me?'

He mustered a grin. 'You know full well I did.'

'I didn't want you to be afraid to look.' The wicked gleam appeared in her eyes again. 'Or *touch*.' She took a deep breath. 'But we need to find Utháki.'

She's right. He sat up, trying to steady the pounding of his heart and settle the heat coursing through his veins. *We need to find him, the seed, and leave.* Azaki smothered a soft pang. *Sorry, Íri.*

'I've got purple all over your face.' Otuko giggled and touched a finger to his cheek. 'I like it.'

Azaki rolled his eyes and glanced round the corner of the passage. 'You would. I'm surprised you've not tried to write your name on me in woad again while I slept.'

She grinned. 'Don't tempt me, Azi.'

'So possessive.'

'Someone's got to make sure that blonde southie girl knows to keep her hands off of you,' Otuko muttered. 'I'm going to be a lot happier once we've made a red oath, Azi.'

'What if I need Íri to heal me again?' Azaki asked. 'Are you going to stand next to us and pout the whole time?'

'You can find a different southie druid.' She pulled an arrow from her quiver. 'A male one.'

'And there was me worrying what you'd think of me for killing Atíko...'

Otuko clenched her fist around the arrow shaft and shuddered. 'I was on the verge of killing him myself. He made my skin crawl. You remember how he used to treat outcasts? What he did to the girls silly enough to let him have his way with them? I'd sooner be dead than in his bed.'

Soft thuds echoed in the distance.

Azaki cocked his head and held a finger to his lips. 'Footsteps.'

She put a hand on his shoulder and leant past him. 'Doesn't sound like one of us, stomping around like that.'

He smiled. 'Still, don't shoot them until after I've checked who it is.'

'If it's the funny and pretty one, I'm going to shoot her anyway.'

Azaki mussed her hair. 'Stop pouting, you. Íri's a little Voréöeasiä princess, she doesn't have it in her to go about stealing other girl's lovers. I don't think she's even thinking about stuff like that, too busy being a good Voréöeasiä and saving the world from Anastagus.'

Otuko narrowed her eyes at him and patted her hair back into place. 'Does she *know* you're mine?'

'Does it matter? She'll probably never see me again after today.'

'I suppose she can pine after you as much as she wants so long as she doesn't get you.' She fingered the tip of her arrow. 'No soft southie will ever understand people like us.'

The footsteps clomped nearer.

Azaki passed his thiokezöeasiä into his left hand. 'Queen of whispering webs, upon your throne of lies, gift a blade of shadow and revel in their cries.'

Otuko nocked her arrow and stepped back. 'Apart from the blonde druid girl, is there anyone I can't shoot?' she whispered.

He gnawed at the inside of his cheek as the footsteps approached their corner and concealed Otuko within his magic. 'The druid with the fish on his staff is Íri's friend, sort of. I'd rather Omotakus, the warrior who had the broken longsword, didn't die either. He's a decent man. I'd like to know he got back home safe and sound.'

'Well, if it's not either of them, they're getting an arrow.'

The figure stepped round the corner and froze. 'Oh, it's you,' Togastakus growled. 'I should've known you'd somehow crawl out of this wretched place unharmed. I'd hoped you'd died. Better you died fighting for the Heart-Tree here, then when you turn against her later. Better for Íriniel.'

Otuko stiffened.

Damn. Azaki grabbed for her bow.

Her arrow flashed past his shoulder, thudding into the faint shimmer of a ward.

The Greenheart stared at the purple feathers as the magic unravelled about him and dragged his eyes up to Azaki. 'You're — you really *are* a traitor... and the Heart-Tree just *lets* you!'

Azaki swallowed and resealed his thiokezöeasiä. 'I'm—'

'He's not a *traitor*. He was never on your side.' Otuko stepped to his shoulder, a second arrow upon her bowstring. 'You won't ever hurt Azi, druid. I'd gut you before you could.'

'Deceive, lady of lies,' he whispered.

The swirling ball of grey mist gathered within the tines of his thiokezöeasiä and burst out in a soft rush. He felt the magic ensnare the small handful of souls still caught within the Theatre of the Worldbreaker, seeping into Togastakus like winter chill into tired limbs.

Togastakus's face darkened and he snapped the shaft of the arrow off. His ward vanished and the head fell to the ground. 'Íriniel will be *devastated*.'

Azaki reached out and pushed Otuko's arrow toward the ground. 'So don't tell her. I'm not coming back, Togastakus. She doesn't need to know. It'd be kinder.'

Togastakus ground his teeth. 'I'm going to tell her. I'm going to kill you, traitor, then I'm going to tell her just what you really were. She'll see I was right all along.'

'That's just selfish.' Azaki side-stepped, leaving a shadow of himself behind.

Togastakus's hand snapped up, wreathed in glimmering blue magic. 'I *knew* you weren't worthy. Maybe now Íriniel will understand and finally join us.'

She might well decide to be a greenheart. Azaki fought down the barbed tangle of emotion threatening to well up from his heart onto his tongue and buried the memory of his dream. *I guess there's really no choice now.* He sent his echo fleeing down the passage beside a shadow of Otuko.

'No.' He put his hand on Otuko's shoulder as she raised her bow. 'Íri would be upset if another of her friends died, even if this one's pretty unbearable.'

'Surge, sea of boundless purity.' Togastakus sent spells hailing all after Azaki's shadow in the mist, sprinting down into the dark as tendrils of water gathered around him.

Azaki waited until the sound of his footsteps faded, then resealed his thiokezöeasiä. 'Come on, Otuko. Let's go find that seed.'

She trailed him along the passage. 'He better not cause us trouble later, Azi.'

'He's Íri's friend, or he was, a while back. Her last friend, really, given I'm leaving her.' Azaki clenched his fingers around the blade in his hand and shoved the sharp knot in his chest deep down inside. 'He'll be trouble, he's never been anything else, but I'll deal with that when it's later.'

'We shouldn't have spared him,' Falaïré whispered. 'Now the little Voréöeasiäki girl will know.'

He sighed. *It'll hurt her less than if another of her friends died.*

Otuko tapped her bow's tip against the blade of shadow in his hand. 'How powerful are you, Azi?'

He shrugged. 'I can usually hold my own.'

'So like a Companion?'

'They all seem to be erudite druids,' Azaki replied. 'I'm just a druid.'

Otuko narrowed her eyes. 'You're *not* a druid.'

'If you see a staff with a proper crown at the top of it, then they're a druid, before that they're just an acolyte and only have spells.'

'And the other one that the Companions are?'

'They seem to have an extra level on someone like me,' Azaki said. 'I could probably handle someone like Kogodakus or Yanastakus to begin with, but after that second unsealing I'd be in hot water. In a fair fight, that is.'

'What about Duratakus's apprentice?' Otuko paused at a fork in the passage and waggled her arrow back forth between the two paths.

He pointed down the left one toward faint light. 'I've only seen him use one spell and I'm fairly sure his staff is just a piece of wood, but I think he's been blessed by one of the Voréoathoki like the eorls and some of the keorls. He's got a knack for surviving things in weird ways and my magic doesn't seem to affect him.'

'If we fill him full of arrows, he'll die.' She reached over her shoulder. 'I've only got four left, though.'

'Four's more than enough.' Azaki let the blade of shadow burst into wisps of dark mist. 'We can always just stab him if he manages to dance or trip his way through those. Blessings aren't infallible. They certainly didn't save Atíko, though I'm not sure what blessing he'd received.'

'And then we'll have the seed.' Otuko grabbed his wrist and tugged him back. 'But that just means Anastagus will get it back.'

Azaki raised an eyebrow. 'The clan's sworn to Anastagus.'

She folded arms. 'I don't care about the clan. It's always been the three of us. I'm only still part of it because Utháki's so stupidly loyal.'

'And if he wasn't?'

Otuko grinned. 'You ought to be grateful he's so stubborn, Azi. If he'd agree to leave, we'd be long gone and I'd be thinking about getting started on having those four children.'

Azaki's stomach clenched. *No, no I'm not used to it.* He breathed out the unease through his nose. *It's just easier not to think about it when she's got her top off.*

'Why does it have to be four?' he muttered. 'Can't it just be a couple?'

She huffed. 'A boy needs a brother and a girl needs a sister. Growing up with just you and Utháki was a nightmare sometimes. You two just don't get some stuff. I'm the one who carries them and pushes them out, too, so I get to choose how many we have.'

Azaki's stomach squirmed and flopped like a landed fish. *I can't believe she was serious this whole time.*

'Anastagus doesn't care for the clan either,' he said. 'He used Kogodakus. He used him up, then left him to die. He'll do the same to us and the clan.'

Otuko frowned. 'Well, Atíko's dead, so the eorls aren't going to be quite so loyal to him now, but he's way more powerful than any of us are.'

'For now,' Falaïré murmured in his ear. 'Our bond will outstrip him. How can a man who only trusts in selfish intentions match the strength of a shared heart?'

Azaki smiled. 'One day, I'll be better.'

'And the seed?' Otuko pulled him close. 'Can we use that? What even is it?'

'We can't use it. It's very powerful, but there's no way we'd beat Anastagus to figuring out how to use it and he'd be unbeatable if he did. Soekus the Lifebringer said so.'

'So we destroy it, then.' She tucked her head under his chin and sighed. 'Sacrifice it to Estrif.'

'Not sure that'd even work.' Azaki wrapped an arm around her slim shoulders and gave her a gentle squeeze. 'We'll plant it in the Silk Gardens. Once it's started growing into a tree, Anastagus can't use it. It'll be part of the Heart-Tree's network of groves.'

Even if that's probably just what the Heart-Tree intended me to do all along. Azaki let Otuko pull his lips down to hers. *I still get most of what I want.*

'A life-debt repaid,' Falaïré whispered in his ear. 'We stay with the girl who saved us and fulfil her dream.'

Otuko's tongue traced his lower lip with the tip of her tongue and let out a low moan. 'Oh, I wish we'd left the clan and got started on having those four babies. Everything would be so much simpler.'

He released a shaky breath and swallowed down the fire her moan had started in his blood. 'I don't think I'd mind the getting started too much, not sure I'm quite so keen on the tiny, helpless nuisance, though.'

She laughed. 'That's what all the boys say at first, I bet, and I'd make it up to you, I promise.'

Azaki chuckled. 'Promises, promises, Otuko. Don't go running that mouth without being able to back it up again.'

A wicked gleam appeared in her eyes. 'Pretty sure my mouth can keep those promises.'

He gulped and tore his eyes away from her lips. 'Right.'

Otuko giggled and held Azaki's gaze through her dark lashes until his face turned hot. 'Unfortunately, this isn't the place for that, Azi. And I want us to make the red oath, too. Can't have you panicking and running off when I get pregnant, or risk some other girl getting her hooks into you.' She glowered. 'I heard Ulika and another warrior talking about you being pretty-faced a couple of years back. She said she broke all your ribs, but once you were a warrior, she was going to make you all hers.'

'Ulika fell into a hole and got eaten by a giant spider. Nothing left but that bit of red hair.' He shrugged. 'Breaking all my ribs really helped me to realise how awful she was.'

Otuko folded her arms. *'Fell...'*

'Well, that or the spider grabbed her and dragged her in,' he replied. 'They do that, I think.'

She glowered. 'Don't lie to me. Utháki told me he threw her in, he can't keep a secret to save his life.'

'That idiot,' Azaki muttered. 'Well, I didn't touch her.'

'I'm sure you didn't.' Otuko snorted. 'But that troll-faced moron couldn't plan his way out of a puddle. It was your idea.' A shy smile flashed across her face. 'You did it for me.'

'You nearly died after she shot you.'

A nasty little thought crept up on him. *Did Ulika know about what you wanted?*

'Otuko…?' he murmured. *'Why* did Ulika shoot you?'

She glanced away. 'As a joke.'

He sighed. 'Look me in the eyes and say that again.'

Otuko twisted around and huffed. 'Fine. I heard her talking about what she wanted to do once you were a warrior and I didn't like it. It made me feel sick, the idea of you and her. She wanted to hurt you and make you run away just so you'd come crawling back to her...' She shivered. 'I told her I'd gut her like a rabbit if she ever touched you.'

'You idiot.' Azaki cupped her cheek with his hand. 'You nearly got yourself killed.'

'Well, it worked out.' She caught his hand under both of hers and pressed her face into his palm. 'She might've decided to mess about with you even before you got your cloak if I'd not. I bet she did with the others that talked to her and vanished.'

'She's dead,' Azaki murmured. 'Long dead. We should forget about her. And Atíko.'

Otuko nodded. 'Good riddance.' She let her hands drop. 'Let's go find Utháki, Azi, and get out of here.'

127

A rumble swept through the passage, throwing Azaki to his hands and knees. A low groan escaped Otuko as the passage lurched left, shifting through the dark rock like a bubble through water.

Azaki pushed himself to his feet and brushed his palms off, squinting into the light. 'You okay?'

Otuko held up a finger and shook her head.

'No?' He chuckled. 'You're looking a bit green, actually.'

'I'll be okay in a—' she gagged and vomited onto the ground. 'Urgh, what is *wrong* with me?'

Azaki gathered up her dust-streaked, ash-blonde hair and held it away from her face. 'Did you let Utháki cook something?'

Otuko hurled another rush of bitter-smelling vomit onto the ground and wiped her mouth on her sleeve. 'If we'd been trying for those four children, you'd be in a cold sweat right about now.'

He picked a splinter out of her hair. 'I think it takes a bit longer than that for you to start getting sick.'

'Yeah.' She shook her hair out of his grasp and hauled herself up on his arm. 'I just don't like all the moving when I can't see it happening. Felt a bit sick a few times, but that was much worse.'

Azaki grinned as the colour returned to her face. 'Well, you're not kissing me now.'

Otuko pouted and grinned. 'I guess that's fair.'

A shadow moved across the light at the end of the passage.

He ripped the falcata free and stepped in front of Otuko, but a second shadow appeared, grappling with the first. 'You ready?'

She scowled and drew the hunting knife from her hip. 'You've gotten too used to that soft southie girl, a little bit of queasiness is nothing.'

Azaki laughed. 'That's my girl.'

'And don't you forget it,' Otuko muttered, pulling a second, identical blade from inside her boot.

'Deceive, lady of lies.' He closed his eyes and felt his magic wrap itself around a handful of souls ahead of them. 'There're six of them, not sure who's on which side, though.'

She shrugged. 'Use your fancy magic, then.'

'Still so jealous.'

She grinned. 'I was tempted to steal that staff.'

'It wouldn't work for you, you'd have to get your own.' Azaki prowled toward the light, one eye on the two shadows still struggling there. 'And then it'd have to bond with you and change shape before you could use it.'

Otuko tapped the blade of her hunting knife against her bow. 'Well, this was a staff once and I'm pretty sure it used to be darker.'

He squinted at the slim arc on her back. 'It's probably died.'

'I'll have to get another one, then.'

Azaki chuckled under his breath. 'You really still want to be able to do magic so badly?'

'Yes.' She folded her arms, hunting knives jutting from beneath her elbows. 'I want it and I'll get it.'

'We like her,' Falaïré whispered in his ear. 'We should keep her.'

Of course we like her. Azaki watched her circling Otuko, silver eyes glowing. *She saved us.*

The two shadows burst into the light, grappling back and forth. One slipped in the pool of red at the entrance and the blur of motion came to an end with a sharp gasp. Utháki tugged his axe out of Omotakus's neck and ripped the broken longsword from his fingers as he fell.

Sorry, Omotakus. Azaki swallowed the flash of heat around his heart and stepped over to the body. A cold weight settled in his chest. *You deserved to go home. Not die here.*

'Azaki.' Utháki bent and wiped his axe clean on Omotakus's blue tunic, stripping the cuirass, greaves, and armguards from his body. 'He was pretty tough for a southie, I think I'll keep these bits of armour and his broken blade as raiding prizes. A bit of work and the blade might make a good knife.'

Azaki brushed Omotakus's eyes closed and gave the dead man's shoulder a squeeze. 'I suppose he doesn't need any of it now.'

Otuko shared a soft look with him and padded to the passage's end as Utháki strapped Omotakus's armour on. 'The other druid's here, the one Estrif's messed with the head of.'

'Getitakus.' Azaki grabbed her hand and pulled back into the dark. 'Don't let him see you, I'm not sure I can stop his magic, especially not now Estrif's blessed him.'

He felt the other three souls his thiokezöeasiä had ensnared fade from his senses as another series of crashes rumbled through the stone. *But he might listen to me after what Estrif said.*

Utháki put a hand on Azaki's shoulder. 'Are you coming back to the clan?'

'I'm coming back to Otuko… and you.'

'And the clan?'

'I won't follow anyone or anything blindly. Not the clan. And certainly not Anastagus.' Azaki bit back a flash of heat. 'You were just *sitting there* and letting Atíko harass Otuko because he's an eorl of *the clan!*'

Utháki flinched and made a quiet rumbling noise. 'I'm sorry, Azi. I didn't understand. Otuko explained.' He shuffled his feet. 'I wouldn't have let Atíko do anything, but Otuko made me promise not to do anything unless she said.'

'Good.'

Otuko pointed her hunting knife into the light. 'And the apprentice?'

'We need the seed,' Azaki said. 'Anastagus isn't interested in the good of the Webbed Pit and he's powerful enough as it is. We can steal the seed from Duratakus's apprentice and plant it in the Silk Gardens.'

Utháki nodded. 'Glory for us and protection for the clan in case Anastagus becomes a threat. Two rabbits with one arrow.'

'You couldn't hit one rabbit with two arrows,' Otuko said.

'I have an axe, not a stick and some string.'

Otuko huffed. 'So, Azi. What's the plan?'

'Getitakus is a useful distraction,' Azaki said. 'Estrif will make sure everyone comes here soon enough. You two stay back and keep quiet, I'll get the seed off the apprentice with Getitakus and whomever else turns up, then give it to you—'

'You're *not* staying behind,' Otuko hissed. 'Not again!'

'Otuko missed you lots already,' Utháki said. 'It's not fair to make her miss you again.'

'Shut up, troll-face. I can speak for myself.' Otuko grabbed Azaki's head in both hands and pulled his forehead down to hers. 'I don't care what happens. Even if you have to leave that little blonde southie girl to be some old warrior's plaything, you're coming back.'

'I couldn't do that.'

Utháki frowned. 'She's a druid. Our enemy.'

'Well, I don't want to fight her and she'd probably turn the two of you to ash, so let's leave her be.' Azaki heard footsteps hurrying toward them from the dark and pushed Otuko and Utháki against the wall. 'After you two have the seed, I'll feign my death and return. Don't wait for me, I'll just catch you up anyway.'

'Only because of this lumbering moron,' Otuko muttered. 'You can't catch *me*.'

'Stay quiet and don't touch anyone or anything.' Azaki shrouded them both beneath the fine grey mist. 'My magic's keeping you hidden, but it can only do so much.'

He stepped into the light, raising his hands as Getitakus twisted about with a snarl. A crimson ring shone around his pupil and red flecks gleamed in his irises

'Just me,' Azaki said.

'Azaki.' Getitakus sagged and some of the crimson faded from his eyes. 'Thank the Heart-Tree. I feared you'd died before reaching the destiny She intends for you.'

Destiny. Azaki glanced round the perfect circle of black sand.

Three other passageways broke the smooth, dark wall.

Akrotera said something like that, too. Unease stirred in the pit of his stomach. *And Estrif.*

'Nope, still alive... for now.' He stepped closer and studied the myriad of gashes and scratches through Getitakus's shredded dark leather cuirass. 'How're you holding up?'

'Tired.' He leant on the shining spear Estrif had gifted him. 'Very tired. But I'll do my part. You'll survive this and get the seed of the Heart-Tree back. I'll rid us of as many of these vermin as I can.'

Another figure burst onto the black sand, rolling across the ground and bouncing back to his feet. Bright blue eyes and cropped, near-white hair flashed over the dark ground.

'I was hoping you'd turn up,' Azaki said.

'Oh no!' The apprentice clutched his pine branch to the breast of his pristine robes. 'The nasty sneaky druid!'

'Better sneaky than silly.'

Getitakus hurled a ball of fist-sized white light at the apprentice, but it curved just past his shoulder and burst against the stone, sending small dark shards flying across the sand.

'You're even worse than the sneaky druid,' the apprentice whined. 'We were just having a chat and you try to kill me.'

Getitakus growled and raised his thiokezöeasiä. His left iris burnt crimson, shining like the red moon. 'You deserve—'

The pine branch's gnarled end slammed into his forehead and he crumpled to the ground.

'Master Duratakus is avenged!' The apprentice's face fell. 'I don't suppose you'd let me get my staff back, sneaky druid?'

Azaki glanced at the heavily glued piece of wood and down at his hands as a faint, warm, orange light settled over him. 'Sure, why not?'

'Thanks, nice sneaky druid!'

Íri sprinted from the same passage the apprentice had come from, her thiokezöeasiä glowing and her eyes aflame. 'Azaki!'

'Where's Toga the Sour?' he asked.

The apprentice caressed the top of his pine branch with his long fingers. 'Is that the really grumpy Voréöeasiä who keeps trying to give me a bath?'

'Yes.' Azaki grinned. 'That's definitely him. Feel free to give him a silly nickname, too.'

Íri glowered at him. 'Are you going to try and fight, or are you just leaving it up to me?'

He edged around until he was next to her. 'I'm actually just amazed he managed to get Getitakus, I'm still in shock.'

'Yep. Right in the face.' The apprentice grinned so wide all his teeth were on show and bowed so low his nose brushed the sand. 'Perfect shot.'

'He threw his thiokezöeasiä at him?' Íri blinked. 'Really?'

'It was a good shot and Getitakus is only knocked out, so no real harm done. In fact, it might be for the best, Estrif's hold on him is only growing stronger.'

Íri sighed. 'Please at least *pretend* to be taking this seriously, the seed of the Heart-Tree is right here.'

'You're not having it.' The apprentice levelled a finger at them and clutched at a bulge beneath his tunic. 'Master Duratakus bravely accidentally struck himself with lightning to protect the seed. I will not allow his sacrifice to go to waste!'

'Toast him?' Azaki suggested. 'The seed will be fine.'

'I've been trying for hours.' Íri let out a little growl. 'He just seems to wriggle out of the way at the last moment.'

'Hmmm, well, no blessing lasts forever.' Azaki slid the falcata back into his sheath. 'Queen of whispering webs, upon your throne of lies, gift a blade of shadow and revel in their cries.'

Íri took a deep breath and thrust a wave of scorching air at the apprentice. He dived across the sand to safety.

Azaki hurled the summoned knife at the apprentice. It struck the top of the pine branch and the hilt bounced off his shoulder. 'Unbelievable, that's the second—'

Something slammed into his side like a charging boar. Pain seared through his ribs as he went sprawling across the sand. Azaki twisted round on his knees and struggled to his feet, every breath sending a lance of agony through his chest.

'Traitor!' Togastakus brandished his lash of water at him, blue light swirling on his palm. 'I *knew* you were a savage!'

Íri swivelled back around and batted the water away with her magic. 'Togastakus, what're you *doing?!*'

Broken ribs. As bad as when Ulika got me. Azaki pressed a finger to them and hissed as the pain flared up. *I shouldn't have spared you.*

'No, we shouldn't have,' Falaïré murmured in his ear. 'If we take risks, they'll come back to bite us, like a wounded beast.'

'He's not a Voréöeasiäki.' Togastakus launched another spell at Azaki. 'He's one of them!'

The blue spell ploughed into the sand at Azaki's feet.

The apprentice watched from the far side, his fingers steepled over the top of his branch. 'Oh dear! All the nasty druids are fighting each other!'

Íri pressed green-wreathed fingers to Azaki's ribs and the pain faded. 'I know. He told me.'

Togastakus gaped. 'But—'

Íri slid her hand under Azaki's shoulder and helped him up. 'He's a good Voréöeasiäki, Togastakus. The Heart-Tree chose him. Who cares where he was from before?'

A soft laugh slipped from the apprentice's lips. 'You're a *really* sneaky Voréöeasiäki, Azaki Kathal.'

Togastakus grit his teeth. 'Then you're as bad as he is, Íriniel, letting the unworthy corrupt our order. I'll – I'll have to take the seed for the greenhearts, before it's tainted too.'

Getitakus struggled to his feet, clutching his face. A dull red glimmer suffused his irises. 'What happened?' He snatched his thiokezöeasiä up. 'Purge, scourge of darkness.'

The phrase changed.

'I got you in the face.' The apprentice pumped his fist in the air. 'That's what happened.'

'Let them fight,' Falaïré whispered. 'We can steal the seed while they struggle and let the little Voréöeasiäki girl believe the greenheart murdered us.'

Azaki smiled, resealed his thiokezöeasiä, and unsealed it once more. *She'd never go with Togastakus after that.*

Getitakus hurled himself at the apprentice as Íri and Togastakus exchanged blows in flashes of heat and washes of steam. Shining spheres shrieked through the air and hammered into the stone walls as the apprentice danced and stumbled through them, leaving small craters and showering the sands in sharp fragments.

Heat seared at the side of Azaki's face as he stalked round the edge of the sand toward the apprentice's back, reweaving Getitakus's truth until his magic drilled into the stone wall away from everyone else. He let the apprentice see Togastakus, Íri, and himself locked in conflict and filled the air full of false spells until the apprentice retreated near the bodies of the warriors Getitakus had slain.

'Be careful, my Azi,' Falaïré murmured as he approached the apprentice's back. 'He's escaped our power before.'

Azaki watched the apprentice duck and weave his way through the empty air and kicked a spear between his legs, sending him tumbling to the floor. The seed bounced free across the black sand.

'Perfect,' Falaïré breathed.

Azaki snatched the seed and strode back across the sand, ducking a pair of blue spells Togastakus sent hissing past Íri. He slipped into the dark of the passageway.

'Azi?' Otuko leant away from the wall.

Azaki placed the seed in her hands. 'Go now. Plant it in the Silk Gardens.'

'You're coming?' Utháki asked.

Heat rippled down the passage and Togastakus thudded into the sand by the doorway. He struggled to his feet and dashed a hand across his eyes. 'Fine, Íriniel! Choose that *savage*.' Togastakus's lip curled. 'If you're not willing to be part of the solution, then you're part of the problem!'

Azaki twisted aside as Togastakus stormed down the passage, muttering to himself and grinding his teeth, stomping his feet so hard the ground seemed to shake. Utháki watched him go with a deep frown.

'One down,' Otuko whispered. 'Azi?'

'Go, both of you. The seed's the most important thing. I can return later if I must.'

She clung to him, pressing her lips against his, and darted away.

132

Utháki grabbed Azaki's wrist. 'She cried for days last time, Azaki. Don't make her cry again.'

'No matter where I am or what I'm doing, I'll *always* be loyal to her.' He glanced down at the three bronze dolphins on the armguard and tugged his wrist free. 'We swore, remember, and even if we hadn't, Otuko saved me. I owe her every second I live.'

Utháki stared him in the eye and grunted. 'You serve the clan and help us your way, then. Last time, you equalled a legend, so I'll vouch for you when you return. Just don't make her wait too long. You two are meant to be together; it's fate. She's loved you since before we swore that oath to look out for her.'

Really? All this time? Azaki chewed at the inside of his cheek. *Otuko should've said. There was nothing for her to be afraid of. I owe her everything.*

'I'd only make her wait if I had no choice,' he said.

Utháki glanced through the passage at Íri, then clasped Azaki's shoulder and strode into the dark.

'Aren't we leaving?' Falaïré slid from the shadows, a smirk upon her lips. 'Or has the little Voréöeasiäki girl's defence of you changed your mind, my Azi?'

'I'm just going to make sure she gets away safely, that's all.'

Her laughter followed him out of the passage onto the sands. 'Are we going to deceive ourselves too, my Azi?' She slipped out of his shadow as he approached Íri. 'The truth's we want both our friends and we'll chase both until we're forced to stop.'

Perhaps. He glanced at where Íri leant upon her thiokezöeasiä, dirt-streaked, dust-covered, and fierce-eyed and felt the gentle strength of the warmth of the orange glow wash over him. *Probably.*

The apprentice's fingers crept to his tunic and he froze, tearing his way free of Azaki's magic with soft laughter. 'Well done, Azaki Kathal. You've grown stronger.'

Getitakus's magic dissipated before the apprentice's raised palm, fading like morning mist. Íri turned her thiokezöeasiä on him, but her heat washed out like a gentle breeze.

The apprentice raised his fingers to his face and ripped away the youthful blue eyes and cropped blonde hair like stray cobwebs. 'Reveal, artificer of falsehoods.'

Azaki's heart sank. 'Do you insist on doing this with all your plans?'

Anastagus dusted black sand from his spider carapace armour with a smile. His deep brown eyes gleamed with humour. 'Yes. It amuses me. And who else can I truly trust but myself?'

Getitakus howled with rage and unleashed a trio of projectiles, but they curved round Anastagus and burst at Íri's feet, hurling her into the wall. She slumped to the ground, blood running freely into her gold hair.

Iri... He sucked in a sharp breath and sprinted toward her.

The arena rumbled and shook, hurling Azaki into the dark sand.

'Your deal with Estrif has ended,' Anastagus said from somewhere in front of him.

Azaki struggled to his feet half a dozen paces from the altar of bronze blades and its marble basin. 'It worked, though.' He staggered to Íri's side and held his palm over her mouth, feeling warm air brush his skin.

Still breathing. He released a long sigh. *Thank the Voréoathoki.*

'What will you do now?' Anastagus glanced across the sand to where Togastakus and Getitakus separated. 'The greenheart is abandoning you, it seems, and as for Getitakus... We both saw him fighting. Estrif's left his mark and it will only get worse…'

Azaki resealed his thiokezöeasiä. 'He was your tool to change how the soft-folk perceive Voréöeasiäki. Kogodakus must've told you about him, they seemed to have known one

133

another once. You took his acolytes to turn him into this where everyone could see what he then did.'

A faint smile passed across Anastagus's face. 'Ah, you realised. Well done.'

'Deceive, lady of lies,' Azaki whispered.

Fine grey mist washed over the dark sand of the arena and he felt his magic thread itself through Anastagus's senses.

Anastagus tensed and ripped his way free once more. 'Even with my thiokezöeasiä unsealed?' The smile slipped from his face and voice softened to a whisper. 'Now I understand. You're Vyfaesiä's gambit. She knows none of the Voréöeasiäki will be able to defeat me, so she gambles her world on you. You are a double-edged sword, Azaki Kathal. You might have the potential to match me, but you have no reason not to join me and help free Olisolamon from her tyranny.'

He doesn't want me dead. Azaki recalled the request for surrender and the note with a brief surge of hope. *If I give him proof I might still be loyal to the clan or him, he might let Íri and I go.*

'But what proof can we give?' Falaïré whispered, her silver eyes flicking to rest on Getitakus. The light in them turned sharp as shattered mirrorglass.

Azaki took a deep breath. 'The tyranny of a giant tree?' he probed as the blood-crazed Voréöeasiäki neared them. 'The Voréoatho of peace and life?'

Getitakus's magic hissed between them and exploded, hurling up a cloud of sand.

'Queen of whispering webs, upon your throne of lies, gift a blade of shadow and revel in their cries.' Azaki rotated his wrist to hide the slim, hand-length blade.

Anastagus swatted the second volley of projectiles aside with his black-gloved hand, but the Getitakus ducked the flash of purple that crackled from Anastagus's fingers and stumbled to Azaki's side.

'Azaki,' Getitakus gasped, the red glow in his eyes flaring and dying like the light of the clan forge when the bellows were worked. 'You must run. I'll fight. Yes. Leave the girl and run. You must survive. I must *fight*. The Heart-Tree chose you for greater things. *Destiny.*'

'We could run and leave the little Voréöeasiäki girl to die.' Falaïré's red-stained fingers curled 'round his wrist, leaving bright crimson marks on his skin. 'But this blood-crazed Voréöeasiäki seems so keen to die for us. Give him what he wants, my Azi. What better proof could we offer?'

Anastagus's expression remained unreadable. 'Well, Azaki Kathal? How deeply mired in self-delusion are you? Can you let him die for your escape? One of the Voréöeasiäki? One steeped in bloodlust, but still one of the Voréöeasiäki. It's him or you. Can you see that truth?'

'I can see *a* truth.' Azaki tightened his grip on the knife and swallowed the lump in his throat. 'It's a bitter choice.'

Getitakus glanced at where Íri lay and brandished the blood-smeared spear his thiokezöeasiä had become. 'She's just one Voréöeasiäki, Azaki. Dying for the world is what she would want. You're meant for more. It's your destiny. Hers is the same as mine. We fight and die, so you'll one day destroy this traitor for good.'

Anastagus has twisted you. Azaki watched the red in the Voréöeasiäki's eyes begin to shine again and hardened his heart. *The more you fight him, the better you end up serving him. Like Yanastakus.*

He forced the knife into Getitakus' temple; it crunched through the bone and he went stiff as stone. The blade burst into wisps of shadow as Getitakus's body thudded to the ground.

134

He had to die anyway. Azaki watched the spear-like thiokezöeasiä crumble into black sand. *He was Estrif's pawn as much as Anastagus's. The bloodlust would've only grown worse.*

'We wanted to prove ourselves useful still,' Falaïré whispered in his ear. 'We have. Everything has a price, remember.'

'Interesting.' Anastagus's fingers flickered with purple light, his eyes shifting from Azaki to Íri's sprawled form and back again. 'Perhaps I should kill you all anyway, just in case.'

Azaki forced himself to grin. 'If you try, you'll never be able to get the seed back by the time I'm dead. It'll be growing peacefully in the Silk Gardens before you catch up to it.'

Anastagus let the violet magic fade. 'Well played, Azaki. Still, I wasn't going to kill you. It'd be far more fitting for you to be the one who helps me tear away Vyfaesiä's lies. I think I'd like her to see that. Her gambit choosing the truth over her lies.'

'I don't trust you anywhere near enough to join you.'

'Not yet.' Anastagus closed his eyes, releasing a wave of green magic across the sand. 'But as I told you once before, only one of the Voréoathoki cares about the truth. Find her and she will set you free forever.'

Íri gasped and jerked upright as the emerald ripple passed over her, the cut upon her head knitting itself closed. 'Azaki!'

'And what about you?' Anastagus took a step toward Íri. 'Soekus's daughter. I've always respected your father. We agreed on many things. Unfortunately, I couldn't make him understand everything.'

'Understand what?' Íri demanded. 'That you're a monster who betrayed his pact with the Heart-Tree?'

'She's no better than any of the Voréoathoki.' Anastagus sealed his thiokezöeasiä. 'Peace and life are part of nature. She doesn't control or embody them. They'd not vanish if we weren't forced to live her lie.'

'Peace isn't a lie!' Íriniel's eyes blazed with orange flame.

'No.' A brief sadness flickered through Anastagus's eyes and in them Azaki glimpsed a younger, kinder man. 'But the Voréöeasiäki are. Everything. From root to leaves. I'll let you learn it for yourselves, though. It's the only way to really understand. One day, you might thank me for prompting you to peel back the veil.'

'We'll *never* believe you,' Íri hissed.

'We'll see.' Anastagus smiled a small faint smile and stared up into the sky. 'Ask your father, he knows some of the truth I found.'

'Liar,' she accused.

'I never lie.' Anastagus frowned up at the heavens. 'The truth can be cold and cruel, but it's *real*. If you live a life based upon the truth, then everything you do is real, no matter it's nature. Imagine the agony of those who die and find they spent their lives devoted to nothing but spun words and shadow. Is that what you want for Olisolamon's people? Didn't we swear to protect them and their world?'

Azaki opened his mouth, but Anastagus's image faded away like smoke in the wind.

'An illusion.' Íri sealed her thiokezöeasiä. 'He's gone.'

'Well, my Azi?' Falaïré bent and touched her red-stained fingers to Getitakus's cheek, leaving five crimson prints upon his face. 'What now?'

'Let's get back to the ship.' Azaki sealed his thiokezöeasiä and tried to smother a hot, ugly flame in his chest. 'We failed.'

'Did we, my Azi?' Falaïré murmured. 'Anastagus's shadow looms, but now we've a way back to the Webbed Pit and the little Voréöeasiäki girl is still safe.'

'We saved the Beacon at the Edge of the World.' Íri wrapped her fingers round his wrist and squeezed. 'We defeated two Companions and almost got the seed back. Now, we should go to the Grey Stair.'

'But Anastagus *won*.' He kicked black sand over Anastagus's footsteps and cursed. 'The people at the beacon see us as warlords. He'll do it everywhere he can. Word will spread. His ugly, selfish truth will get everywhere.'

And the next boy drowning on hate won't be saved by an Otuko, he'll be found by an Anastagus.

'Let the Hands of the Heart-Tree worry about that, Azaki. There's nothing else we could've done. Don't let his lies get to you.'

'I won't.' Azaki stared west as if he could see through the dark stone to where Otuko and Utháki were leaving him behind once more. His heart hung like a fistful of lead beneath his ribs. 'I'm sick of Anastagus. All of this is his fault. He started everything.'

He takes people like the boy I once was and turns them into monsters like Kogodakus.

'Well, you ought to thank him for meeting me, at least,' Íri said as they limped towards the steps.

But if I'd not met you and Soekus, I'd be with Otuko, guilt-free. Azaki gnawed at the inside of his cheek and swallowed a tangle of thorns. *We'd be warriors, maybe even married if she'd told me what she wanted.*

He forced a smile. 'They do say good things come in small packages and you *are* tiny.'

She snorted. 'Is that your way of admitting any girl stupid enough to be with you is going to be disappointed?'

Azaki laughed as they stumbled up the steps together and through the passage toward the distant light. 'What would it matter? Have you seen anyone even remotely interested in me?'

She rolled her eyes. 'Well, *Anastagus* seems interested in you…'

'That's a truly disturbing thought, Íri. Thanks for that.'

Íri limped past the taloned toes of one of Estrif's vast effigies, her gold hair cast pink and orange by the setting sun. Azaki stumbled along beside her, gripped by a deep, cold ache.

'Are you okay?' She touched the back of her hand to his forehead. 'You feel all clammy.'

'I've felt better.'

'You've looked better, too, though it'll be dark soon, so that'll be an improvement anyway.'

Azaki chuckled. 'At least the Lady of Betrayal hasn't yet—'

Something hissed past his neck.

A shadow staggered from the dark behind the feet of Estrif's statue and into the sunset. Warped, puckered scar tissue covered the left side of its face and neck and a grey tunic hung in tatters from a girdle armoured with circles of scorched spider carapace. The figure's brown eyes blazed with rage and he clutched his winged thiokezöeasiä with white-knuckled hands.

Duratakus survived. A slow, hot trickle crawled down Azaki's stinging neck and red soaked into his shirt and dread coiled around his heart. *Damn.*

'I will not fail him,' Duratakus muttered as the wind picked up around them. 'I can't.'

'Blaze, beacon of virtuous ire,' Íri whispered, her hands trembling.

Faint orange flame swirled in her eyes.

She's exhausted.

The heat haze strained into the howling wind. Duratakus's scars smoked and he bared his teeth in a soundless scream.

'We need to get around him,' Azaki murmured, drawing the falcata from his hip. 'If we can get around him, I can hide us once the sun's set and we can get back to the ship. I'll give you a chance to hit him. Hit him as hard as you can.'

Íri drew in a deep, wavering breath and the glow of her thiokezöeasiä's crown flared up. The heat haze curled around the crown, folding into a shivering, shimmering spear tip.

This is going to hurt. Azaki lunged, gritting his teeth.

Duratakus flinched back and slashed his thiokezöeasiä across. The wind slammed into Azaki, hurling him across the stone. His right hand crunched beneath his side, exploding into searing pain, and the falcata slipped from his grip.

Duratakus went flying down the slope away from the river in a trail of smoke.

Azaki dragged himself upright with a clenched jaw, fighting the dull ache in his limbs. *Good riddance.*

'Azaki?' Íri snatched his falcata up. 'Let me heal you.'

'Start running.' He spared a look at his throbbing, bent, broken fingers. 'And save your magic, Íri. We might need it for more important things.' Azaki staggered back to her side and let her sheath his falcata.

Her eyes lingered on his hand.

'Go.' He gave her a nudge. 'I've had worse.'

'Fine.' Íri resealed her thiokezöeasiä and broke into a run down the slope. 'Don't blame me if they end up all crooked later.'

He matched her pace, watching the curve of the orange sun sink over the horizon as they hurled themselves down the gravel hillside toward the shining curve of the river.

137

Azaki twisted around and glimpsed a shadow upon the slope. 'He's chasing us, Íri.'

'Of course… he's chasing… us,' she gasped, swiping her sweat-drenched hair off her face.

Azaki glanced to the river and back at the shrinking gap to Duratakus. *We're not going to get across that before he catches us.*

'You really need to do more exercise,' he said. 'We're being outrun by a man who managed to hit himself with lightning and fell off a mountain.'

They laboured across the gravel dunes to the river's edge as the last of the sun slipped behind the edge of the world.

'Go.' Azaki cast the Lady's Shroud and dragged the shadows up to her neck. 'This'll keep you hidden for a minute or two until you're out of my reach.'

'What?' Íri's green eyes flashed. 'Why would I be out of your reach?!'

'Because you run like a snail and need a headstart.' He forced a grin and turned toward where Duratakus stumbled over the dunes. 'I'll catch you up... probably.'

'But…' She threw her arms round his neck and dragged him into a tight hug. 'You better catch me up, or I'm going to toast you in the afterlife,' she murmured into his jaw.

'I'm too pretty to toast.' He gasped at the flash of pain as green light flickered in the corner of his eye and his fingers crunched back into place.

'You'd be prettier toasted.' She drew back a fraction and chewed her lip. 'Azaki…?'

'No time.' He watched the colour rise on her cheeks until his spell covered her. 'Go, Íri. Now.'

He watched the river ripple and splash as Íri crossed, kneeling and scooping a few palmfuls of water into his mouth. The soft gnawing of exhaustion faded a little as the cold water filled his stomach.

'Are we leaving her?' Falaïré stepped in front of the last rays of light as he turned back toward the slope. 'Was that our goodbye?'

Azaki sighed. 'Either way it works out, Iri'll need the headstart.' He flexed his healed fingers. 'I hope Duratakus is as tired as I feel, or it might not work out at all.'

'Our power will be enough,' she breathed. 'We're enough.'

'I don't think I've enough strength left to unseal it.' Azaki let himself feel the ache, deep and cold as a winter night, settling on him like heavy midwinter snow. 'Yeah, I'm fairly sure I can't.'

'We won't know unless we try,' Falaïré murmured as she faded away.

Duratakus ground to a halt atop the dune rising from the water's edge. 'I remember you.'

'Anastagus is such a gossip.' Azaki shook his head. 'You'd think he'd be more careful about concealing our connection.'

'I saw you fight against us at the beacon and in the arena. My master may think you'll still be useful, but I don't trust you. You're from the Webbed Pit, the Spider's clan, betrayal's in your blood. Best to just be rid of you.'

Nothing for it, I suppose. Kill or be killed.

'Come and get me, then.'

Duratakus grinned, splitting the scar-tissue at the corner of his mouth and sending a drop of blood trickling down his chin. 'Why would I get within your reach, when I don't have to?' He held his thiokezöeasiä out horizontally and rose into the sky.

'Damn it.' Azaki cast the Lady's Veil, threading his magic through Duratakus's mind. 'That's just unfair.'

The air above Duratakus's empty hand shivered. Azaki hurled himself to his right as the shimmer streaked toward him. The spell bored a deep, smoking hole through the gravel bank into the dark stone. A second and a third hissed past Azaki's shoulder into the river.

I really do need some more spells. He cast Azaki's Web upon Duratakus as he gathered a fourth spell. *Something that's actually dangerous.*

Duratakus snarled and clawed at his face. The spell on his palm burst, slicing a thin red line through his scarred left cheek, and he broke free of both illusions. 'No more tricks!'

Azaki tightened his grasp on his thiokezöeasiä and watched Duratakus hovering overhead. How long can he stay up there for?

'Lure him close,' Falaïré whispered in his ear. 'Once he's tangled within our snare, he cannot fly away.'

The air upon Duratakus's palm swirled and distorted once more. Azaki recast the Lady's Veil thrice, but Duratakus's fixed stare never left him, and Azaki's magic faded out amongst his thoughts.

Damn. He threw himself flat into the gravel as the wind screamed past his head.

A great gash stretched across the ground behind him, torn into the gravel and carved into the stone beneath.

Azaki leapt to his feet and jumped away from a second spell as it scored through the gravel where his feet had been. 'Queen of whispering webs, upon your throne of lies, gift a blade of shadow and revel in their cries.'

He concealed the small knife behind his forearm and dodged a third spell, darting up the slope toward Duratakus. *This'd better work.*

The edge of the fourth spell caught Azaki on the shin in a flash of agony. He glimpsed bone as he doubled over, tears springing to his eyes as he clenched every muscle in his body against the pain.

Duratakus swooped closer.

Azaki cast Azaki's Web over him and threw the blade of shadow. The knife caught Duratakus in the thigh and he cried out, wobbling in the sky and collapsing to the ground. Azaki drew the falcata and dragged himself up the slope, gritting his teeth at the searing pain in his shin, closing the gap between them as Duratakus tugged the blade out of his leg. He hurled it back, but it burst into wisps of shadow in the air between them. Azaki lunged, aiming the tip of his sword at Duratakus's ribs, but he leant aside and the blade nicked his hip.

'Heaven's sightless wroth, high skies' lash; become guard-less blade, poised to slash.' Duratakus clenched his fist and a shimmering blade of wind extended from it.

Azaki braced himself behind the falcata. The wind blade swept past his bronze sword and sliced a burning line down his ribs.

'Damn,' he hissed, pressing the back of his hand to the shallow cut.

Duratakus limped forward, slashing wildly.

Be patient. Azaki back-stepped across the gravel, keeping his weight off his throbbing shin as sweat began to gather on Duratakus's brow. *That can't be an easy spell to sustain.*

The wind blade's tip scored a line down the length of the falcata and the shimmering edge began to unravel.

Azaki held his ground at the river's shore.

Duratakus's slashes sped up as his spell came apart and the wind blade screamed as it cut at Azaki's torso over and over. He stumbled back into the cold river, slipping on the rocks beneath its ripples.

Lore of augmentation. Azaki clenched his jaw and forced the dregs of his magic to his muscles, matching Duratakus's unnatural swiftness, turning him round a blow at a time until they stood in red-clouded water, drenched to the waist and gasping for breath.

The wind blade came apart around Duratakus's fist and Azaki lunged, driving the falcata through Duratakus's raised forearm. He gasped and wrenched his arm off the sword, falling back into the water. Azaki stepped after him, blade raised.

A shadow flickered in the corner of his eye and he reeled back.

Duratakus came up from the water, swinging his thiokezöeasiä round in a red-tinged spray. A soft snick echoed over the sound of the river and the top half of Azaki's thiokezöeasiä fell into the water.

'No,' he whispered, snatching it up. A bright, blazing point of fury ignited somewhere near Azaki's heart. 'Falaïré…'

Duratakus thrust his wind blade-tipped thiokezöeasiä forward, but his leg gave out and he fell to his knees in the cold water. Azaki hammered the blunt edge of his falcata into Duratakus's face, crunching through his nose, and drove the blade into his stomach to the hilt. Hot blood poured over Azaki's fingers as he tugged the blade back out and shoved Duratakus away. He moaned and clutched at the gushing wound beneath the river surface, his magic guttering out as the water turned red around him.

'It takes a while to die if you're stabbed there.' Azaki staggered to the opposite bank. Raw, hot fury coiled on his tongue as he clutched the pieces of his thiokezöeasiä to his chest. 'And it'll *hurt.*'

The throbbing in his shin, the burning lines upon his ribs, and the ache in his bones faded beneath the heat searing through his veins. He watched Duratakus crawl out of the river on the far bank and curl up on the riverside. Blood trickled out from under him into the gravel.

I promised. Azaki limped up the gravel bank toward the coast, hot tears trickling down his face as Falaïré's words rang in his ears. *But now it's just me again.*

Twenty-Three

The sun crept above the edge of the world, spilling red light across the horizon. Azaki forced himself on as its faint heat soaked into his numb, aching limbs.

'Want to lend me a hand, Akrotera?' he asked the rising sun. 'Or you, Vyfaesiä? This is meant to be your damn world fragment and I've had more help from Estrif and Akrotera than you.'

Pain lanced through his right leg with every step. The black, cracked scab oozed little crimson trickles each time his weight came or left the limb and his shirt crusted to his chest over the wound upon his ribs.

'Not far now.' Azaki hugged the two halves of his thiokezöeasiä to his chest and fixed his stare upon the boulder-strewn summit of the tor. 'Just this one, then the next one, then the ship.'

The Heart-Tree could bring Falaïré back. He clutched the pieces of his thiokezöeasiä tighter. *She must.*

Something tore into the gravel beside him on the slope, sending up a cloud of dirt and spraying him with small stones. Azaki blinked through the dust and staggered round to stare down the slope.

Duratakus plummeted out of the sky into the gravel, dragging himself upright and gathering another spell on his palm. Dark, dry blood covered his stomach and damp rags lashed his right thigh and forearm. Azaki snatched a fist-sized rock from the ground and hurled it at Duratakus. The stone struck the wound on his raised arm and he howled, slumping back onto the gravel.

'Go and die!' Azaki snatched up more rocks. 'Just go and *die!*'

Duratakus clawed his way to his feet and raised his wing-crowned thiokezöeasiä. 'Scream, invisible spectre,' he snarled.

Azaki hurled the stones one after the other. The first two struck Duratakus on the head and shoulder, forcing him to his knees. The third bounced off the spider carapace armour covering Duratakus's waist as the wind began to rise.

Damn him. Azaki stumbled into a run, forcing himself up the slope toward the summit. The pain flared up in his leg and black spots swirled before his eyes as his lungs strained. *I hate him. More than Kogodakus.*

He squeezed into the gap between two boulders and stared south toward the lake, hunting for a sail. The shining ribbon of the inlet came to meet the spread of stone columns beyond the next small hill, an unbroken spread of sparkling waves.

Azaki's heart sank. 'Íri...'

Have you abandoned me, Vyfaesiä? He slid to his knees and groped for the hilt of his falcata. *I suppose with the seed already heading to the Silk Gardens, I'm no further use to you.* He released a long sigh. *And I kind of hoped betrayal was just for the Princess of Whispers.*

A spell burst against the other side of the boulder, showering him in dust.

'Queen of whispering webs, upon your throne of lies, gift a blade of shadow and revel in their cries,' Azaki whispered, ducking round the boulder to hurl the knife.

The blade stuck in Duratakus's uninjured foot and he let out a cry.

Azaki scrambled back behind the rocks as spells crashed into the far side of it. 'Queen of whispering webs, upon your throne of lies, gift a blade of shadow and revel in their cries.'

The shadows dissolved upon his palm as the last dregs of his magic failed.

'Maybe I should've gone with Otuko after all, Falaïré.' He winced as another pair of spells slammed into the boulder at his back, sending fracture lines snaking across it. 'I never really thought we'd not be enough, though, not after all the tight situations we've wriggled out of.'

And now you're gone. Raw despair clutched at his heart with sharp, cold claws. *I don't want to return to being the hate-warped, empty boy Otuko found. I don't want to. I don't.*

Duratakus's spells crashed against the boulder. The cracks gaped wider and dust clung to the blood trickling from the scab on his shin.

Azaki clenched his jaw and thrust his sword into the ground. 'Queen of whispering webs, upon your throne of lies, gift a blade of shadow and revel in their cries.'

The blade half-formed upon his hand; one edge straight and sharp, the other fading to a soft curve.

He leant round the edge of the rock and threw it at Duratakus, but the wind sent it sailing past him down the slope. 'Damn it!'

Another spell hammered into the rock and little pieces of dark stone pattered down around him.

How unfair. He blinked away his tears and stared at the bronze falcata thrust into the ground between the two halves of his thiokezöeasiä. *Is it really so much to ask for one good thing, Vyfaesiä?*

'Falaïré…' Azaki took a deep breath and pressed the pieces of his thiokezöeasiä together. *'Please?'*

He pushed the halves against one another until the skin tore on his palms and blood trickled down his wrists. His arms shook and ached, his breath catching in the back of his throat. A last, desperate shred of hope lingered in his heart.

'Please,' Azaki whispered. 'Please.'

His arms gave.

The pieces of dark wood clattered to the floor and rolled away into the crevice beneath the fractured boulder.

'Fine.' He slumped against the rock. 'I'll die here, then. Otuko's going to cry and Íri will be mad. Why can't I ever have just one good thing?'

A shadow flickered in the corner of his eye and a smooth, cold weight slid into his sticky, stinging hands.

Ebony wood lay upon his blood-smeared palms.

'Falaïré,' he whispered, clutching his thiokezöeasiä to his chest.

She leant out of the shadows of the boulder, her silver eyes glowing with mirth. 'You look awful, my Azi. Isn't the little Voréöeasiäki girl around to heal you?'

He dragged her close and crushed her against him, drinking in the faint, sweet scent of athoëasirki. Her cool skin felt smooth as spider-silk beneath his torn palms, her lips soft as snow in the crook of his neck.

Falaïré laughed. 'We're not done yet, remember.'

No. We're not done. Azaki closed his eyes and smiled, breathing out his relief through trembling lips. *It'll always be us.*

Another spell crashed into the rock and light spilt in through the cracks, falling across his thiokezöeasiä. Bright flashed in the corner of his eye and an array of lines and spots of light swirled upon the other boulder as he turned his thiokezöeasiä round in his hands.

A circlet of jagged mirrorglass rose from its top, countless, small pieces jutting out like a ring of thorns and eight long, sharp shards rising above them like the tines of a crown. The same shining circlet sat upon Falaïré's ebony hair, gleaming bright as stars.

Azaki tugged his eyes away from Falaïré's mirrorglass crown. 'Why's it different?'

She eased free of his embrace and pressed her left forefinger to the tip of one of the shards. A bright bead of red welled up on the ball of her finger. 'A broken heart might heal, but it'll never be the same.'

'As unhelpfully cryptic as always.' He grinned and fought down the lump in his throat before it turned to tears. 'You're not going to tell me what's changed, are you?'

Falaïré's red lips curved into a smirk. 'The Voréoatho may not grant us another chance, my Azi,' she whispered. 'Guard our heart more carefully.'

He clenched his jaw. 'Nobody will ever break my thiokezöeasiä again. I'll kill any of Anastagus's followers who try.'

She laughed and touched her red-stained fingers to his cheek, leaving hot, wet prints upon his skin. *'We'll kill anyone who tries.'*

Azaki snatched his falcata from the ground. 'Deceive, lady of lies.'

A ball of grey mist gathered and swirled between the eight mirrorglass tines of the crown, bursting out past the boulders. The drain dragged him to his knees, but his magic snared Duratakus like a fly in a web.

'Run,' Falaïré breathed in his ear. 'We've nothing left. The truth we've spun won't last long.'

Azaki glanced at where Duratakus hurled another spell into the rock and rammed the falcata into his sheath. A fierce, twisted heat welled up about his heart. 'This isn't over,' he muttered, staggering down the far side of the hill toward the stream and the inlet. 'One day, Duratakus, I'll look down on you as you die.'

He hauled himself up the slope of the last hill, slipping and sliding in the gravel with tired, aching feet, gripped by the throbbing, stinging pain in his shin and chest. A great weight of exhaustion pressed down upon him like the fist of a Voréoatho.

I'm far enough. He let himself slide down to where the gravel met the hexagonal columns and sealed his thiokezöeasiä.

A distant howl of rage drifted to his ears on the wind and Azaki allowed himself a small smile as he limped along the line of strange stone shapes.

The longship floated beneath him where the columns crumbled away into the water; its white sail with the black sword emblem strained in the wind and the taut rope stretching from its stern to where a single column rose from the lake trembled.

'Azaki!' Íri dropped her thiokezöeasiä and sprang to the side.

He lowered himself down the column into the water, gritting his teeth as his shin stung like he'd salted the wound and pulling himself along the line to the side of the ship.

Íri seized his wrists and dragged him over the side.

Azaki slumped on the deck and clutched his thiokezöeasiä to his chest. 'Hi, Íri. I hope you weren't too bored waiting.'

'Bored!?' Íri's tone climbed an octave. 'I was worried out of my mind!'

'Well, I made it back.' He rolled over and grimaced at his mutilated shin. 'Not exactly in one piece, but close enough.'

She gasped. 'Is that… *bone!?*'

'You can use it as an excuse to touch me later.' Azaki hauled himself up on the side of the ship and tucked his thiokezöeasiä into a coil of rope. 'We need to leave before Duratakus notices us.'

Íri dragged her eyes away from the blood oozing from his broken scab and summoned a slim blade of fire, severing the rope. The ship lurched toward the end of the inlet.

143

'Less sail.' He groped for the rope fastening the sail down. 'We can't sail this by ourselves at full speed.'

'Idiot.' She batted his hand away. 'Don't move. The bone's sticking out!'

Azaki slumped back down to the deck and poked a finger into his scab. 'I can't wait for it to go foul. This time it'll be me shivering and sweating instead of Otuko, only she's not here to look after me.'

Falaïré slid her slim, small feet into his lap. 'Perhaps we should learn to heal things, my Azi. Eventually, this little Voréöeasiäki girl's not going to be there…'

He grinned. 'I need a lot of new spells, but I'll add it to the list. First, I want—'

She lunged forward and seized hold of his shin. 'We want to not *die*.'

White-hot pain flared up his leg.

Azaki gasped and pried her red-stained fingers off. 'What—'

Falaïré's eyes burnt, shining silver flame around smouldering dark. 'You sent the little Voréöeasiäki girl away. If she'd been with us, we might have never been separated or hurt.'

'But—'

She curled the crimson-drenched fingers of her right-hand into a fist. 'When you thought you were dying, what was it you wanted? The little Voréöeasiäki girl? The little warrior girl? Or us?'

Azaki glanced at where Íri wrestled with the rope on the other side of the longship. 'Us.'

Falaïré's eyes softened. 'We can't have *everything* we want, my Azi. If you keep choosing to risk what you want most for lesser desires, you'll eventually lose it. And where will we be then?'

Íri darted across the deck. 'Where are you hurt?'

He pulled his eyes away from Falaïré's. 'Mostly, you know, that gaping wound in my leg. Otherwise, a lot of bruises and cuts. I'm fairly sure it's just the pain that's stopped me collapsing.'

'Anything else serious?' Íriniel's fingers lit up green and she touched her palm to his shin. 'This… Did you *walk* on this?! Smear the dirt into it with your own hands?' She plucked out a piece of gravel as his new skin shed the scab. 'There are *rocks* in you.'

'It hurts pretty much everywhere. And yes, I walked on it. Hopping wasn't really an option.' He inspected the small pile of gravel she picked out of the scab. 'The rocks are just a happy coincidence.'

She shook her head. 'Clearly I shouldn't have left you. What happened to *I'm a tough raider from the Webbed Pit?*'

Falaïré laughed in his ear. 'See,' she whispered. 'Even the little Voréöeasiäki girl thinks she should've stayed.'

Azaki rolled his eyes. 'It worked out alright, didn't it?'

Íri ripped his shirt away from his chest.

He hissed and clenched his teeth. 'I was quite attached to that shirt.'

'Yes. Literally.' She traced her finger down the edge of the cut. 'This is infected.'

Azaki pushed her hand away and poked at it. 'Yeah, it's probably not meant to be oozing a cloudy yellowy-green.'

Íri stuck her hand out. 'Knife.'

He grinned. 'You mean you're going to use my—'

'Do you really want me to change my mind and let you die of blood poisoning?' She extended her hand closer. 'Come on.'

'Queen of whispering webs, upon your throne of lies, gift a blade of shadow and revel in their cries.' Azaki grimaced at the drain on his strength and passed the half-finger length weapon over. 'Try and do it in one go, please.'

She bit her lip and tugged his shirt over his head. 'Hold still.'

'I'm too tired to try and escape.' He offered her a grin. 'A good thing you didn't manage to get your hands on Toga the Sour in such a defenceless state.'

Íri snorted and drew the tip of the blade down the cut.

A line of fire seared down his ribs.

Azaki clenched his jaw as a wave of pus-tinged blood washed down his chest. *'Ow. Very much ow.'*

She reached out and squeezed his fingers. 'Sorry.'

He watched as the fresh cut knitted itself back together beneath Íri's green wreathed palm. 'Not even a scar.'

'No number of scars will make you handsome or dashing. I'd give up, if I were you.'

'Says the girl with a thing for sulky-faces and goatees.'

Íri scowled. 'If there was even *any* truth in that, there'd be no chance now.'

Azaki patted her on the head and mustered half a smile. 'There, there, Íri. Your heartbreak will fade. In time, you'll come to love again.'

She brandished the knife at him, but it burst into shadows as his spell failed. 'He tried to get me to go with him to Grey Sails Grove and join his greenhearts. There's a blue spiral all up his thiokezöeasiä now and when I said no, he stomped off across the lake surface like he was walking on stone.'

Azaki dragged himself across to grope for his thiokezöeasiä. 'Best to avoid that grove, then. No doubt Toga the Sour will fill it full of grumpy, purist Voréöeasiäki like him.'

Íri's eyes were fixed upon his thiokezöeasiä.

He waved the crown from side to side and laughed as her eyes followed it back and forth. 'Something wrong, Íri?'

She reached out to touch a finger to his thiokezöeasiä's crown, flinching back and sucking at the ball of her finger. 'Sharp.'

Azaki inspected the tips of the eight mirrorglass tines. 'Yes. Very. That's actually going to be quite inconvenient.'

Falaïré's soft laugh rang in his ears.

'How'd it get like that?' Íri asked.

'Well, Duratakus broke it, then—'

'The Heart-Tree fixed your thiokezöeasiä?' Her eyes went so wide all the white showed around her bright green irises. 'She made your bond even stronger?'

'Don't say destiny or greater things.' Azaki frowned. 'Getitakus kept saying that as he told me to leave you to Anastagus's mercy and flee.'

And Akrotera. And Estrif. His stomach knotted itself. *And for some reason the Lady of Betrayal hasn't killed me.*

'What happened to him?'

'He died. Quickly, though.'

'I guess it's for the best.'

Azaki cocked his head. 'Really? That doesn't sound like the Íri I know.'

Íri clenched her fists. 'He wasn't acting like a Voréöeasiäki should. I saw his eyes at the end and they'd turned red as blood. He'd've ended up like Kogodakus, or worse. I guess you were right about Voréöeasiäki being capable of good or bad like everyone else is.' She took a deep breath. 'Forget him. Do you know who the only other Voréöeasiä in living memory to have their thiokezöeasiä returned by the Heart-Tree is?'

'Please don't tell me it was Anastagus.'

'Worse.' She smiled and leant in close. 'Valia the Creepy.'

'Fantastic.' He stifled a shiver. 'But I thought you didn't like me calling her that.'

'I don't. It's rude. But it was worth it to watch you squirm.'

'It's a good thing I'm too tired to squirm much.' He let his head thud back against the side of the ship. 'Where're we headed?'

'The closest coastal village to the Grey Stair.' Íri pointed across the lake past the prow. 'If it's under siege, we ought to go help.'

'I suppose so.' Azaki hauled himself to his feet on the side of the ship. 'Good thing you didn't leave me behind, it'll be much easier to sneak through a siege with my help.'

She huffed. 'I wasn't going to leave you. I was about to go back after you and scold you for dawdling.'

'In my defence, I had a large piece of leg missing.' He grinned. 'I knew you'd miss me too much to abandon me, even if I was a bit late. I did worry for a moment when I couldn't see the ship, though.'

She struggled with her smile. 'Get some rest, Azaki. I'll make sure we stay on course for a bit.'

I could use a nap, I guess. He watched the mountains shrink as Íri wrestled with the rudder and sighed. *I'm sorry, Otuko. I've not made it back to you this time, either.* He swallowed a hot, bitter rush of guilt. *Please don't cry. I don't want to be the one who makes you cry.*

'The seed's planted in the Silk Gardens,' Falaïré whispered in his ear. 'The girl who found us said she'd leave the clan with us. What need have we of the Webbed Pit?'

'None,' he muttered, sagging back onto the deck as legs threatened to give way. 'But Utháki—'

'What friend would deny the happiness of those he proclaims to love,' she murmured. 'He'll come south with us, or he'll betray us. A chance at having both is better than no chance, my Azi.'

Azaki allowed himself to imagine Otuko beside him in the peaceful, green, southie lands. A faint smile crept onto his lips. 'I can't say it's so bad. Maybe it'd be worth trying, though I fear she's quite keen on those four grey-eyed children.'

Falaïré rested her head on his shoulder. 'So long as we don't risk greater desires for lesser, why not?'

The bronze keel grated on the pebbles as the wind drove the longship ashore among scorched beams and the burnt out hulks of small boats. Small, brown birds pattered along the empty beach on long legs, gulls perched and nested in the nooks of ruined huts.

'Another raided village.' Íri swept her hair behind her ear. 'I hope the people got away to the Grey Stair in time.'

Azaki jumped down onto the pebbles and stomped through the foaming edge of the surf to where the tangle of seaweed and driftwood lining the beach ran beneath the longship's prow.

She passed down his thiokezöeasiä, then hers. 'Can you?'

'Help Voréöeasiä Princess Íri down another long drop?' He grinned and leant their thiokezöeasiäki against the prow. 'It'd be an honour.'

She snorted and dangled her legs over the edge. 'Get ready to catch me, then.'

Azaki caught her round the waist and put her down on her feet. 'Good thing this one's a pebble beach too.'

'You wouldn't drop me.'

He shot her a smile and lured Itaki down from the mast with half a walnut. 'No, but I might pretend just to make you scream.'

'I wouldn't scream, I'd hit you.' She plucked her thiokezöeasiä from against the boat and picked up his too, studying the mirrorglass crown. 'Does Otuko actually put up with this without hitting you?'

He laughed. 'She's the *reason* I'm like this, but no. She's equally violent as you.'

'At least I know who to blame.' Íri set off up the beach. 'Come on, Azaki.'

'So keen to get walking. Who are you and what have you done with Voréöeasiä Princess Íri?'

Colour rose on her cheeks. 'The faster I get to the Grey Stair, the sooner I'll have some more bearable company.'

Beyond a crumbling line of pale sandstone and long, rustling grass, a dozen charred, ravaged buildings squatted round a square of blackened mud. A short, square stone tower rose out of the mud, leaning toward a screen of trees at the village's perimeter.

'It's a real shame there's no walking equivalent of *Row Your Boat*.' Azaki clambered up the bank at the edge of the beach and offered Íri a hand.

She let him pull her up. 'Don't even think of trying to make one.'

'Row?' Itaki fluffed his wings up on Azaki's shoulder and cocked his head. 'Bail. Íri. Íri.'

Azaki chuckled and hummed the tune to *Row Your Boat* until Itaki bobbed his head. 'I know what I'm teaching you next, tiny fiend.'

Íri folded her arms and set off through the ruins. 'What a pair you're going to be.' She shook her head. 'Itaki missed you. He'd chewed halfway through that cage you made trying to get out and find you.'

'Good thing I made it back, then.' Azaki picked his way through the mud on large stones and bits of wood until he reached the middle of the square. 'He gets bitey when he's upset.'

Íri prodded him in the foot with her thiokezöeasiä. 'I'm going to take a brief break.'

'You're tired already?' Azaki raised an eyebrow. 'It's only been a few minutes.'

'No, I need to pee.'

'Okay. I'll be here teaching Itaki a new song.'

She shook her head and drifted away round the back of the tower.

He watched Itaki preen and glanced north past the burnt ruins toward the distant mountains. 'What would you do, little monster? Go north or go south? If I want, I can go back to the Webbed Pit now.'

'Íri.' The parrot fanned its red tail feathers and busied himself preening.

'Listen to the bird,' Falaïré whispered in his ear. 'It gives good advice.'

'Does he? Or does he just repeat the words I've taught him?'

She laughed. 'If we go back to the Webbed Pit, we know what we'll have.'

'Otuko. Uthàki. A good chance of being named keorl and leading raids, then eventually eorl, provided the Princess of Whispers doesn't kill me. Recognition from those who spurned us.' Azaki shuffled his feet as his stomach clenched and fluttered. 'Grey-eyed children. Giving Otuko her dream.'

Falaïré circled him. Red dripped from the fingertips of her right hand into the mud. 'Anastagus's pawn, too...'

'Maybe for a bit.' He gnawed at the inside of his cheek. 'Not for long, though.'

'And if you go south?' She swept her ebony cascade of hair round over her shoulder onto her chest, her crown of broken mirroglass shining upon her brows. 'What then?'

'The Heart-Tree's pawn. Íri.' Azaki sighed. 'The recognition of being one of the Voréöeasiäki.'

Falaïré's silver irises sharpened. 'Is that all?'

'No. I like how green and peaceful it is. Otuko might well come with me. Uthàki… maybe.'

'And no Anastagus.'

'Is being the pawn of a Voréoatho any better?' Azaki asked. 'We can outgrow Anastagus if we want to enough. You said so yourself.'

She smirked. 'You became the pawn of a Voréoatho the moment you took up a thiokezöeasiä. Regardless of what you choose, a fragment of her spirit, me, will always be with you.'

'Well, I don't like Anastagus.' He grimaced. 'I *really* don't.'

'Why not?' She caught his chin in her damp, red-stained fingers. 'His truth is as true as any other.'

'He's selfish.' Azaki wrestled with the distaste curdling on his tongue and coiling in his gut. 'He finds people when they're hurt and alone, and he saves them, but then he uses them up and leaves them behind once he's done with them.'

'We're just like him,' she whispered. 'Only… *not*.'

He narrowed his eyes. 'His ugly, self-interested truth is nothing like our beautiful web of infinite truths.'

'Then don't be his pawn.' Falaïré touched the pale fingertips of her left hand to his cheek. 'Give the girl who saved us and the warrior boy a truth that brings them south.'

'I'm not sure they'd be welcome.' Azaki frowned. 'I don't want them to live surrounded by people who ignore or look down them again. That's an awful life and it'd turn them into awful things.'

She slipped round behind him as Íri re-appeared. 'We can try, though. We won't know until we do.'

Azaki stared into the mirrorglass fragments of his thiokezöeasiä's crown. *We chase what we want. What else is there?*

A shadow flickered in the corner of his eye, obsidian-dark; its many reflections flitted through the mirrorglass fragments like wisps of ebony cloud.

'Azaki?' Íri waved a hand in front of his face. 'Let's get moving.'

He nodded. 'Sorry, I was thinking.'

She paused. 'About home again?'

'The Webbed Pit was never really home. Otuko and Utháki were.' Azaki watched the ground beneath his feet as they crossed the line of the burnt palisade and moved into the trees. 'Do you think I could get her to join me?'

'Join you?' Íri stopped. 'She can't be one of the Voréöeasiäki, Azaki. The Heart-Tree hasn't chosen her.'

'But she could come south?' He studied her bright green eyes until she turned away to stare at his thiokezöeasiä's crown. 'Íri?'

She frowned at the pieces of mirrorglass. 'Why just Otuko? Why not your other friend? And why're you asking *now?*'

'Utháki's funny about clan loyalty. As outcasts from birth, Otuko and I never really got into it as much, but he'd probably never leave the clan. His mother died just to give him a chance to be part of it.' He shrugged. 'I'm asking now, because until recently I didn't think she'd agree.'

Íri tore her eyes away from his thiokezöeasiä and chewed her lip. 'Does Otuko wear woad on her face like the warriors of the Clan of the Sword Spring?'

'Sort of.'

'Purple woad.'

Falaïré laughed in his ear. 'Uh oh…'

Íri's eyes flashed. 'That's where you went!'

He gnawed at the inside of his cheek. 'Yes. The eorl of the Webbed Pit I saw when scouting has a habit of using his position of power to *persuade* younger warriors to sleep with him. He chose Otuko to escort him to the Theatre of the Worldbreaker, so…'

'You were jealous.' Her lip trembled. 'You killed him.'

He blinked. 'I didn't want him to be able to take advantage of her and he's one of Anastagus's strongest supporters in the clan. Trust me when I say everyone's better off without him.'

She took a deep breath and turned away. 'I guess it doesn't matter. She could come south if she wanted. It's not unknown. As long as she lives by our rules, she'll at least be tolerated.'

Azaki smiled. 'That's good. I owe Otuko a lot. Thanks, Íri.'

'Don't mention it.' She stalked off through the trees, walking as if Estrif himself was on their heels.

Is she mad I killed Atíko? He hurried after her, stumbling through the bracken and brambles that sprawled beneath the birch trees. *He's her enemy, too.*

'She doesn't like it when we don't tell her things, remember.' Falaïré slid through the undergrowth beside him, the shadows of her dress flowing round the leaves and vines like water.

Azaki frowned. 'Right. She thinks it means I don't trust her.'

Íri ground to a halt at the edge of the copse of birch trees where a thick, grey fog hung.

He hastened to her side and put a hand on her shoulder. 'What is it? I'm sorry for not telling you. I - well, I'm used to keeping the truth to myself, I guess. It's how I was raised. Lies were my armour.'

'I'd rather you'd told me, but I can understand why you didn't.' She turned her face away, then covered his fingers with hers. 'I stopped because of the mist, not you.'

Azaki peered into it, straining his eyes. A dense silence lay in the fog and the hairs on the back of his neck prickled. The mist parted, fading away in grey tatters, but the weight of the quiet remained.

'I don't like this place,' he said.

Íri edged closer to his side as the fog retreated, her fingers tight around her thiokezöeasiä.

Endless mounds rose from limp dead grass and bone-white, leafless trees, marked by flickering purple ghost-lights. Bronze longswords rose from each and every one, thrust into the dancing violet flames as if the ghost-lights bled out from within the knolls.

'The Field of Swords,' Íri whispered. 'The Cult of Mūru worship here. This place was supposed to be haunted by the Shadow of the Last Doorway himself before the Heart-Tree spread Her groves across the world.'

'Given I've already unexpectedly bumped into Akrotera and Estrif, and somehow avoided the Lady of Betrayal's vengeance so far, I think I'd rather not take risks with any more of the Voréoathoki.' Azaki glanced down the treeline. 'Is there a way around?'

'Not until you reach the Marsh Road. It'd take almost a week longer than crossing.'

The last of the mist curled back, revealing a dark grey smudge rising upon the horizon.

The Grey Stair. Azaki watched the distant smoke, trying to judge the distance. *At least a couple of days away if we go straight across.*

'We don't have time to waste, do we?' He placed one foot onto the dead grass and grimaced as a deep chill crept over him. 'Ladies first?'

Íri's lips twitched. 'It's not chivalrous to let ladies go first if you think it's a trap.'

Azaki grinned despite the ice crawling up his spine. 'I guess I'll go first and see what happens. I warn you now, though, that if I end up as some kind of spectre, I'll haunt you forever.'

She snorted. 'I'd just ignore you, I've gotten good at it.'

'I'd follow you back to the Heart-Tree, move all your bookmarks, and rearrange your bookshelves.' He chuckled. 'It'd drive you mad.'

'And yet you'd still be less annoying than you are alive.' She stepped down next to him and grimaced. 'It's much colder, that's weird.'

Azaki strode forward through the grave mounds, taking care not to step on any of them. 'I guess we keep going and see. Either we'll make it through or we'll end up as cursed spirits.'

'I don't want to be a cursed spirit.'

'Well, look on the bright side. If we do end up as cursed spirits, it ought to really annoy Toga the Sour.'

'Why?' Íri shot him a way look, a hint of colour rising on her face.

Azaki cackled. 'Because we'd be together for *all eternity*. He'd literally die of envy.'

Her cheeks reddened. 'I don't think it'd be very romantic.'

'No. Probably just a lot of floating around scaring innocent travellers.'

'You'd probably enjoy that.'

'I definitely would for a bit, but I wouldn't want to do it forever.'

'Mūru would probably find you so annoying he'd grant you immortality, just so he'd never have to deal with you again.'

'I could *live* with that.'

Íri groaned. 'Yes, that's the exact sort of thing I mean by so annoying.'

'Mūru hates both the Volōmothí and the Volōmotistí with every fibre of his being,' Falaïré whispered. 'Best to avoid the unenviable fate of those damned to his grasp. Even truth cannot save us from the hatred of one of the Voréoathoki.'

The purple flames fluttered, froze, and flickered into a frenzy. A shadow slid through the corner of Azaki's eye, sending ice trickling down his spine and through his veins.

I don't like this at all.

'Stay strong, my Azi,' Falaïré murmured. 'Our fun can't end so soon, we've far too many tricks left to try.' Her lips brushed the nape of his neck, curving into a small smirk. 'Our broken heart has been healed. We're stronger than before.' Her cool fingers tilted his chin up toward the heavens. 'The stars are waiting.'